Abraham's Bay

& Other Stories

Abraham's Bay
& Other Stories

Jack Greer

DRYAD PRESS • Washington, DC

The paper used in this publication meets the minimum requirement of American National Standard for Information Sciences — Permanence of paper for Printed Library Materials, ANSIZ39.48

Cover image, *Pirates Bay*, is a painting by Kevin Fitzgerald, from the private collection of Nell Beal.

Book and cover design by Sandy Rodgers
Photograph of Jack Greer by Skip Brown
Text is typeset in Sabon 10.5 over 14

"Night Sea" originally appeared in *Pembroke Magazine*.

Dryad Press
P.O. Box 11233
Takoma Park, Maryland 20913
www.dryadpress.com; publisher@dryadpress.com

Library of Congress Cataloging-in-Publication Data
Greer, Jack.
    Abraham's Bay & other stories / by Jack Greer.
      p. cm.
    ISBN 978-1-928755-12-8 (alk. paper)
      1. Voyages and travels—Fiction. 2. Islands of the Atlantic—
Fiction. I.
      Title. II. Title: Abraham's Bay and other stories.
    PS3607.R473A63   2009
    813'.6—dc22   2009033028

for Bobbie, David, and Jenna

&

for Merrill and Sandy

Contents

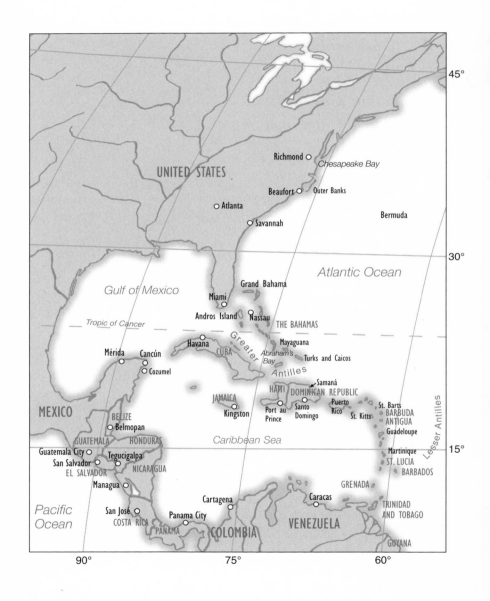

45°

Richmond ○ Chesapeake Bay

UNITED STATES

Beaufort ○ Outer Banks

○ Atlanta

Bermuda

○ Savannah

30°

Atlantic Ocean

Gulf of Mexico

Grand Bahama

Miami ○

Tropic of Cancer

Andros Island Nassau

THE BAHAMAS

Havana ○

Greater

Mayaguana

Mérida ○ Cancún ○

CUBA

Abraham's Bay

Turks and Caicos

○ Cozumel

Antilles

Samaná

JAMAICA HAITI DOMINICAN REPUBLIC

MEXICO

BELIZE Kingston ○

Port au Prince Santo Domingo Puerto Rico

St. Barts
BARBUDA
ANTIGUA

○ Belmopan

St. Kitts

Guadeloupe

GUATEMALA HONDURAS

Caribbean Sea

Lesser Antilles

Guatemala City ○ Tegucigalpa ○

15°

Martinique

San Salvador ○

ST. LUCIA BARBADOS

EL SALVADOR NICARAGUA

Managua ○

GRENADA

Pacific Ocean

Cartagena ○

Caracas ○

TRINIDAD AND TOBAGO

San José ○ Panama City ○

PANAMA COLOMBIA VENEZUELA

GUYANA

90° 75° 60°

Preface

The wind first found me when I was about twelve years old, on the shores of the York River, in the southern Chesapeake Bay. There my grandmother built a small cottage, where we spent every summer. I didn't really know my father's side of the family — he left when I was three — but my mother's mother gave me a place where the wind could reach me.

On summer nights, without a flashlight, I walked through soggy bottomland down to my grandmother's dock and sat dangling my legs over dark water. A night breeze often blew from the south, a soft breath from far off. The wind came from beyond the river mouth, from beyond the Bay. It was a wind born offshore, a sea wind. It carried the sweet smells of the Atlantic, and more. It brought the breathing air of far-away lands. It whispered the promise of what rides on the wind itself.

It called from where the wind begins.

I learned to sail, the only way I knew to ride the wind. As a teenager I sailed up and down the river and then, in my twenties, up and down the Chesapeake Bay. In our thirties, my wife and I sailed with our young son out of the Bay and into the ocean, up to Newport and Block Island. And in our forties, we headed south, down the U.S. coast to Florida, and then east, into what the charts call the Southwest North Atlantic.

Out of our travels among those swells came these stories.

It was a time before cell phones and the Global Positioning System (GPS) became commonplace. Before so many mega-yachts berthed at islands like Antigua and St. Barts, before big development hit remote ports like Puerta Plata in the Dominican Republic. Now, in Puerta Plata, a modern marina offers wireless

Internet, a swim-up bar, and a Vegas-style cabaret. At the time of these stories, a handful of sailboats visiting Puerta Plata secured their sterns to an old commercial pier, where frayed wires dangled and concrete crumbled.

Satellite navigation was just coming in then, but it was rudimentary and depended on transit satellites that wandered in and out of range. Only a fortunate few could afford the first expensive GPS systems. Communications meant single sideband short-wave radios, or VHF (very high frequency) radios that reached less than twenty miles. On the remote islands of the Bahamas it meant rowing ashore to a Bahama Telephone Company (BaTelCo) station, with its diesel generator and tall thin radio tower. There was no email.

Though it was a different time, some things have not changed. In summer the south wind still blows up the Chesapeake. The east wind that howls along the north shore of the Dominican Republic still eases at night, as if to let a small boat pass by.

The technology has changed, but the unspoken messages borne on the wind are the same. And those who cannot help but hear, still listen.

Abraham's Bay
& Other Stories

Starting from Beaufort

THE BEACHES OF NORTH CAROLINA'S Outer Banks lay
empty. Gone were summer's bright umbrellas and children
wading in the shore break. The sea turned gray and winter made
its first forays south on the dark wings of northerly winds.

Behind fish-shaped Shackleford Banks lay the town of Beaufort. As autumn arrived the small port drew sailors from up and
down the coast. Facing east like pilgrims, they steered sailboats
through cuts into the Atlantic, then set their course for Bermuda
or the Caribbean. They hurried ahead of winter gales, careful to
skirt shallows that reached far out to sea.

On an afternoon in early November, Jerry Wheeler and his
wife Rachel leaned over the side of their small white sloop,
using a hand drill to bore holes in the stern. The final bracket
for the windvane. White fiberglass dust drifted over the water.
They globbed pasty caulk around the heads of large stainless
steel bolts and slid them home through the hull.

This was their push-off day, though they felt too tired to
leave. Beneath gloomy skies, they struggled to finish the last of
what they had come to call the List. Not the last, really — the List
grew daily of its own accord, and so could never be finished —
but the last of those things they agreed must be done before they
could leave. Before they could turn the bow of their sprightly
thirty-foot sloop, *Courageous*, toward the sea.

For now they merely climbed into their gray rubber dinghy,
the two of them in their ragged jeans, and steered toward the

Beaufort docks. They wanted to check the Weather Channel one
last time and to see their friends. A tough autumn tide pulled
Courageous against two anchors. Many boats had already
cleared out, and slips stood empty.

Jerry felt antsy. One by one he watched boats come down the
Intracoastal Waterway, then push off for the islands. Everyone
spoke about it the same way: go east across the tumultuous Gulf
Stream, then sail southeast to the 25th parallel, where it meets the
64th longitude line. There turn south in search of easterly trade
winds and drive down Highway 64 to the British Virgin Islands.
He knew there were dangers, like the Anegada reef that lay east
of the Virgins. For centuries it had claimed boats slightly off in
their navigation. Not to mention the Gulf Stream itself, tropical
storms, and two weeks of sailing on the open sea. But he fixed on
that intersection where latitude met longitude, as if he expected a
sign there, an X marking the spot, so he would know where to
turn. Anything other than those trackless miles of ocean.

He pushed open a bright green door and they stepped inside
to get a beer. Over the bar the Weather Channel played continually in this sailor's pub. Bart stood propped by a stool.

"Hey, Captain Jerr. Rachel. Are we ready?"

"Ready as we're going to be," Rachel said, holding up one
finger for a beer.

Bart nodded and they all looked up at the TV. Dirty blonde
hair hung down Bart's forty-year-old neck, stubble like hay bris-
tled his cheeks. His T-shirt said "Back Street Pub." Though not
tall, he edged out Jerry, who was short and dark, with a cropped
beard almost black. "Rough this time of year," he said toward the
TV. "Sixty-foot schooner got rolled in the Stream few years
back."

Jerry and Rachel clutched their mugs and watched cold fronts
muster on the screen — muster and march, like Sherman, to the
sea. Day after day they saw the same pattern: a cold front
dropped down from the northwest, headed straight for the
Eastern Seaboard. Each surge of sailors waited for the cold front

to pass, then pushed off. Those who stayed behind watched as the next front marshaled on the map. Such a simple bent line, this cold front on the weather chart, but it stood for a fierce wind that came out of the Great Plains, troop train on a southeast run, building steam before it crashed headlong into the coast.

Of course it was not so much the coast it crashed into as the Gulf Stream. "When it's blowing thirty or forty here it's blowing fifty or sixty on the Stream," Bart said. "It's the temperature difference. Cold air. Warm water. Worst thing," he went on, "is that it's a north wind. Goes straight against the current coming from the south. You get humongous waves then. Square waves."

Rachel asked if that's what rolled the sixty-foot schooner. "Naw," Bart said, "that was probably a rogue wave. Had one of those off shore just a few weeks ago. Hit an aircraft carrier so hard it rippled the flight deck. Popped a couple crew straight overboard. Wave musta been fifty feet high."

"An aircraft carrier?" she said. Jerry turned to look at his wife. The first thing people noticed about Rachel was her neck. It was graceful, almost sculpted, and gave her a sense of elegance, of dignity, even in the frayed T-shirt she now wore daily, and the blue jeans stained with boat varnish. She looked younger than her thirty-eight years, with deep brown eyes, and no one believed that they had an eighteen-year-old son.

"Yep," Bart said. "About a hundred miles off Hatteras is what I heard." Bart appeared to find strange pleasure in such things.

Jerry's full name was Jeremiah. His West Virginia father had wanted something Biblical. Instead he got a curly haired daughter-in-law who studied Buddhism and a son who went by Jerr. In the bar's mirror Jerry saw himself and looked away. Despite his dark hair he appeared pale — pale, bearded, and thin. They had already been on the boat for two months, but he had hardly seen the sun. He'd spent so much time underneath things, installing new bladder tanks for fresh water and for diesel fuel, new hoses, new intakes, new pepcocks. He had installed a new depth sounder and knot meter, running wiring beneath berths and under floorboards, then back through the engine compartment where all wires joined in a great tangle of oily dust, all color codes gone black. He had made a new mount for the LORAN unit and installed a new radio, drilling a hole through the teak deck and running the wire all the way to a new antenna at the masthead. While swinging at the mast top, he had installed a tri-color running light and anchor light with confused four-way wiring that kept not working. He had also installed a new satnav, an instrument which he regarded with awe and mistrust, running the wire back through the engine compartment again, banging his head and his knuckles as he struggled to connect the stumpy white antennae (uncomfortably phallic) now erect at the stern rail.

"Did you hear that?" she said. "They said a 'strong' cold front. What does 'strong' mean, exactly?" She had put her beer down on the bar and now wrapped both arms around his right arm. She felt soft. At times she had that quality of softness, like a feather mattress where he could lie down and sleep forever. Other times, when angry, she grew hard, all edges sharp.

"I guess that means we'd better be well off shore before it hits," he said. The beer gathered in the pit of his stomach like sea foam. They both knew this was it: the cold fronts would grow stronger as the season turned, and then the time of the gales would have begun. The "weather window" would close, the window between the threat of hurricanes that stretched from the heavy heat of summer through September and October, and the certainty of gales that began in November and grew wild in winter. Do not leave Beaufort before November 1, everyone said, when a late season hurricane could form near the islands and head north. Then again, they said, sometimes they formed even after November 1.

"I wouldn't wait too long," said Bart. "The gales are on their way."

When they returned to their boat, they agreed to nap for an hour. It would be a long night as they set out to cross the Gulf Stream while good weather lasted. Rachel stretched out in the V-berth, pushing aside the storm jib in its big red bag. He lay on the berth in the main cabin, across from the settee. Soon he could hear Rachel's breath come slow and even, but he could not sleep. He forced himself to close his eyes, as thoughts of what he had not yet fixed streamed through his mind. He thought of his mother.

His mother was thirty-six when she died of leukemia. Jerry, an only child, turned thirteen only a few days before, on May 22. That long summer he stayed with his grandmother, Edna Baines, in her old house on the Rappahannock River in Virginia. The humid air was thick with loss. His grandfather, a country doctor, had died many years before, and his grandmother lived alone. That summer she bought a small white johnboat with a fifteen horsepower outboard. She never said it was for him, but it was.

His father rarely visited that summer. He wasn't doing well. A brittle man, he seemed to split when his wife died. Where he went that summer remained a gap in family history. Possibly he just wandered.

That summer Jerry turned to the water. Every morning he ate his orange slice of cantaloupe and his sugar-frosted cereal and headed down to the dock. He took a fishing pole with him and a crab net. He took oars so he could poke along the shallow banks, or he started the engine and roared up the Rappahannock, throwing spray all the way to the Tappahannock bridge.

It didn't matter whether he scooped soft crabs from eelgrass or dangled a line for croaker in deep water. Only that he was on the river under his own power, the sun spangling the waves, the air rich with sea smell.

When summer ended, both he and his father returned to Martinsburg. The house felt empty, but his friends were in Martinsburg, his things, his memories. His father played the part of parent in the only way he understood, as rule-maker, and nursed his own wound in silence. Without his mother, much of the softness of home life hardened. He scraped against his father's harsh discipline.

All through the school year Jerry longed to return to the river. The johnboat, stored under a canvas tarp, waited. When summer arrived, he left for his grandmother's. As he hurried toward the water, she insisted he take a life jacket, warned him not to speed. But she let him go. She trusted him. In all those hours alone he learned the geometry of every creek and cove. He worked his way down the river toward Windmill Point and the Chesapeake Bay and dreamed of open ocean.

Back in Martinsburg, he sat in his room on dreary winter weekends and read of clipper ships, of far-off shores, of wind in the rigging. In college he discovered Joseph Conrad and Herman Melville and, later, the writings of solo sailor Bernard Moitessier. He started a journal and copied lines from *Lord Jim*: "he had traveled very far, on various ways, on strange paths, and what-ever he followed it had been without faltering, and therefore without shame and without regret." He wanted to travel that way. Without faltering. Without regret. He wanted to strike out like Conrad for the wide world and to peer with Whitman into his own soul.

What do you need camerado?

Rachel stirred in the V-berth. Was she awake?

He opened his eyes and looked at the cabin ceiling, varnished wood. Though the sloop had a fiberglass hull, the cabintop, the decks, the cockpit were all wood, teak and mahogany. Beautiful, but a lot of work, and always the threat of rot. This past July Fourth, he had found it. As he pushed a screwdriver along the edges of the cockpit floor to scrape away wet residue, the blade went right through. He had no choice but to replace the whole cockpit floor. Not an easy job, since once he ripped out the old floor he had nowhere to put his feet. It was like trying to replace a bathtub drain while standing on the sides. He spent all of August in the sticky Chesapeake heat pouring resin on his shoes, swatting mosquitoes, and dropping stainless steel screws into the bottomless bilge. At last the cockpit floor was in, covered with too much resin in hopes that it would never rot again.

So here they were. A mountain boy at heart, he had spent his grandmother's inheritance on this boat, and now doubt crowded his mind. He could almost hear his father's voice, *What are you doing, young man?* His father, who now sold furniture part time in Martinsburg.

There was no turning back. He and Rachel had both committed to this dream of going to sea. They had schemed for a year off without pay, a year away from Martinsburg, where for fifteen years they both taught high school — he English, she French. Every day as he worked his way through period after period and paper after paper, his thoughts returned to this vision of the open sea. So at the end of August they transferred all their worldly belongings to a rented storage space, a hollow cave with damp concrete floor. They imagined others who'd parked their furniture there after divorce, bankruptcy, or death. Then they pulled down the metal door, secured it with a padlock.

The keys to their two-story home they turned over to a young couple who'd rented the house for a year. In their old Honda station wagon stuffed full of clothes, books, and equipment, they pulled out of Martinsburg and headed down to Galesville, Maryland, where they kept their boat.

All the work on *Courageous* they'd planned for the summer remained undone because of the cockpit repair. As August ended and September began, they crawled around each other and over all the gear that got in their way as they drilled and banged and tried to install everything to make the boat, never designed for off-shore work, ready for sea.

He gave up on sleeping and stood up, lightheaded. He walked to the chart table and ran his fingers over oiled teak. Pulling the mic from its holder he clicked on the VHF and listened to make sure no one else was on 16. Then he pushed the transmit button.

"*Wanderer, Wanderer,* this is *Courageous.*" Nothing. He waited a moment then repeated his call.

The radio speaker crackled. "*Courageous,* this is *Wanderer.* Channel 10?"

"Channel 10." He flipped the dial.

"Hey, Jerry, what's up?"

"We've made our decision," he said. "We're leaving tonight."

"Why didn't you leave this morning, so you'd have all that daylight?" Bart asked.

"Just put the steering vane struts on today," he said. "Been working all day. For months, actually. And now we've got to go — there's a cold front coming."

"There's always a cold front coming," Bart said.

Rachel came out from the forward cabin, rubbing her eyes. "Tell him there's a full moon tonight," she said. "The weather should be good."

He said as much to Bart, who agreed they should have a good window to get across the Stream. He wanted to know what time they were pushing off.

"About three hours. The tide shifts before nine. We're going to the gas dock, then we're off."

"Me and Carla will come down to see you," Bart said.

"Tell him that would be nice," Rachel said. "I'd like to see Carla before we go."

When they hoisted anchor two hours later, he paused on the foredeck to look back at Beaufort. He thought of the warm glow of the pub. Of everyone gathered around the television telling tales of past adventures. He thought of the dollar bills stapled above the bar, with the names of boats written on them (one of them said *Courageous,* their 30-foot Swedish sloop). Now they were setting out on their own adventure. In two weeks they'd be sitting in a bar in Tortola, telling their own tale. Still, he felt a sense of foreboding. As if he were seeing all this for the last time. He was glad they'd made out a will before leaving Martinsburg.

Their son, now beginning his first year at the University of Maryland, would get everything.

He struggled with the anchors — one Bruce, one CQR, both tangled by the tide that ripped up and down the inlet and by a wind that seemed forever contrary. By the time they got to the gas dock, the day's last light was heading west. They were exhausted. The owner, just closing up, let them top off their tanks. "We're heading for the islands," he said.

The mustached man looked at him. "It's rough out there," he said.

"They'll be all right." He turned to see Carla standing by the pump. Bart was already walking down to have a look at the boat.

Rachel looked at the mustached man and then walked off to join Bart.

Jerry filled three plastic five-gallon jugs that he'd lash to the lifelines near the shrouds, while Carla stood watching him. Only one generation removed from Brazil, she spoke better English than Bart. She leaned against the pump, her olive skin barely covered by shorts and halter top. A good ten years younger than Bart, she was almost skinny, with dark Latin hair and alluring eyes — hazel and full of light. "It's late to be taking off, isn't it?" she asked, leaning back to stretch her arms over her head and suppressing a yawn.

"We'll be at sea for two weeks," he said. "What difference does it make what time we leave?"

"Yeah," she said. "I guess." She pulled one of her halter straps down and examined something near her armpit. "Damn mosquitoes," she said. Diesel fuel spilled onto his shoes.

"Damn," he said. He moved to the next jug.

"Sure you're awake?" Carla asked.

Bart walked over and said, "Looks like you're all set." He and Carla each grabbed a heavy jug and carried it to the edge of the dock. *Courageous* pulled at her lines. "I know I asked you this before, but did you think about taking along any crew? Two weeks is a long time at the wheel."

"Why, do you want to go?" Rachel asked hopefully.

"Oh not me," he said. "Unless you're paying. I've got to finance my own trip, remember? We should be heading for the Bahamas sometime before Christmas. But there are people around. You know. I could probably find somebody. I'm sure I could."

"Thanks, Bart," he said. "We're going to go it alone. We sort of planned it this way."

"Sure," Bart said. "I understand. You'll do fine."

"Well," Carla said, "break a leg." She leaned down from the dock and kissed him on the nose.

"Bye, Bart, and thanks for everything," Rachel said, pecking him on each check. He shook Bart's hand and said good-bye.

"Looks like you're all set," Bart said again. He took hold of the bowline. "Don't forget to stay close to Radio Island on your way out. Bad shoal on the left." Jerry nodded. Bart stood above them on the dock, his blonde hair shaggy, his four-day beard unshaven. As charter boat captain, he'd made many trips from here to the islands, one of them in a small hurricane, and experience surrounded him with a halo of confidence, of knowing. In his cut-off jeans and T-shirt he looked completely at ease.

The engine already in forward, *Courageous* edged from the pier. Bart threw the bowline onto the foredeck, and Carla moved along the dock to put an arm around his waist. They waved and shouted words of farewell. Then they receded into the dim shoreline and vanished.

"This is it," Rachel said.

He looked at her as she stood on the foredeck, coiling the bowline. They wouldn't be needing that line — for a thousand miles. "This is it all right," he answered and gave her a thumbs-up sign. She couldn't see it in the dusk.

Now he leaned left and right to see around the dodger. The moon climbed above the horizon's haze and shone full on the water. Its light carved clear silhouettes of daymarkers. On their starboard side Radio Island loomed, dark castle with broken pilings. He wanted to steer away from that ragged bulkhead and whatever structure that was on land, but he knew deep water favored this side. To the left a broad sandbar lay only a few feet beneath the surface. Bart had run aground there himself and had a tough time getting off.

"Should we be this far over?" Rachel called back.

"I think so," he said.

"Do you see the pilings?"

"I see them."

After they slid past Radio Island, he had an awkward moment of uncertainty. Where was the channel? He remembered the shifting channel coming into Beaufort from the Intracoastal Waterway, where boat after boat hit bottom, giving the local prop and shaft shops plenty of business. The biggest problem all along the ICW, especially near sounds or ocean cuts, was the side-setting current. He would aim straight at a channel marker, but the one behind would steadily head east. Or west. Until, boom, they were on the bottom, still staring straight ahead at the marker.

As they made the trip south down the "ditch" from the Chesapeake to Beaufort, he'd been conscious, as he maneuvered in and out of guts, cuts, and canals, not only of the currents but of a presence to his left, a shadow rarely glimpsed but always there. The shadow was the Atlantic Ocean. The Big Pond. The sea that stretched from the Old World to the New, 3,000 miles, where waves coming from north or south or east took their time gathering strength and mass until they lazily slammed into aircraft carriers or flipped sixty-foot schooners.

He had never seen the Gulf Stream. In fact, neither of them had ever been offshore, with the exception of a summer's trip to Block Island and Newport, their only overnight at sea. He was a West Virginia boy born and bred and, in the summer, a Chesapeake Bay sailor, nothing more. He felt at ease guiding *Courageous* up and down rivers, just as he was now guiding her out

Beaufort inlet and between harbor buoys — but beyond these blinking buoys all lights vanished. Once they left the shallow continental shelf, no lines could reach to anchor either buoy or boat. The bottom dropped down a steep cliff, five hundred feet, then a thousand, then two thousand, then three. By the time the boat passed over the ancient sea bottom, the depth finder (if it could reach that far) would read 6,000 feet, then 12,000 and more. They would be flying far higher than the Blue Ridge Mountains in their five-and-a-half-ton bird. Heaven help them if they fell from that sky.

Rachel looked back. In the moonlight he looked pale. She turned and stared ahead again, the bow wave whispering beneath her. The lights of Beaufort and Atlantic Beach slowly fell behind. Soon they would pass the last harbor markers and be free of land. Liberated. She had dreamed of this all her life, since curling up in bed with those books by Richard Halliburton that her father gave her, and since that trip she'd taken to Europe, her junior year in college, on the *S.S. France*. She remembered how everyone stayed below at night, to dance and drink, but she went on deck to stare at the broad Atlantic. Something pulled her toward the sea, to this open space, something that made her free.

For a long while she stood on the bow, staring at the full moon. The night held calm, and with the moon so bright the sea looked benign, warm, luminescent. At last she made her way back to the cockpit, bringing the bow line with her and stowing it with other lines in the locker. She could hardly find a place, with so many things jammed in. "We're loaded to the gills," she said.

"You got that right."

"How're you feeling? Tired?"

"I'm okay," he said. "How about you?"

"Bushed. I'm going to go below and get some sleep. We might as well start our watches now, or else we'll both be exhausted."

"Good idea."

"Are you strapped in? I wouldn't want to lose you."

He held up the nylon line for her to see. This was the first time they'd worn lifelines, hooked to stainless steel cables that he'd run the full length of the boat. He'd put a short line here in the cockpit as well. The tether felt unfamiliar and gave him the sensation that he was inviting disaster by preparing for it. "Go ahead and get some sleep," he said. "I'll motor for a while. The batteries need charging, and there isn't much wind to speak of."

"Call me if you need me," she said. She came to the binnacle and kissed him on the mouth with full lips.

She disappeared down the companionway and he held the wheel, steering generally east. The important thing was to get across the Stream — before the next cold front hit. With a thousand miles of ocean ahead, and with who-knew what winds and currents, it seemed futile to set a course just yet. The Stream would sweep them north until they got across it. The main thing was to cross the Stream, then they could get a fix and set a course.

At the same time, this abandonment of dead-reckoning unsettled him. All his sailing life he had depended on the compass, on his sense of set and drift. But now he would have to rely on the satnav, a new experiment for him — one reading had placed him five miles inland, in the suburbs of Morehead City. And on celestial navigation, which he'd never practiced outside of a classroom. Even in class his answers weren't all that consistent. He worried how, with the boat pitching up and down, he was going to plot a course with a plastic sextant and whether he could remember the sequence of formulas. Height of eye and all that.

He glanced to see how fast he was going, but the companionway doors — swung open on their hinges — blocked that part of the bulkhead. Actually, what difference did it make? Anyway you looked at it, it was going to take them two weeks to get there. Two weeks. He hoped the steering vane worked — they didn't have an autopilot and couldn't afford one — because otherwise they would be pretty tired of steering . . .

Against his right knee a small circle of light turned his skin a sickly shade of amber. The amp light. It had been on for about two weeks now. The mechanic wasn't sure, but he thought the generator part of his Dynastart had gone bad, which was okay as long as the starter worked, and as long as the free-standing alternator worked. He'd stared at the mechanic, at the alternator. What would you do? he asked. "Me? I dunno. I guess I'd just keep toolin along."

So here he was, tooling along, the amp light throwing its constant caution sign, heading into the Atlantic Ocean, everything depending on the alternator — the navigation lights, the knot meter, the depth finder, the radio, the cabin lights, the LORAN, the satnav . . . everything. He'd tried to rig a third battery, just in case, but he screwed up the wiring and ruined the new battery, and the battery switch didn't always make contact now either. He tried to keep all these thoughts suppressed in his mind, because there was nothing he could do. The only thing was to go for it and hope everything worked. He headed east, with an unexplainable phrase running through his head: "whistling in the dark."

The last buoy disappeared astern, the only beacon still visible the lighthouse on Cape Lookout, behind them, far off on shore. The sea stayed calm, but he knew when they entered the Gulf Stream the waves would become unpredictable. In fact, he could see up ahead what appeared to be a breaking wave already. It was not too large though, and he lined the bow up to take it head on. When it struck, the wave sent a shock through the whole length of the boat and jarred his brain. He had hit the bottom. The boat arched sideways with the next wave and came down with a crash. Now waves seemed to break all around him, and when he looked up he saw the piercing eye of the lighthouse.

Wham! the hull hit the bottom again, and Rachel scrambled through the companionway, holding the door that banged loose as the boat rose on the next wave and slammed against the bottom. "What's going on?" she cried. "Damn," he said, throwing the engine in reverse and giving it full power. "Damn. Call the Coast Guard," he said. "Tell them we're on Cape Lookout

Shoals." As he said this a beam of light swept across her face. He had failed her.

Now the lighthouse seemed to suck them toward shore, and waves and current worked together to pull them farther onto the bar. Wham! the hull hit hard, and then the boat leaned on its side, pivoting on the sand with a prolonged screech, as if in agony.

With the companionway door banging out of the way, he could see that the depth finder was not on. Nor was the knot-meter or the satnav or the LORAN. What had he been thinking?

"The Coast Guard wants to know our position," Rachel said. Her voice seemed remarkably calm. "Do we have a LORAN fix?"

"No," he said. "We don't." The hull rose and slammed against the bottom again. "Rachel," he said. "I think we may have lost the boat."

She looked at him and said nothing. "What should I tell the Coast Guard?"

"Here, let's trade places. I've got her in reverse. Just try to back her out of this mess."

Rachel put the mic down and pulled herself into the cockpit. She could hardly believe her eyes. The soft and gentle sea now broke in whitecaps all around.

"Coast Guard, this is *Courageous*, do you read me?"

"Roger, *Courageous*, what is your position?"

"Stand by. I'm getting a LORAN fix." He switched on the LORAN, which took forever to cycle through its routine check.

"*Courageous*, there are two people on board, is that correct?"

"Roger, Coast Guard."

"Do you have your life vests on?"

"Roger Coast Guard." He looked around to see where one was.

"*Courageous*, do you have a life raft?"

"Affirmative. We have a life raft."

"What color is it?"

"It's . . . orange, I think."

"Do you have a position yet?"

"I'm working on it," he said.

"Roger. Standing by."

He stared at the LORAN and tried to think of what to do, but it was hard to think with the boat slamming against the sandbar. The LORAN was old, an early model that he'd gotten from a friend for free. He hardly ever used it — he didn't really need it in the Bay — and he was having a hard time remembering how to operate the damn thing. It used TD's and therefore required a chart with overprinted LORAN lines. A new LORAN, which displayed longitude and latitude would have been a thousand times better. He struggled to read small numbers printed on the chart beside the LORAN lines, all in different colors. The chain, that's what he needed. He punched it in and hit the auto button.

"*Courageous, Courageous, Courageous,* this is the United States Coast Guard Fort Macon Group, do you read me?"

"This is *Courageous.* Go ahead."

"Do you have a fix yet, Captain?"

"It's coming up now." He felt like smacking the LORAN, but wait, here were numbers, logical numbers, appearing in an ordered sequence, one after the other . . . He read the numbers to the Coast Guard before he had even decided which chain was the best one to use. In fact, their only chart with LORAN lines was one that covered the whole southeast coast. The numbers told him only that he was in the vicinity of Cape Lookout shoals. He knew that already.

"*Courageous,* this is Fort Macon Group. Captain, these are some pretty strange numbers."

"Roger, Coast Guard. We have an old LORAN unit. Some of those numbers should be good, though." He looked up through the companionway at Rachel. Her tongue was stuck in her cheek and she leaned to one side, as if willing the boat away from the shoal. She wore a fixed, almost angelic expression. The banging stopped.

He reached up and switched on the depth finder, and the knotmeter too. "What does the depth finder say?" he called. She looked at the bulkhead for a moment and then sang out, "Eight feet. Ten feet. Fourteen feet."

He sprang into the cockpit. "Take a heading of two nine zero," he said.

"*Courageous, Courageous*, this is United States Coast Guard Fort Macon Group."

He jumped back down the companionway. "Roger, Coast Guard, I think we're off."

"Repeat that, Captain. What is your status?"

"I think we're off. We're in fourteen feet of water."

"Twenty-two," Rachel sang out.

"Correction, twenty-two feet of water."

"What is your heading, Captain?"

"Two nine zero," he said. "Two hundred ninety degrees."

The radio stayed silent for a moment, once more a small gray box with the words "Standard Horizon" on the front. Then it spoke again, "That looks good, Captain. We have you at an estimated position of approximately fifteen miles at a bearing of about one hundred degrees from the Beaufort Inlet, on the edge of the Cape Lookout Shoals."

"Roger, Coast Guard, that sounds correct. I was trying to get too much easting I guess."

"What is your destination?"

"We were heading for the Virgin Islands," he said. The idea now struck him as crazy.

"Do you have any damage?"

"I'll check. Stand by."

He hung up the mic and pulled a flashlight out of the drawer. If there was one thing he knew, it was this boat. He knew every support, every seacock. He lifted the floorboards one by one and looked in the bilge, looked for water coming in, looked for stress cracks. Sure enough, several of the wooden supports that held the floorboards had popped loose from the hull where fiberglass tabbing had broken. Near the chainplates he saw stress cracks and some separation where the deck met the bulkhead — had that been there before? He flashed his light in all the lockers, under the V-berth, the settee, the starboard berth.

"Coast Guard, this is *Courageous.*"

"Go ahead, Captain."

"Some floor supports broke loose. I can't see anything else."

"Are you taking any water, Captain?"

"Negative. Don't see any water."

"Do you require any assistance at this time?"

"No, Coast Guard. We'll call if anything develops."

"Roger, Captain. We could check back in exactly one hour to make sure everything's all right. Should we do that?"

"That would be good. Thanks."

"What is your current heading, *Courageous?*"

"Still two nine zero. We'll hold that course for a while until we regroup. We may want to return to Beaufort to check the bottom of the hull."

"Roger, Captain. We'll speak to you in one hour."

"Roger. Out."

"This is United States Coast Guard Fort Macon Group out."

He hung up the mic again and climbed the companionway steps. The lighthouse on Cape Lookout flashed. Rachel stood at the wheel, glancing alternatively at the lighted compass, the depth finder, the horizon. She appeared in control, her curly hair blown back from her face. He was in awe of her.

"I blew it," he said.

———

They tacked off the coast until dawn and then sailed back into Beaufort Inlet, anchoring in Town Creek and crawling into the double berth to sleep. They had spent months preparing for the launch date, and now time seemed to unravel, with no clear pattern. Beaufort harbor changed. As the last of the boats preparing for the November jump left, the town's energy dropped a notch. They hauled *Courageous* at the local yard and looked for damage. Along the bottom, the sandbar had abraded paint and gelcoat, and a quarter-sized chunk of fiberglass was gone. They patched it, but it wasn't anything to worry about. The glass was thick at the bottom of the keel.

Courageous went back in the water and they anchored in Town Creek, their confidence shaken, trying to decide if they were ready to set out again. They called their son in College Park and told him that they hadn't left after all. They said they would call when they set out again. He sounded relieved that they were still on solid ground and not at sea. Then they called their friend Nan, the designated contact, who was confused. She didn't understand what had happened. They said everything was fine and that they would call when they had firmed up their plan.

"Firmed up your plan? I thought you'd been planning this for years. What's there to firm up?"

They said they would call her. They climbed back in the dinghy and rowed out to the boat. *Courageous.*

"Well," he said. "Let's get everything buttoned down again."

The very next morning, while they ate hot oatmeal and made a new list, the VHF radio announced a gale warning. It was the first time local forecasters used that word. They thought about what to do. Their anchorage was as protected as they were going to get in this area, so they threw out a third anchor and let out more line. That evening the sky grew dark and the wind cold. By nightfall the wind hit a steady thirty knots in the harbor — who knew what it was blowing offshore . . . Near them, a sleek white sailboat dragged anchor and quickly ran aground by the commercial fishing dock. Another boat threw them a line and tried to pull them off, to no avail. As the tide ebbed, the grounded boat lay on its side, white walrus, stranded and squirming in shallow waves.

After the gale passed, the sky tried to go blue, and they began working on the boat again. He refiberglassed the floor supports to the hull, and reinforced the area where the deck and bulkhead had separated slightly. He also looked at the amp light again, but he couldn't do anything about it. The boat would never be perfect, he realized — they were still as ready as they would ever be. But as they planned their next departure, the radio called for a second gale, and they hunkered down. The night was gentle and deceiving, but the next day wind whipped across the harbor, even colder this time. Again they put down their third anchor. The boat shook in ponderous gusts.

With the passing of the gales something changed. The light grew thinner, the sea darker. Night winds, no longer balmy, bore the edge of winter. Still, they knew if they could get past the Stream, the water and then the air would warm, and they would get a little farther south every day.

They prepared to leave again, topping off fuel and water tanks. But as they stowed their food and clothes, the radio called for a third front, with strong winds from the north. They returned to their same spot and put down all three anchors. His hands felt raw against the wet anchor lines. Harbor mud covered his yellow foul weather gear. In the shuddering cabin they huddled by the VHF radio. The Coast Guard announced regular updates on channel 22, and they switched the dial to hear reports of boats in trouble off shore. One sailboat, *Bodacious*, was hit by large seas, damaged and adrift. "It sounds like mayhem out there," Rachel said.

He looked at her through the steam of hot chocolate. "I think it would be better to head down the ICW," he said. "Once we get south we can set out from there."

"Do you think so?" she said.

"It's getting too cold," he said. "We need to get south."

She stood and looked through the narrow portlight, as if to see whether he were right. Wind pushed small waves across the harbor, crests folding into foam. "White caps," she said, "even in the harbor." The sky dropped a shade.

They tried to call Bart on the radio, but got no answer. It turned out he was away, doing salvage work. When they got hold of Carla she said, "What the hell are you doing here?" They told her the whole story. "Damn. What a month this is turning out to be. Bart's on *Dauntless*. They're holed up in Oregon Inlet. They were trying to get a menhaden boat off the banks. Then the weather came up, and they had to split. The Coast Guard told them not to come in at Oregon Inlet, that it was too rough, but they said the hell with that and they came in anyway. It must be pretty bad out there."

Yes, he said, it must be.

They agreed to drop by the boat when they came ashore. Mostly they had been on board, they said. They hadn't really gone much of anywhere.

"Well, if you got time on your hands, you ought to at least see the marine museum," Carla said.

They ambled into town and into the museum, a place they'd passed many times.

Rachel lingered by the collection of books about the Outer Banks, the Graveyard of the Atlantic. He stood staring at the models of boats, at the miniature masts and centerboards and rudders, and as he stared he shrank until he was a small boy again, looking at ship models in the Mariner's Museum in Newport News, where his mother had brought him. The ships had fascinated him then, seeming more than real, the shouts of sailors in the air, the wash of waves at the bow, burying the dolphin striker. He was at sea, with the wind in the rigging and he at the crosstrees. What land lay ahead, just over the horizon, he could not say. Hispaniola, perhaps, or the Lesser Antilles, or the Gold Coast. All he knew was he was at sea, with the spray over the windward side, the deadeyes wet and dripping and the ratlines taut from the strain of wind.

He looked at the models again and saw the caulking, the screws, the bent planks, the rust, the rot. He had lost the sea. It was no longer in him.

"This is the chart we should have had," Rachel said, and he joined her to look at it.

It was true. They had charts of the entire ICW; they had charts of the islands, from the U.S. Virgins clear down to Venezuela. But this piece of the puzzle, the crucial middleground between land and sea they did not have. He pointed to a single three-foot hump on the fringe of the shoals. "I bet that's what we hit," he said.

"We could have easily missed that," she said. "Then we would have made it."

"Until the gales came," he said.

"Maybe we would have been out far enough."

"Maybe," he said.

Anchors and nets and shards of hulls regarded him, holy relics from the sea. He was the recanter, the defector, the apostate.

"Thanksgiving is next week," Rachel said. "Do you think we'll still be here?"

"Who knows?" he said.

"Carla invited us to eat with them on *Wanderer*. Bart's back. I thought it was nice of them to invite us."

Yes, he said it was.

For Thanksgiving they moved *Courageous* into a slip. Wind rattled the halyards of other boats. Water sloshed against the bulkhead. He hopped up on the dock and walked to the end. The wind. How many times had he stood at the ends of docks, or even on the balconies of apartments, and felt the wind in his hair and dreamed of going to sea. But was it really the sea where he wanted to go, or did he long for something else, to return to the inorganic, as Freud might have said, and not the real sea at all . . .

The moon was waning now. Clouds raced through the fading light like white caps on the crests of waves.

"It's cold."

Jerry turned to see Rachel standing behind him. She came closer and he put his arm around her. "It's the wind," he said.

"I bet it's howling out there."

He tried to imagine the waves piling up in this north wind, there, in the Stream. Was that the inorganic he was looking for?

"Bart and Carla have dinner ready," she said.

He kept looking out over the harbor, as if he could see beyond it to the sea itself. She tugged at his arm, and they turned and walked back down the dock and climbed aboard *Wanderer*.

Bart and Carla sat in the shelter of the dodger and stood as they saw their company coming. "Let's eat!" Carla said. He followed everyone down the companionway. The kerosene lanterns cast a yellow light, and the cabin felt warm from the stove.

"She's been cooking all afternoon," Bart said.

"Yeah, and Bart's been a big help . . . "

Bart looked at him and opened his mouth as if he'd been goosed.

They crowded around the small teak table and Carla kept bringing food, until they had no place to put it. She'd made a turkey in the propane oven, and stuffing and peas and mashed potatoes. He and Rachel had bought cranberry sauce and a bottle of Cold Duck that they opened and poured all around.

"To good friends," he said.

"And the devil and the deep blue sea," Bart added.

Bart turned his attention to the turkey, which he'd already begun to carve. "White meat?" he said to Rachel.

He knew that Bart had been arrested by the Coast Guard once. A strange thing, really, since Bart had graduated from the Virginia Military Institute in Lexington and had considered a career in the service. But he'd become a delivery skipper, piloting boats from the East Coast to the Caribbean, and then down through Central and South America. And at one point the cargo he carried was not legal. The Coast Guard had intercepted him at sea, had put him in chains. In chains.

When everyone had finished Rachel said, "I brought dessert." Carla looked skeptical, but Rachel reached into her small blue duffel as if performing a magic trick. "All right!" Bart said. "Snickers!"

They returned to the cockpit, huddled behind the dodger and out of the wind. He and Rachel hunched together because of the cold, while Carla kept shifting her weight; only Bart seemed at ease, his feet — in old running shoes — propped by the companionway. "Well," Bart said, "what's the plan?"

"We're still thinking about it," he said.

"We're still thinking about the big passage," Rachel said.

"Sure," Bart said.

"Problem is," Jerry said, "gale season has arrived."

"You still might find a window. I've left here right on through December."

"Really?" Rachel seemed interested.

"Heck, year before last we left with snow on the deck — remember that, Carla?"

Carla was finishing her drink and so didn't answer. She just looked at Jerry over the rim of her cup.

"So you think we could still make it all right?" Rachel said.

"Sure. You could make it all right."

Carla lowered her drink and said, "Why don't you join us in the Bahamas?"

"The Bahamas," Jerry repeated. "Aren't they a little too close to Florida? Crowded?"

"Less crowded than the Virgins," Bart said. "People think of Nassau, but the Bahamas stretch seven hundred miles into the Atlantic. Hundreds of islands. Places with no people at all — just iguanas."

"Sounds remote," he said.

Rachel looked at Bart. "Where will you and Carla go?"

"We have to think about the finances," he said. "But if we go south we'll probably jump off from Palm Beach and head for Cat

Island. We hung out there last year. Nice place. Low key. Local folks really hospitable."

"We made good friends there," Carla said.

"That's a long way down the ICW," Jerry said.

Carla shrugged.

———

Their heads light with food and wine, they walked back to *Courageous*. The sloop lay snug in its rented slip. They stepped aboard and pushed open the companionway hatch — it squealed in the cold. Down below they plugged in the electric space heater they'd bought the day before. As they watched, its silver sinews turned red.

"What do you think?" he said. "Should we head for the Bahamas?"

"But what about the Virgins?"

"We can head east from Florida," he said. "See how far we get."

She looked at the chart of the Atlantic that lay open on the settee table. He tried to take her hand.

She started to say something more. In her eyes swam reflections of the cabin light. Pushing past, she went to the head and closed the door. He collapsed on the starboard berth and stared at the bookshelf above the settee. His eyes wandered over the titles until they fixed on a book Rachel had given him years before, when they graduated college. *Gypsy Moth Circles the World*, by Sir Francis Chichester. He got up and pulled the hardcover book from the shelf. The dust jacket pictured the fifty-three-foot ketch *Gypsy Moth IV* heeling with a single jib as it rounded Cape Horn through towering waves. On the inside flap he found Rachel's tight handwriting. She had dedicated the book to him and to their own adventure, their dream of taking to the sea. Back on the berth, he lay the book on his chest and closed his eyes. The electric heater hum filled the cabin. He felt the boat rise and fall on unimaginable waves. All night wind rattled halyards against the mast.

The next morning, at dawn, the diesel blew white smoke from the stern of *Courageous*. Beaufort lay quiet, waiting for winter. They pulled lines from pilings and felt the hull slide out of the slip. The bow swung into the harbor. They stood at the wheel, the two of them in their winter vests, and steered south down the long, sheltered ditch.

At Sea

IN LATE NOVEMBER OF THAT YEAR a powerful storm swept through the Bahama Islands, reaching as far south as Conception Island below the Exumas. The storm brought deep snow to the Midwest and sent gale warnings up south of Hatteras. There pounding seas sank the ninety-foot commercial tug, *Winchester*, five men pulled off at the last minute by a marine helicopter dispatched by Fort Macon. Nat Taylor misjudged the strength and speed of that storm, putting out from Port Everglades for the Berry Islands in a Peterson 44, just ahead of the front. With fifteen years experience as delivery captain and live-aboard cruiser, he had outfitted *Zealot* with all the usual gear — including satellite navigation and radar — and had become over the years a respectable marine electrician, carpenter, and plumber. He knew *Zealot* was a good boat.

His mistake was not so much in timing the arrival of the storm as in anticipating the strength of the south wind that preceded the front. He wanted that south wind, since it would lengthen the swells of the Gulf Stream, swells which grew steep and dangerous in a northerly blow. What he didn't count on was the strength of gusts from the south, some thirty knots and more, presses of wind that lay his boat over and, along with the northerly track of the Gulf Stream, set him off course. He found himself beating back against the Stream to get his rhumb line, a slow and tedious slog that put him behind schedule and in the path of the cold front. Normally more cautious, Nat would have preferred to wait out unsettled weather, and as the wind began its inevitable swing from southwest to west to northwest he cursed his own impatience.

He argued with himself about what had lured him onto these building seas, to make this mad dash across the Florida Straits and above the Great Bahama Bank. Wasn't it, he asked himself with considerable irony, a woman he hardly knew, who, with her girlfriend, was a guest aboard the huge motor yacht *Out-of-Sight*, now anchored at Great Stirrup Cay?

As he braced himself against the wheel, it occurred to him that his entire life, his less-than-brilliant career in college, his on-and-off business dealings, some of which he preferred to not recall, not to admit to, had all led to this mad quest. Holding the wheel and staring into the chaotic night, he felt like a traveler who had topped a hill so that he can see at last where he has come and where he is heading. And all he could see was water.

Pan-Pan Pan-Pan Pan-Pan came the scratch of the radio, almost lost in the whistle of the wind. He set the autopilot and slid along the cockpit to the companionway. *Hello all stations. This is the United States Coast Guard. Break. The sailing vessel* Last Try *is reported damaged by high seas and adrift at latitude . . . North and longitude . . . West. Any vessel transiting the area should keep a sharp lookout and report all sightings to the United States Coast Guard. Break. This is the United States Coast Guard out.* He could never catch the latitude and longitude in these announcements but it sounded like *Last Try* lay well north and west of his position. Probably right in the axis of the Gulf Stream. Grabbing the edge of the dodger he stuck his head up to see if he could spot anything and took a face-full of spray. Nights like this always reminded him of boxing, the sea weaving and dodging and then planting a right cross when he forgot to duck. He looked again, wiping water from his eyes with an open palm. Total darkness, the gibbous moon captured by the cold front's advance guard. Now began that slow wait he often endured on night passages, when all his mental energies focused on the east, as if he

could will the rise of the sun. He could endure anything in daylight.

Only tonight his energies did not center entirely on the sun;
he saw, as he took the wheel back from the autopilot, the face of
the woman he had come to know over these last weeks, as if her
face too were rising in the east as *Zealot* labored to bring the
Berry Islands over the horizon. This vision strengthened him and
buoyed his spirits more than the hot coffee he sipped from his red
thermos. For a time he felt exhilarated, confident, the reefed
main, staysail, and mostly rolled genoa enough to power him
eastward, and he knew if he could hang on through the night the
west wind would send him flying along the Northwest Providence
Channel, just above the Great Bahama Bank, toward the northern tip of the Berry Islands and Great Stirrup Cay. There this
woman waited — though not for long, since in a few days' time
she and her friend would ascend the hollow and fragile-seeming
ladder of a chartered airplane and leave him to this tropical landscape, to its turquoise emptiness and clarity. They would return
to the concrete and asphalt realities of Washington, D.C., a city
that she described as "an architect's caprice." She seemed a rare
sea bird that only winged south for one month each year, and he
pushed the boat so as not to miss the season. Again the wind laid
him over, the stern skidding sideways, and again he knew he
would have to shorten sail.

Setting the autopilot, he clipped onto a jackline and crabbed
forward, water hissing past the leeward rail at his feet. His hands,
doomed to super slow motion, groped to find the correct cleat, to
loosen the proper line, to wrap the right winch, each attempt
halted and postponed by the rising pitch and fall of the boat in
the waves. He leaned toward the mast to retighten the main halyard but found that he had forgotten the winch handle and he slid
back to the cockpit to retrieve it. After pulling himself along the
handrails to the mast again, he found the pressure on the mainsail too great and crawled hand-over-hand back to the cockpit to
further ease the mainsheet. By the time the main hung trim from

its new reef points he fell exhausted beside the wheel and sat in a stupor as the autopilot tried to steer the boat through rising seas. For long undulating moments he watched as the autopilot raced to catch up with the wild sway of the boat while one wave after another lifted, turned, and dropped the hull. Unlike a helmsman, the autopilot could not anticipate the larger waves and like a dumb beast reacted too late to forces that pushed it off course, unaware, without understanding, wasting the wind.

He took the wheel for a few short moments but then engaged the autopilot again so he could roll in the rest of the genoa jib. Now *Zealot* settled into a steady pounding under double-reefed main and staysail, and he thought again of a boxer taking body blows, saying to himself, *I can stand this.* When he took the wheel once more he lost patience not only with the autopilot but with himself: like the autopilot he had moved through his life reacting too late to every force that found him, dumb to whatever magnets guided his mind. He was lacking some knack for life, and he wondered now whether this person he had come to know pointed toward a truer pole.

Though the Gulf Stream had pushed him predictably to the north, once near the banks currents became less clear, so he returned the wheel to the autopilot's robot hand and forced himself below to the nav station. The storm's decibels dropped as he climbed down into the cabin, but the small basket full of bananas over the counter swung wildly and the water he'd left in the galley sink sloshed back and forth with each rising and falling wave. Normally accustomed to the motion of the sea, he felt a sudden queasiness and looked longingly at the half-opened companionway hatch. He knew he had to check his course carefully: the Great Bahama Bank lay barely submerged to the south, with its scattered sand bores and coral heads, invisible in the darkness. Hitting a reef in this weather would mean almost certain death, sharp coral driving holes through the fiberglass hull and tearing a life raft — and its occupant — to tatters.

Nat had made the trip to the Berrys before, usually stopping at Bimini or Cat Cay but sailing right past Great Isaac and its towering light when in a hurry to get east. And tonight he was in a hurry. He had passed Great Isaac at about 19:00, steering north to clear Northeast Rock before setting a course to the southeast, toward the light at Great Stirrup Cay (which he hoped was working). Why in the world *Out-of-Sight* had chosen this particular island was beyond him. As far as he knew only a cruise liner or two made regular stops there to let troops of tourists ashore for a brief rum-inspired bash on the beach. Otherwise there was nothing there but a lighthouse and a military tracking station.

Just as the satnav came up with its bright green numbers — a brilliant digital idea — the staysail began whacking at the cabintop. Reluctantly he stuck his arms back into the wet foul weather gear and threw the companionway doors open to the howling night. The staysail had gone crazy in the veering wind. He adjusted the sheet and the sail strained with the load, the boat shouldering the waves. For crying out loud, he yelled at the black wind. Almost in answer he heard a long rushing hiss, a serpent let loose in the night and his own reptilian blood lost all heat — another vessel, a large ship perhaps . . . *Hisssssss*. Then he saw the pale white tumbling crest of a mothering wave that had gotten itself crosswise to the sea, bearing down from a northerly direction and reaching for his chest he felt the absence of his life harness. Lunging for the cockpit, he managed to dive through the companionway as the wave hit, a mountainous rush of water following him down the hatch as he sputtered and cursed. Damn! he yelled. Damn! He knew better than to leave the companionway open in this weather, and yet here he was, up to his crotch, swamped like some novice sailor, water washing in every direction, soaking the berths, the table, everything that was his home. For a moment he heard the electric pump whir in its effort to clear the bilge, but then it stopped, leaving a sickening absence of sound. The batteries had shorted out and that meant the ship's whole electrical system. Everything. Son of a bitch! he yelled, smacking the water. Along with the bilge pump died all the lights — the cabin lights, the nav station lights, the bright green numbers of the satnav — all vanishing like so many up-raised hands disappearing into the darkness of a slough or bog. Or like a boat vanishing beneath the surface of the sea.

This is serious, he thought. He leaned forward in nearly waist-deep water in total darkness. He felt around for his life harness, holding his breath as he crawled along the cabin sole grasping for the line. On the third try he found it but as soon as he stood a wave lifted and dropped the boat and slammed him into the chart table. For a moment small lights wandered through the darkness, almost a relief in the pitch black. He tried to rise but as the boat wallowed water sloshed through the cabin, throwing him off balance and splashing his opened eyes. Am I being punished? he wondered, and for the first time since his early teenage years the word came to him: *predestination.* He remembered the minister explaining this to him before admitting him to the confirmation class (his mother's idea). Presbyterians, he had said, believe in predestination.

Was this it then? Had his childhood, his protracted adolescence, all his tentative choices and (he confessed) half-hearted relationships led him to this, this . . . destiny? For the past several days he had entertained the fatuous notion that all his missteps, all his bad plans, had changed, been redeemed, the moment he had met Bea, but now he felt the future threatened by one fact that seemed difficult, no, impossible to dispute: his boat was sinking.

He fumbled with the life harness, his back braced against the chart table, legs spread, as if preparing to parachute from an airplane, and once he'd snapped the clip into place across his breastbone he waded to the companionway and pulled himself up and out. In the cockpit the noise of the slatting sails almost deafened him — of course the autopilot had died and the boat had swung around into the wind, almost close-hauled but sliding backwards, a good way to break the rudder . . . After clipping a line to his life harness, he grabbed the wheel with one hand and with the other cranked as hard as could on the port-side winch, sheeting in the staysail and bringing the bow out of the eye of the wind;

then he locked the wheel, the main pulled all the way in. Now he was hove to, with a boatful of water. He searched for the flashlight he'd left on the cockpit seat, but it had either washed overboard or was sloshing around in the flooded cockpit. Instead his hands found the long bilge pump handle dangling from its lanyard and he shoved it into the familiar fitting on the side of the kickpanel. As he began to pump, he caught himself looking at the dim white box secured on deck, the white box that contained his life raft, and he knew that part of himself was ready to throw the thing overboard and pull the pin. Easy now, he said out loud. Easy now, as if he were calming a restive horse. He paused long enough to make certain the companionway was secure then returned to the pump, wondering . . . how many hours will it take, how many strokes to pump it dry? But there were no choices to be made now, no reason even to think, only himself and the pump as he tried to find the rhythm of the waves, back and forth, back and forth, an ex-Presbyterian bobbing before the wind.

As he pumped he recited to himself the things he didn't like about this situation. He didn't like having no running lights in a seaway on a dark night. He didn't like the water standing in the cockpit, the boat so low on her lines that the scuppers wouldn't drain properly. (He knew that any water making its way over the coaming and into the cockpit would stay there and soon sink him.) He didn't like losing the autopilot — or the radio. (For a moment he thought of the urgent message he'd heard earlier — with no way to alert the Coast Guard there would be no such message about him.) And most of all, he thought, rocking forward and backward on the pump handle, he didn't like losing the satnav and the LORAN because now he didn't know where he was.

For a brief moment he considered altering his course, assuming he could keep the boat afloat. He could head back toward the Florida coast, where the harbors were well maintained and well marked, but this would mean battling not only the northwest wind but also the axis of the Gulf Stream, an unpleasant proposition. Retracing his steps to Great Isaac or Bimini in this weather at night was downright impossible, even if he could navigate well enough to find out for certain where he was. Like so many harbors in the Bahamas, they were reef-ringed and tricky, better approached in daylight.

How how how had he brought himself to be here, his boat now feeling no more substantial than the white faces of foam that regarded him from every wave, whispering *predestination.*

⁓

Ida Taylor lifted the thin bow of a Venetian blind and looked at the black lake of the parking lot. Though small, her condominium in the Mount Vernon townhouses of Richmond, Virginia, had about it the weight and scale of the large homes owned by her mother and father and their parents before them, who had run a small furniture business in Richmond. As she often did, she thought of the business, how it had grown as the result of her grandfather's prodigious energy and discipline, but just as World War II had seemed to rob her spirit, all the young men (including her fiancée) leaving to cross the oceans, so it sapped the strength of the family. The business shrank and finally shriveled like the snake skins she used to see at her grandfather's gentleman farm in Goochland County. The farm was gone, the business gone, her parents gone, and she grown old. *Older than the hills*, she would tell her daughter, Celia.

The television droned on, the Wheel of Fortune, a show she hated but watched anyway. The wheel of fortune had left her pretty much alone, only her cat Patience to keep her company and those biweekly visits from Celia, regular and uninteresting. Now now, she said out loud, turning from the window, as if to speak to the cat, it doesn't pay to be bitter. The cat responded by nicking the sofa with exposed claws — she fanned at it with a rolled *People* magazine.

Nat had moved to Florida. For years she had comforted herself with the opinion that Nat was "finding himself," or perhaps even sowing those wild seeds which would one day sprout like chrysanthemums in her tiny townhouse yard, bearing, she felt sure, grandchildren. But as his years at sea accumulated with his letters in the bottom dresser drawer, she began to fear that he would never "return to his roots." This year, when her neighbor Florence Patilla pestered her with questions about her son, she answered that he had decided to move to Florida. After announcing this matter-of-factly and tolerating her neighbor's "Oh that's nice," she went into the bathroom and cried, cried as if her children had just left home, as if her husband had just walked out the door with that fake alligator suitcase to seek happiness between the legs of a trollop. Now she told everyone that Nat had decided to move to Florida, which helped put a stop to their questions and gave her something more definite than this open-ended waiting, even if she didn't like the idea very much. In fact, it brought upon her that emptiness she had tried to deny since her ex-husband Joe had first taken up with that slut Raylene — a regret sour enough to make her sick to her stomach.

Almost as if to call back the men who had left her she rose and walked, with some stiffness, to the bookshelf and reached for the cracked spine of a photo album. This was not normal: Ida Taylor did not moon over her personal past. With her quick breath, a cumulus cloud of dust rose from the book, testimony to its place, sedentary, on the shelf beside *A Stillness At Appomattox* and volumes about Virginia and the Civil War, more evidence of a past she couldn't fathom. The night had grown dark, the lack of light as heavy as snow on the roof, the temperature plunging after the passage of a strong cold front, the whole country taking early the first scythe blade of winter.

With rigid fingers she twisted up the thermostat before returning to the turquoise arm chair. She turned the yellowed pages of the album, the old-fashioned kind, with glue-on points dried and losing their hold pasted at the corners of shiny black-and-white photographs. There he was. Joe Taylor, a handsome man in military uniform, back from the war. He had grown a thin

mustache and with his wavy hair combed back and his pronounced cheekbones he resembled Errol Flynn or even Clark
Gable, with smaller ears. Gazing at the photograph, which now
took on the shimmering lambency of a pond's surface, she knew
that despite the umbrage harbored for these thirty years, time
would have taken him anyway, stealing his hair, slowly turning
that muscular frame into a set of rigid bones hung with soft flesh.
Only his high cheekbones had remained until the end, like rocks
protruding from an eroding headland.

Rocks. The album slid from her lap as she jerked awake. She
blinked in confusion at the images of Nat in diapers, Nat in his
Little League uniform, Nat in his high school graduation gown,
as if she'd been given someone else's family album, someone else's
son. The wind howled, the sliding glass doors rattled, something
trembled behind the curtains. What an awful night, and how
unlike her to sit up and doze in her chair — she hadn't even taken
her medicine or brushed her teeth. She knew she must look awful,
her eyes no doubt veined with red, her hair matted where she'd
slept. What if Nat should drop in unannounced, the way he did
sometimes? She stared at his graduation picture, at the bright face
with its hint of unhappiness around big brown eyes, until the
black graduation robe fluttered and filled the apartment, blown
by the wind.

He lunged forward and back, his whole body pumping. His last
satellite fix — the last one he'd been able to record — had put him
on course for Great Stirrup, but he feared that the north wind had
driven him south. If he could keep his boat afloat, he should be
nearing Great Stirrup around 7:30 in morning according to his
calculations, and though it would be too light to see the beacon,
the lighthouse and tracking tower would still make good landmarks for taking a bearing.

He thought of the shallow anchorage at Panton Cove, where
he could find some shelter from this north wind. It seemed that

sailing so often came down to this — launching out only to begin desperately seeking shelter. The first hints of fatigue came to him now, like thin cirrus clouds ahead of a cold front. With a crew of one, exhaustion would prove as fatal as plague aboard ship, so he slowed and paced himself, trying to think of something other than the metal lever in his hand to which he now felt both indebted and enslaved. He pictured this woman, Bea, with her dark curly hair and dark eyes. The first time she said her name he thought simply of the letter "B," and in a way that was how he thought of her. But she had told him her name was short for Beatrice, an old-fashioned name, and he stumbled over all those syllables. Beatrice Rothenberg. Unlike anyone he had ever met, she had a wildness in her eyes, her hair a tangle of curls in the wind, her face beautiful and olive-skinned, with long dark eyelashes and full lips. A tautology, Bea, Beatrice, B. As he brought her face into focus it became older, softer, and soon transmuted to the features of his mother. He'd meant to call his mother before he set out on this trip, and now sharp regret followed the circle of his stomach lining, as if he'd swallowed his own childhood.

His childhood. Seamless days of basketball, softball, football, absorbed by spheres, round or oblong, rubber or leather. He'd been good enough to get by, his determination making up for what he lacked in talent and size, and so he avoided the agony of being chosen last. As he worked the pump, he conjured up summer days in Richmond, stifling heat that brought a kind of security, and though he didn't think of himself as someone who dwelled in the past, he surrendered to this boyhood remembrance. His eyes stung in the wind. Heavy with its own weight, another large wave curled and broke, a fat flood of water rushing over the boat and into the cockpit. He stopped pumping, standing in water for the second time tonight, and listened with his whole body for the movement of the hull — just as a heart surgeon might hold the muscled mass in his hands, waiting to see if the next beat would come. The next beat came. Though heavy with her burden, *Zealot* wallowed on through the waves, the water level mercifully lower than the companionway and bridgedeck. The cockpit drained (slowly, lugubriously) through the scuppers. He threw himself back into the pump, trying to pace his movements but finding it difficult to restrain a new burst of anxious energy.

He hoped these unbidden childhood pictures would divert attention from his back and the gathering tension and soreness taking root there, but when he tried to tap his memory again, to regain, for instance, the feel of an outfielder's glove — the sweat and grit as it slid over his left hand and that leathery smell — he came instead into a shadowed stretch of memory, as if a player had stepped behind the bleachers and out of the mid-day sun. The baseball glove had come as a gift from his father, an important thing, since when Nat was three his father had left them and moved to Baltimore. (There, according to Nat's mother, he lived for a time with a woman who, in his mother's words, "earned her living on her back," though whether or not this was true he never knew.)

What had come to him with the unmistakable edge of truth, again from his mother, was a pronouncement she made one particular Saturday morning. Their small family, the three of them, had come together unintentionally at the end of a difficult week, he and his sister sprawled before cartoons on black-and-white television, his mother prowling the living room, aggravated at the clutter over which she apparently had no control, a southern lady forced to live amid chaos. Absorbed in the omnipotent flights of Mighty Mouse, he woke to his mother's rages as if they had no motivation but appeared inexplicably, violent eruptions of ancient volcanoes. He's never done a damn thing for either of you, she said, glaring at him and his younger sister with narrowed eyes, a sentence connected to a line of thinking he had missed in his animated reverie. Trying to pay to her the attention she seemed to want, he said: He sent me my new glove (nervous because he usually kept his mouth shut when his mother got like this). Ha! she spat back at him, as if vindicated. I bought that glove with my own damn money, wrapped it up and forged the bastard's name just so you'd have something from him. Then her hardened face collapsed and she left him sprawled with his sister in the ruins of the living room, the glimpse of regret in her eyes all he needed to assure him that she spoke the truth.

His father. As a child he had hated him from a distance, but as an adult he wondered whether his father were really as worthless as his mother continually claimed, or just an ordinary man trying to find his way through life and simply not succeeding that well, a man of mediocre talents, ordinary convictions . . . like himself, perhaps.

Idiot! he yelled at the oncoming waves. Idiot! But he kept pumping, postponing as long as possible the moment that he would throw back the companionway hatch cover and try to see the dark water and judge whether he'd made any progress at all.

———

This time the photo album slid to the floor unheeded, spilling the past onto the oriental rug, as if memory were an egg, broken to expose its rich privacy. Ida Taylor heard, felt, nothing. She had let go of the small room where heat registers hummed and kept her warm. Like a passenger on a trans-Atlantic flight (like herself on the one trip she had taken to Europe, too nervous to enjoy), she held her back erect in the chair though asleep, one part of her mind checking the status of her body as a pilot glances at the plane's controls, okay? okay? okay?, while another part of her awareness (not quite consciousness) traveled through remnants of perception, a survivor after a hurricane or a heavy bombing (Joe had been a bombardier), exhausted but unable to stop walking through the ruins, picking up whatever was left and marveling at the new combinations of the remains: a doll long forgotten now seated on the crushed three-piece suit of the man she once loved, a picture of her two children among the jacks and balls of her own toy chest, as if her childhood playthings already contained the trappings of her eventual motherhood. Rigid, asleep, she kept up her search through the darkness behind her eyes as if on a vigil. As the night wore on she became exhausted with this sleep, her dark search circular, moving around and around the rubble left by time but with part of her attention focused elsewhere, the eyes of a fisherman's wife as she makes her compulsive circuit of worry on the roof around the endless gambit of the widow's walk.

———

It was bad, real bad. Not the water in the cabin, which he'd pumped down nearly to the floorboards, but the absence of a fix and no lighted markers except a two-second flashing buoy charted at about 78 degrees 18 minutes, which he would probably never see, even if it was working. Too overcast for a look at the stars, much less a sexton shot. What he would give for his old battery-powered radio direction finder! It had seemed so out of date once he'd gotten satnav and LORAN — and now GPS was beginning to overtake them as well.

A series of heavy waves pummeled the boat, more body blows. He eased the jib sheet and brought the sail around to the starboard side, and *Zealot* was sailing again (even if water still sloshed over the cabin's floorboards). He couldn't afford to drift off course any longer — and his back demanded a break from the pump. And more than that something urged him to take charge, to take the wheel, to get this damn boat somewhere. Steering hard among the building waves, he continued to navigate in his head. Estimating his position after lying to for approximately an hour and a half (two hours?), and based on the only positive fix he had (from his satnav), he figured Great Stirrup lay almost due east — so he charted a course well to the northeast to avoid the shallows that filled in on this side of the Berry Islands. On that mental chart — the only thing he could see clearly in the darkness — he watched waves trudge out of the north to break on coral banks that stretched away south in the blackness, down to the no-man's land of the reefs ringing Andros Island.

Though he had set himself a compass course to the northeast, he also steered largely by the feel of the sea, the red compass light extinguished along with everything else, the cresting waves too large and too steep to ignore, and the compass dial, when he could see it, wildly swinging with the waves. Again he asked out loud, addressing a breaking whitecap that galloped down wind like a spooked mare, *How did I get here?* But the question blew back into his mouth, as insubstantial as cotton candy his mother used to buy him at the Virginia state fair. The more important question, with the two-second flashing buoy not there and the darkness an unrelenting hand before his eyes, was: *Where am I going?*

———

Ida's eyes jerked beneath closed lids. Strands of gray hair poked from beneath her ear lobes, as if windblown.

———

Now the waves began breaking regularly in long lazy cascades and for some reason he felt slightly relieved. Large breaking waves: it wouldn't get much worse than this — he would be okay as long as he didn't hit anything. Hit. The word stuck in his mind like a stone, and he recalled the couple he'd heard about when he traveled north several years ago, an older man and woman in a forty-one foot Morgan. They'd crashed into a jetty in a big wind (at the Harbor of Refuge at Lewes, Delaware, wasn't it?). They had both died on the rocks.

For hours he held his course, or just north of his course for safety's sake, looking for a flashing buoy, or failing that, for the distant light of Great Stirrup Cay. If only his satnav were working . . . Locking the wheel, he went back to the bilge pump. If he could get the water out, let the batteries dry off, perhaps everything would work again. Less likely things had happened. But the boat failed to keep its course and he jumped back to the wheel, then alternated in quick succession: the pump, several rapid thrusts; the wheel, wrestled back on course; the pump; the wheel; the pump. After a while he couldn't remember which he had in his hand, the wheel or the pump. His mind surrendered all authority to his muscles, which seemed to know whether to turn or thrust.

When the pump at last began to suck air the handle lost its resistance and he crashed into the coaming like a drunk. In some ways he felt drunk, sick drunk, the way he felt when Ned Broder first handed him a six pack of Richbrau and like a fool he drank it. Pulling himself up as the boat began its inevitable swing to windward, he felt that he had never fully emerged from that adolescent drunkenness, the beer containing not hops and yeast but some narcotic never purged from the body, not even by puking. And though he prided himself on never succumbing to seasickness he puked now, barely able to reach the spray cloth before whatever it was he had last eaten — tuna fish probably, he couldn't think — erupted from his body of its own volition, its own will to return to the sea. For a long moment he stared at seawater, bubbles stationary as the boat flogged in irons, the surface ascending and descending in its merciless rhythm, and then he pulled himself back to the wheel, spinning the circle of stainless steel until the sails filled with a violent slap and the compass swung and spun back toward the east.

With the bilge dry (and with the dim hope that his electronics might begin to work again), he should have felt encouraged, but in his exhaustion he considered what would be lost if the boat went down. Since he had no insurance, the monetary loss would prove total, the sea taking back what he had earned from it through sweat and cunning over the course of a decade. He did not think of himself as part of what would be lost, perhaps because he still had some slight faith in the life raft and radio signaling device (EPIRB) designed to effect his rescue, but also because he could not regard himself clearly at all, the continual slamming of the boat weaning away his capacity to imagine himself. His consciousness was becoming oceanic, only the solid contours of the boat clear against swirling confusion. He considered the details: the wheel, the compass, the dangling reefing lines which needed tightening (he could only stare at them, unable to move).

What would be lost. He thought of the half dozen composition books on the shelf above his berth. These were not the logs of his sailing but of his mental life. They were letters to himself, asking, "Where are you, and When will you come home . . . " They were letters to his father, now claimed by a wasting disease that brought him too soon to old age and death. He had spoken to his father over the years, man to man, but their conversations stayed on the surface. He never asked the hard questions. He never asked, "How could you leave your own children." He never asked, "What kind of man are you." It was these warped notebooks, stained by condensation, he thought of saving as hope faded of finding a light to steer by.

Never mind. He would continue along the Northwest Providence Channel, rough but deep, very deep, and maybe find the lee of Grand Bahama Island if he had to (a lee, that is, if the wind ever went northeast). The wheel felt like iron in his hands as the boat rose and heeled on waves he gauged to be at least ten-feet high (and he a truck driver, astronaut, railroad engineer, tearing down the rails at break-neck speed, the last long-haul, hell bent for leather). Suddenly defiant he yelled, *waaaaa-hooooo*, the shout of a soldier charging his hail of bullets. If Beatrice Rothenberg was out there in this black shapeless ululant maelstrom he would find her.

Ida looked down the long nave of her mind. Wasn't that her son, drifting like a ghost away from the altar? He was leaving, and she feared he would not come back.

He leaned over and with his wet, fig-skinned fingers tightened the lever that locked the wheel. When he banged against the binnacle, taking a wave, the dim red compass light came on. There was hope. He fumbled with the lifeline that had become tangled around his legs and scrambled through the companionway, careful to slide the hatch cover shut behind him. A single cabin light was trying to come on, flickering like a firefly thrown against the bulkhead, and he could see the chaos of the main salon. Books had spilled into the middle of the floor and now lay soaked like wet leaves. Rolling around them, errant billiard balls, raced the grapefruits and oranges he'd bought just before he left. He surrendered everything to the pitch and roll and grabbed the handrail by the nav station. With an index finger that felt inexplicably limp, he pressed the switch of the small computer. Nothing, and then a dim green row of Xs and Os. Pressing the other buttons did nothing to change the cryptic message. He switched on the LORAN, which soon flashed a yellowish row of Fs, as if grading his performance over and over. His radio did nothing, but still he felt guardedly optimistic. Turn everything off, let it dry out and try again later. Once he felt that the wires had dried enough he would try starting the engine and that too might drive out some of the moisture. Then he could figure out where he was — maybe this was what appealed to him about sailing: this continual effort to find himself.

The boat swerved into the wind again, and cursing he threw back the hatch and stormed into the cockpit, yelling, All right already! He bore off, filled the sails, and locked the wheel. On a whim he tested the switch for the autopilot. The tiny red diode blinked. The engaged pulley whirred erratically, then stopped — probably a blown fuse (he'd forgotten to unlock the wheel). He ducked below and shut off all three batteries, something he should have done to begin with, and waited for them to dry.

As the boat headed up again, he scrambled back to the wheel. The wind caught the sails, and *Zealot* heeled over hard. He would have to reef the main once more, should have reefed it already. Easing the sheet he locked the wheel again, clipped to the jackline and went forward. Always when he went forward he entered a different world, the deck plunging beneath him, the bow asserting itself into the rage of the sea. Here, not at the helm, not in the cockpit, was where the boat fought for itself, in a riot of white water. At times he rejoiced in this carnival of spray, as a cowhand might raise one arm and whoop, but tonight he lacked the energy, his attention focused on slowing down, managing the beast of his boat, coaxing it toward the safety of deep water where first light (if it ever came) would show him the way to safe harbor.

For once he welcomed the inevitable swing into the wind so he could bring down the main and put in the third and final reef. After this the only thing left was to furl the main altogether — perhaps he should do this now, he thought, but he wanted to keep some speed, to be sure of his headway. He cleated the reefing line, the rope burning his fingers as the sail bucked and jerked in the wind's eye. He tightened the halyard, coiled it, and stepped back from the wildly swinging boom. With the sails reset, the boat finally responded to its angled rudder (the wheel still locked) and bore off, the staysail backwinded. He would have to hurry back to the wheel — as soon as he set the vang. Back, back moved the bow, the boat now taking seas on the beam with a violent rolling. He held the hand rail, unable to do much else until the boat regained some stability as it resumed its slog over the seas.

At last he set the vang and checked the lines before making his monkey crawl back toward the cockpit, watching (not wanting to see) the white crests of breaking waves on the beam, discernible even in the darkness. As the boat continued to fall off, waves edged toward the port quarter, and when he reached the dodger, careful to hold on as he rose to climb around, the stern veered suddenly northward in a breaking sea. The wind crawled behind the mainsail, and the boat began to jibe. He held on and ducked, but not far enough, off-balance on the lurching deck as the boom, held down by the vang, shot across like a baseball bat and clipped him at the cranium, the usual dimness of his mind suddenly white.

He fell senseless against the netting of the leeward lifeline, soaked by spray, and the boat plunged on with the helm locked down.

⸺

She leapt to her feet and breathed. Her heart had begun those rare but frightening palpitations that threatened to go on interminably — no, not interminably but until that final termination that would leave her sprawled on the floor alone, no one to call an ambulance, not her daughter curled up and fast asleep next to that cold fish, Marty, not her husband twice removed from her, once by life and once by death, nor her son . . .

Something was wrong, not only with her heart, something was terribly wrong, she had felt it even before she fell asleep, felt it as soon as the sun went down and this steady moaning of wind began rattling the shutters and pressing against the sliding glass door. She stood waiting for her heart to rediscover its God-given rhythm, staring without comprehension at the photographs on the floor, her children at all ages, as though she had many children, all (whether with toothless grin or awkward squint into the sun) now bearing mute photographic witness to — what? her death? She moved forward, legs stiff, photographs nagging at her ankles. Step. Balance. Step. Balance. Needing a goal she headed for the kitchen to take her medicine — that combination of vitamins, minerals, tranquilizers and blood thinners, none of it really heart medicine, certainly not nitroglycerin, not yet — as if this could cure her.

The kitchen remained a long way off but she tacked toward it, until she brought the doorposts within reach. There she rested as her heart finally slowed, the kitchen seeming to soothe her. She walked to the counter and methodically brought down different bottles, taking from the refrigerator the ubiquitous jar of ice water, a fixture in every home she'd had. Despite the odor of chlorine, the water soothed and doubtless did more good than the medicine. She collected her thoughts. The first thing to do, she figured, one hand flat on the counter, her engagement ring tilted to one side on its wrinkled finger, was to call Nat. She looked at her watch. 2:30. Never, not even during his wild high school and wilder college days (and nights) had she called him at such an hour, though she might sit or lie in the dark and wait, wait for the sound of the car in the driveway, the fumbling key at the door. But now she checked the number in her dark blue book, lifted the receiver and dialed direct. It wouldn't kill him to have his mother wake *him* once before she died. Electric circuits leapt the distance that seemed to her so long, past the Carolinas, through the marshes and clayey midlands of Georgia to Florida, the state that had swallowed her son. Crisp rings and the sound of the receiver, lifted. Hello. This is Nat. "Nat. Nat. You don't know how glad . . . " I'm not here right now — I'm off on a quick sail to the Berry Islands. Should be back in about a week — around Sunday. Please leave a message and I'll get back to you then.

Bleeeeeeeet.

How cruel to leave his voice behind. She stood open-mouthed, wanting to say, "This is your mother — " but uncertain of what other message to record, she heard the machine bleep again and knew the conversation was over.

Of course it would not be that easy, Ida thought, just to call him; otherwise her intuition would have proven all wrong. She had some act to perform. What was it? She called information. What city? Fort Lauderdale, Florida. What listing? The United States Coast Guard. She wrote the number carefully in the back of her book.

"Coast Guard. Port Everglades."

"Hello, um, Coast Guard (she said this as if it were someone's name). I would like to ask you what I should do if a boat — that is if I think perhaps a boat might be missing or overdue. Or in trouble." She strained to sound other than she was: an elderly, overanxious mother concerned for her son.

"Stand by."

And so she stood by. She stood by the calendar that Nat had sent her with different shots of sailboats for each month — though she didn't care for boating herself. She stood by the blue address book, increasingly filled with names which no longer belonged to the living, names she did not in any way mark with an X or a check or a penciled cross, because she knew that eventually she would have no names left. She stood by the clear plastic square with a snapshot gleaming on every facet. Her daughter. Her son. Her daughter. She left the top space blank, saying she meant to fill it but secretly saving it, saving it for her first grandchild. She stood by.

"Coast Guard Port Everglades. Go ahead."

Go ahead. Go ahead. She feared she would again remain speechless, mute until the receiver clicked her off. Go ahead. She would have to sound specific. He said he would be back by Sunday. This was Sunday. He clearly meant next week. Go ahead.

"Hello?"

"Yes, hello, I would like to report the late arrival of the Yacht *Zealot*, uh, forty-two, no forty-four feet long, one mast. Due at the Berry Islands today."

"Did you say *Zealot*? Where in the Berry Islands exactly?"

"Oh, I'm not certain." She felt her credibility slip. "I guess it depends on the wind."

"A sailboat you say."

"Yes."

"Do you know the registration or documentation number?"

"Oh no, I'm afraid I don't." Why, why did agencies, public and private — from the local police to the bank manager — make you feel ignorant about your own life? "I believe it is registered in Florida. Fort Lauderdale is his home port."

"Did he leave from Fort Lauderdale?"

"Yes. Yes, he did." (What if he hadn't . . .)

"When?"

"Yesterday morning." She felt her skin: it seemed to move.

"It's 2:45 now. Do you mean Sunday morning or Saturday morning?"

"Oh . . . Saturday. Yesterday."

"Ma'am, I don't know if they've had enough time to reach the Berry Islands in a sailboat by now. And I don't think there's any place for them to check in if they have."

"It's only one person. My son. His name is Nat Taylor. Maybe he left Friday morning."

A short but painful silence followed. Then the voice came back: "Stand by."

———

Only the aboriginal rhythm of the sea, taken over for everything, a saline solution in his vacuous skull, his hollow bones. Memories no longer washed in the tidal rip of his thoughts but took directions of their own so that the most important and the least important moments of his life emerged not in front of him, nor behind him, nor around him but instead of him, complete, the total occupancy of the space once known as himself.

———

Ida held the phone as though it were someone's hand, the hand of a young Coast Guardsman perhaps, who would, despite his youth, search for and find her son. Then the voice came back to take her phone number. "We'll call you with an update in the morning," the voice said. "You should get some sleep." She said she doubted it, but only to herself, because already the voice of the Coast Guardsman had returned far away, back to Florida.

———

He opened his eyes only once to see the deck covered with small creatures, their eyes bigger than his own as they scurried about, trimming the sail, securing the lines, turning the wheel. One of them touched his head with a tiny hand as it passed and plunged his thoughts into darkness.

A tide of impulses took the shape of a question in his mind: What was the relation of Beatrice Rothenberg to the sea? The question did not take such a simple shape — less a syntactical structure than a mental wash: the shape of her legs against a pounding surf, her arching neck soaked by spray, her belly in a clot of kelp. Where was the truth in this? How could he disentangle the body of Beatrice from the sea? How could he drain the sea from B? His own body rolled and writhed with the agony of this conundrum. He could deal with the ocean. He could deal with women. But he could not grasp the sense of this Beatrice-sea. It was beyond him.

During the long dark night he tossed between the waves of this teasing duality, his mind numb with the senselessness of it. Then he had an idea. The idea began in his eyes, though lidded. It spread along his optic nerve, branched out into his cerebellum, his hypothalamus, filled his whole cranium. He had never had such a brilliant idea.

The idea was daybreak. He blinked and tried to raise himself from the deck, to do one early-morning push-up, but his strength eluded him and for the immediate present (and it was very immediate) he had to look at the world sideways. He could not comprehend what he saw.

Early morning light — the moment the sun touches the horizon — and a vast sea of small remnant whitecaps. The sea was not dark blue but turquoise, the color of the bank.

The boat drifted sideways, moving slowly with the wind, which had diminished to a warm breeze. Large clouds slid overhead, the tail end of the cold front, most of the gray gone out of them. He pushed up. His legs took him forward before he even thought, "I am going to put the anchor down." His hands knew the simple routine: he unlashed the shank of the plow and pulled the chain from the hawse hole. The weight of the anchor yanked the chain from his hand and formed a cascade of links over the bow roller, stopped only by his foot. Without a snubber at hand, he cleated the chain itself and let it pull against the rubber roller, good enough for now. Anything and everything was good enough for now.

He had arrived. He had survived the Beatrice-sea.

He did not need the depth finder to know he was in shallow water. The color told all. But where was he? His head throbbed as he watched the turquoise grow more brilliant with the rising sun. The anchor caught, and *Zealot* swung around into the wind. The triple-reefed main, now luffing, looked surprisingly small. He saw that the mainsheet had fouled on one of the jib winches and on the engine throttle. The jib sheet likewise had snarled near the blocks, as though whipped by wind from every compass point, and with the sheets thus fouled the boat must have hove to in the night.

Rubbing his pounding head, he dropped the sails, then went below and poured the remainder of the coffee, barely warm, from the red thermos. Crossing his fingers, he switched on the batteries and climbed back into the cockpit and turned the key. The diesel engine turned slowly, slowly, then caught and began to sputter and smoke from the exhaust port in the stern. He descended into the cabin again and looked at the instrument panel, where the voltmeter and ammeter told him that the alternator was charging — the system seemed to be back. He heard a familiar whir and realized the bilge pump was working, sucking water from beneath the floorboards.

Feeling as if he were pressing his luck, but unable to wait any longer, he hit the switch for the satnav. A row of eights appeared, but when he hit the reset button the machine began to cycle, and soon it flashed the asterisk that meant it was receiving a signal from an over-flying satellite. Soon he would have a fix. He grabbed the binoculars from their case by the chart table and climbed on deck, where he plopped down in the swaying cockpit and began scanning the horizon, searching for a clue to where he could be. At first he saw nothing but that blue-green water, then he spotted some kind of craft, far off, heading away from him. He saw what appeared to be a marker, a fixed structure, in the wake of the receding vessel, almost due west. What in the world could that be? Where was he?

He climbed back down to watch the satnav — it had collected several asterisks now, and a fix should be imminent, if it worked. Meanwhile, he turned on the old LORAN set and programmed in the only TD line he could read from the chart. The LORAN seemed as confused as he was, so he returned to the satnav, and there was the fix: 25 degrees, 29 minutes North; 78 degrees, 22 minutes West. He bent over the chart, his fingers trembling, and marked where the lines intersected. The Russell Light. He was just east of the Russell Light.

How was this possible? How could he have been blown onto the banks in the middle of the night and survived? How could he have missed the coral? The breaking waves? He felt a queasiness in his stomach and climbed to the aft rail, leaning over, unsure at first, and then certain he was going to throw up.

———

Ida opened her eyes and stared at the fabric of the sofa where she'd fallen asleep. Daylight had broken over Richmond, a certain silence signaling that the wind had died. She was listening for something else though — what was it? The phone. She was waiting for the Coast Guard to call.

———

Nat knew where he would go from here. He would head for the Northwest Channel and from there he would leave the banks and make for Chub Cay — only about another fourteen miles. At Chub Cay they had a telephone, the only telephone in this part of the Berry Islands. He would call her.

He hoisted anchor and motor-sailed toward deep water.

When Nat finally arrived at the Chub Cay marina he was

ready to pay any price for a slip. His head hurt and he blinked at the brilliant day as if he doubted its reality.

"What happen' to you?" a muscular man asked, as his big hands took a line and tossed it over the nearest piling.

"What?"

"Ain't that blood?"

He reached up and felt a crusty patch along the side of his scalp. "I got hit in the head," he said.

By afternoon, sitting in the bar, he had told his story many times. At first the men in the marina did not quite believe him. Then, gradually, as they began to see the truth in his eyes, they commenced to comment on it — offering opinions on how he had come onto the banks unscathed in the dark. Or had it been just after dawn?

"After dawn," one of the men said. "The only-est way possible."

"And then you passed out," another man said. There was general agreement.

"I was already passed out," Nat said. "I was knocked out around, I don't know, two or three o'clock in the morning I guess. That's all I remember."

"You must have woke up," the first man said.

"Did you dream?" This question came from a different quarter, from an older black man with a close-cropped white beard. The other men looked at him.

"I was out cold," Nat said.

"Did you dream?" the man said again. Nat wondered whether the old man might be deaf. "Did you see anything?"

"Did I see anything?" This question seemed an odd one to ask someone who had been knocked unconscious, but as a flaw of wind tousled the green casuarina trees in front of the bar it occurred to him that he had seen something. And it seemed to him as well that he understood what the man meant by his question — and that the man already knew the answer. "I think I hallucinated," Nat said.

"What did you see?" the old man asked.

"I saw . . . small creatures — like meerkats maybe, or some kind of bird — with big eyes. They . . . "

"What did they do?" the old man pressed him.

"They did everything. They scampered all over the boat. They took the wheel and steered. They trimmed the sail. They did everything."

"They brought you here," the old man said, satisfied.

"Chickcharnies," another man said. "Chickcharnies," they all echoed, and it was this explanation they accepted unanimously, as though someone had come up with the obvious answer to a question which had only moments before seemed unanswerable.

All afternoon they drank Clique beer and told stories. Nat heard of men, women and children, some from Andros Island, tricked by chickcharnies, creatures who evidently delighted in baffling the islanders by misplacing things or spreading rumors. As the people spoke — several black women had joined them now — he watched them, their teeth white as they smiled, aware of what a handsome race they were, and he began to feel that he had not only crossed the Gulf Stream in a norther but had passed through some other barrier, and landed in a strange and exotic place not marked on any worldly chart.

By late afternoon, the pounding in his head had eased (perhaps because of the beer), and he stood suddenly and announced that he had to make a telephone call.

"Who is she?" one of the women asked with a white smile.

"Excuse me?"

"Where is this 'person' you got to call?" The young woman's large eyes flashed mischief — everyone picked up her taunt and passed it around, until all he could see was a circle of smiles.

"Yes, it's a woman," he said. "She lives in Virginia. Richmond, Virginia. It's where I'm from. It's my home."

As he rose to walk toward the building with the telephone, he saw a bulky white boat struggling to back between the pilings of a narrow slip. On the stern he saw the name, *Out-of-Sight*. And there, trying to help with the lines, a beautiful dark-haired young woman, who looked not only familiar, but more than familiar, as if her arrival had been predetermined, staged almost, as he emerged from the bar. But he did not believe in predestination, any more than he believed in chickcharnies, and he continued on toward the telephone, to call his mother. He had a feeling, new in his life, that everything else would take care of itself.

White Shadow

T HEY KNEW BETTER THAN TO LET a cold front catch them on the banks. With the sun going down and black coral heads fading into the Bahamian shadows, they had no choice but to find the best place they could for the night. So far the wind was still east but already had some south in it. Shortly after nightfall she knew it would go south altogether, before the norther came through. They dropped anchor by Hawksbill Cay, close in behind several large rocks, to give them protection from the north. Once morning came with its relief of light, they could head for a better anchorage at Staniel Cay, most likely with a following wind.

Janie Truxton had made this trip before on *White Shadow* from West Palm Beach to the Exumas, bringing money and supplies from the States, and taking contraband back north. Contraband was a word that had come to her only recently. Usually she had just said herb or weed, words she had grown up with, but her words were changing.

"Back down on her!" he yelled, paying out anchor chain. Jed McAllister could yell. Normally he gave hand signals, signs they had worked out over three years of sailing together, so that they often glided into an anchorage without exchanging a single word. But this evening something was eating at him. His face scowled with irritation and worry. Probably he didn't like the idea of anchoring here in the open, angry at himself for getting so late a start. But something else ate at him as well, a shadow.

As she stood at the wheel in her unraveling cut-off jeans, waiting to see if both anchors would set (Jed had put out both the

Bruce and the heavy CQR), she thought how odd it was that they had not even given this thirty-three-foot sloop its shadowy name. The boat had originally belonged to a doctor in Fort Lauderdale. Probably the doctor had found the name romantic or racy, and had not intended anything sinister.

"Cut!" Jed yelled again, drawing a flat hand across his throat, and she pressed back on the throttle until the engine rattled and stopped. Then came the sound of wind and surf around rocks.

"Do you think we'll be okay here?" she asked when he came back to the cockpit.

He pulled off the yellow work gloves he used for chain work and threw them toward a corner of the cockpit. "I guess," he said. She looked at him. In his khaki shorts with all those snaps, he still had that swashbuckling air she'd found appealing from the start, at the Two Turtles bar in George Town. His carefully trimmed beard and dark eyes gave him the look of an English buccaneer, only lately she had noticed a few white hairs on his chin, and this suggested to her an unsuspected frailty, as if he were blanched underneath.

"At least we're not alone," she said. Out on the banks, about a mile away, a Bahamian sloop dropped anchor and was now lowering its sail. With its delicate lines, the sloop seemed a figurine. The presence of another sailboat — a local boat — gave her some assurance that they'd anchored in a safe place. Because other than that slender shape she could see no sign of human life, only water and the silence of Hawksbill Cay. In the failing light the island's bluff made a dark presence. She felt they'd come under the wing of some black mythical bird.

Below, the cabin moved with the breath of an easy ground swell, but not wanting to miss the twilight, she grabbed their Bahamian guide and returned to the cockpit. She knew this subtropical evening, its gathering clouds tipped orange and turquoise, would fade fast. Jed, hands rusty from the chain despite his gloves, finished securing the snubber lines and then stood leaning against the mast. There he took bearings on rocks and shore, so he could tell later whether the anchors held.

Perhaps they had anchored here once before; she couldn't remember. There were so many cays along this stretch of the Exumas, and the ones she knew best in this area were Warderick Wells, a little further south, and Normans Cay, just north, where Jed sometimes conducted business. Between Hawksbill and Normans lay Shroud Cay.

According to the guidebook, Hawksbill had few occupants, few houses. She could see none from here. It also had, the book said, a cairn at the top of the bluff, and lifting her eyes she wondered that she had not noticed it before. A white stone marker taller than the tallest man. A cairn. While Jed tightened the furling straps on the main, she ducked below to pull the paperback dictionary, dog-eared and water-stained, from the starboard bookshelf. The word "cairn" was Scottish and referred to a heap of stones placed as a monument or landmark. But this one looked more like an obelisk, the Greek word for a four-sided tower coming to a pyramidal point. Obelisk, the dictionary said, also meant dagger.

"Look," she called to Jed. "Did you see that cairn?"

He raised his head for a moment and then went back to work. "Sure," he said. "I've seen it."

"I think it looks more like an obelisk," she said.

He continued to work, coiling reefing lines that dangled from the boom.

She took the binoculars from their holder and scanned the island, looking up and down the ridge. Other sailors had told her — complained to her even — that the Bahamas, unlike the Lesser Antilles, were flat, but "flat" did not describe the Bahamas she had come to know, with their ridges and cliffs, and with their jagged edges, as twisted and dark as volcanic rock. The sea had carved the Bahamas from hard oolitic limestone. Waves smashed against those limestone shores just as they did against the boulders of Maine; and much of this shoreline was rocky and forbidding, unlike the flat sandy beaches of Florida. No, though low-lying, the Bahamas were not flat, and the delicate cassuarina trees and short scrub brush gave the cliffs and ridges the look of mountain ranges in miniature.

When the cairn came into view through the glasses, it startled her — ghostly white in the dusk, aloof from the bluff's dark gray. It appeared to keep watch from its high perch, silent and foreboding. Unlike the reassuring beam of a lighthouse, the cairn's dim whiteness sent a more obscure and less sanguine message, less like a navigational aid than a gravestone. She shuddered. The wind had already begun to swing south and die.

"What about dinner?" Jed asked, coming back to the cockpit.

She put down her book and looked at him, at his short ponytail, wrapped with a rubber band. Should she confront him now or later?

"We're fresh out of fish," she said. "How about stew out of a can?"

"Suits me," he said, and then he disappeared down the companionway.

A white shadow, she thought. She looked at the cairn in the near-dark and saw how it seemed to glow even without sunlight. The thought came to her that black slaves once worked these islands for white masters and that her family, originally from Virginia, had descended from freed men. Darkness came.

———

From the propane stove pale steam rose from the stew. She stirred and thought. First they had made only a few deals, taking marijuana from a friend in the Bahamas to another friend in West Palm Beach. Only later did she realize that Jed had planned this all along, this shuttling back and forth. For her it seemed a casual thing, taking some weed from one friend to another. Then the meetings became more secretive, more serious. Jed would disappear for hours at a time and then not tell her what was up. She became less like a partner and more like an unwilling accomplice. Because what was *up* was the white shadow, cocaine.

She poured the stew into two blue plastic bowls and took them to the settee table. Jed was already in his seat, waiting, reading an old boating magazine by the dim light of a twelve-volt bulb.

"We ought to put on a back-stay tensioner," he said, stirring the stew with his spoon. "It wouldn't be that hard."

She waited a moment, then spoke. "What happened at Norman's Cay?" she asked.

He looked up at her, his blue eyes narrowed. "What do you mean?"

"Something happened, didn't it? I could tell by the way you acted when you rowed back to the boat. Where was Larry?"

"Larry is all right. Don't worry about Larry."

"Who should I worry about?"

"Don't worry about anybody. It won't do any good."

"Did you make a deal?"

He looked at her again, taking a slow mouthful of stew, the steam lifting from his bowl like a spirit. "Not exactly," he said.

"Did you change your mind? I wouldn't blame you if you changed your mind."

"Not exactly," he said again.

She dropped her spoon on the table. "Then what, exactly?"

"I don't think you want to know."

She watched him eat his stew and turned the words over in her mind. I don't think you want to know. She no longer knew what he did. It was as if she did not know him. That was the thought that now ran through her mind: she no longer knew him. "Maybe I'd better know," she said.

"Maybe you'd better not know." He ran his palm over unshaved cheeks.

With the dim light on the side of his face, and with the small diamond earring gleaming white in his ear lobe, he looked less like a buccaneer than a pirate. Perhaps that's what he was. "Was anyone hurt?"

"Let's just put it this way," he said. "They thought we were trying to take their money."

"Was anyone . . . "

"I believe 'cocksucker' was the word they used. They weren't being very civilized."

"What happened?"

"Are you sure you want to hear this?"

"What. Happened."

"One of them pulled a knife on us. Three of them, two of us."

"And?"

"Larry had his bag with him, the long bag, with the machete in it."

She knew of this machete, a stainless steel machete he had bought in Viet Nam — he was always bragging that it wouldn't rust — and now the sudden urge came to her to stop listening. She could picture the rest.

"Larry did it," he said. "Not me."

"Not you."

"No," he said. "Not me."

Not you, she thought. You are not you. Perhaps you were never you, and I only made you up, with your earring and your beard and your Francis Drake smile, and your body. And soul.

She pushed away the bowl and stood up. The short walk to the companionway and up into the cockpit seemed long, and when she emerged from the cabin the intensity of the darkness dazed her. She waited a long time for her eyes to find the world. Out on the shallow bank a single dim light flickered, the kerosene anchor light of the Bahamian sloop. Odd that he would anchor out there, away from the island, with no protection. She wondered if he knew a cold front was coming.

To the east the island added its weight to the darkness, as only land can, always darker than the sea. Up on the ridge the cairn faded into dusk, but when she looked at an angle, she could still make it out, the vaguest of ghosts, an ashen shadow against the night. She picked up the binoculars and looked.

After a while Jed came up and sat across from her. "The cold front should come through some time after midnight," he said. "Then as soon as we have enough light we can head down to Staniel Cay."

"Then what?" she said.

"Then what . . . then we keep heading down to George Town, what else?"

"And then we go back to West Palm Beach again?"

He rubbed his hands together, and suddenly it was cold, even here in the Bahamas, where she had come three years ago from New York, seeking warmth. "Are you having a change of heart?" he said. It could have been a probing question, almost a gentle question, but he asked it with impatience. A change of heart. Was that like a change of life, isn't that what they called it? It would be coming soon enough for her, this change of life, and then there would be no children, all captured in that narrow plastic he always wore and discarded, and so now all she had was this, a change of heart.

"I guess I am," she said.

"No one's keeping you on this boat against your will," he said. "But if you do leave, you'd better keep your mouth shut."

That was when she looked up at the cairn and saw the lights. A row of lights, like torchlights, heading up the ridge toward the cairn, and then they were gone. "Did you see that?" she said.

"See what?"

"Those lights. On the hill."

He turned and looked, suspicious, taking the binoculars. "Someone with flashlights?" he asked.

"They looked more like torches," she said. "A line of torches heading up the hill, toward the cairn."

"Torches?" he said. He searched the ridge with the binoculars for some time but could see nothing but the cairn. "Torches?" he said again.

"Yes," she said. "As if a line of mourners were climbing the hill to pay their respects to the dead."

"The dead? What dead?"

"At the cairn. The ones marked by the cairn."

He clicked on the flashlight and looked at her, letting his eyes move over her face in the glow, probing. Her unruly dark hair was pulled back, sharpening her coffee-colored features. She was getting older, he thought, though she was still a beautiful woman, especially when she let her kinky hair fall all around her face. He wondered what she was driving at.

"Did you see any lights or not?" he asked.

"Yes. I know I did. A row of lights, heading up to the cairn. Then they disappeared."

"They disappeared . . . Well let me know if you see them again." He shut off the flashlight and returned down the companionway, to read his magazine again or perhaps to sleep.

We have a machete too, she thought. We keep it under the cushion of the settee, wrapped in a sheath of cardboard and sprayed with oil to stop rust. She thought about the machete as she kept watch. Anchor watch, with a cold front coming. Except tonight she kept watch over the cairn. Or perhaps it was watching her.

More than once she saw a glimmer of light along the ridge, but always fleeting, and she couldn't be sure. She stared through the binoculars until she began to see fine grains of light everywhere, like white dust, but could discern nothing. She closed her eyes to rest, but when she finally opened them again, the stars had turned and a sharp ache crawled along her back where she'd leaned against the coaming. The wind had shifted, too, to the west, and the cold front was here, a dry front, with little or no rain, just a spirit of wind down from the United States, making its long journey across the Great Plains and down through Georgia and Florida — how had it found them this far south?

Only the cairn had not changed. It had not shifted, lurched, or left. It remained high over the water, the highest thing here, facing all directions, but mostly west, since it stood on the western side of the island, and watching the west wind come to it, she began to think that perhaps the cairn had called this storm from the continent, in retribution.

Waves began to build from the west as well. Already they slapped the rocks *White Shadow* had nestled behind, off to the north-northwest. Maybe the rocks would break the force of the waves and shelter them. Out on the banks the sloop's anchor light flickered, as the kerosene lantern swung with the waves.

She looked one last time at the cairn, then worked her way down into the dark cabin, threw herself onto the bunk beside Jed's shadow. She wished she could be somewhere else, even in her old apartment in New York, in the East Village, with all its noise and squalor, anywhere that would be hers alone. But there was nowhere else to sleep here on the shallow and open banks, only *White Shadow*, the graceful sloop under whose spell she had fallen with its promise of freedom.

When she woke it was still dark, but the world had changed. The cabin lurched left and right, everything banging back and forth, back and forth, until the galley cabinet burst open and pans spilled onto the cabin sole, a nerve-jangling crash and clatter. She reached over and felt for Jed. Not there. Tired and frightened, she got up, staggered aft, the floor a wild seesaw. She put the pans back in the cabinet, trying to wedge them so they wouldn't knock the door open again. Then she climbed the companionway, holding with both hands as the boat rocked, a circus ride. Jed stood in the center of the cockpit, holding the boom and shifting his weight to port and starboard with the rhythm of the waves.

"The front's come through," he said when he saw her.

"Yes," she said. "I noticed."

The anchorage was transformed. The swell now rose beneath them and crashed astern on the island's jagged bank. The rocks to the north, she now saw, gave them little protection, with waves bending past in their onslaught toward the shore. They were in a breaker zone.

"The long-shore current is keeping us sideways to the waves," he said. "I thought about rigging a bridle, but I think it's too rough."

It was rough. The wind had built from the northwest and now sang in the rigging. The island raged behind them, a lee shore. She looked up to see how the Bahamian sloop was faring, but the anchor light had vanished. She lifted the binoculars from the cockpit floor where they'd fallen and looked for the sloop, but it had gone. "I wonder where the Bahamian boat went?" she asked.

"Who knows?" he said.

"What should we do?"

"Nothing much we can do. We know there's coral out there — no way we can move before day break. It's about 3:30 now. We'll just have to tough it out for a few hours. Then we can leave — if I can get the anchors up."

She thought of the chain, over a hundred feet of it on each anchor, bucking with finger-snapping force in these breakers. She wondered if their old diesel engine would be able to get them out of here.

She looked back. The cairn stood on the ridge. The breakers foamed white.

―――

Out of the night thoughts came to her like waves. She lay on the berth with Jed beside her, dead weight, and felt the boat slam back and forth in the breakers. In the galley drawer forks and spoons and knives slid, chang, chang, chang, chang. The hull yawed with the pull of the anchor rodes, a horse breaking from its trainer. Larry Nashville he called himself — who knew what his real name was. What had he done with the machete? How had he used it? And Jed, the abettor, the shadow, ghost at the grave.

Wind sang its hymn in the rigging.

She carried a torch up the steep ridge, called to the grave of the suzerain. The cairn gleamed in the torchlight and she raised her machete against it. Chang, chang, chang. As the blade struck the stone, sparks flew, small bright stars that rose toward the sky. These were the souls of the dead, and as the machete chipped and splintered the hard stone, blood began to flow, but whose blood she could not say.

Wham! A large wave broke against the side of the hull and she started awake, aware that even in her sleep she had been gripping the side of the berth. Jed still slept. She could see the cabin. She could see the chart table and the companionway steps and the portlights like gray pearl. Day was coming. She struggled up, then crashed to the other side of the cabin. She gripped the hand rail that ran overhead, pulled herself to the companionway.

In the predawn light she could see very well where they were. She could see the breakers coming in from the west with the strong wind, folding onto the island. She could see the boulders send up spray as they took the force of the waves. It seemed that the rocks ahead gave them some protection after all. There was no sign of the Bahamian sloop or of any other person or boat, only the cairn at the top of the ridge. She remembered a word from college. *Adamantine.* She wanted a cup of coffee very badly.

Working her way back down the companionway ladder, she braced herself at the galley. By placing the kettle in the sink she kept it from flying around and pumped water from the tap. She held the kettle in place using the fiddles on the propane stove as she heated water. But once the water was steaming, she scalded her hand trying to pour through a coffee filter. The cup slid back and forth, and coffee grinds spilled into the sink. After several tries she got enough water through the crumpled filters for two cups of coffee. Jed, awakened by the aroma, climbed from the berth to join her. He stood like a monkey, hanging by one arm from the overhead rail. His khaki shorts were wrinkled and his white T-shirt said, "Family Island Regatta."

She pointed toward the hot cup in the sink and then went up to the cockpit. The cockpit seats tilted left and right, making it impossible to sit. The best place to stand was in the center, one hand on the boom above, knees bending from side to side. For a long while she watched in silence, sipping hot coffee, steam in her face. She felt Jed standing behind her.

"We'll be able to leave soon," he said.

She looked up at the cairn.

"I'm going to get the engine ready," he said. She knew that without the engine they'd never get out of here. They were too close to shore to tack off, and besides, rocks and coral heads blocked their way to either side. She knew, too, that in this wind they could never pull the boat to the anchors by hand. The only thing was to motor straight out against the waves.

One thing was certain: she didn't want to stay here.

Jed checked the oil, turned on both batteries, and sat at the wheel, pausing before he turned the key. When the groan of belts against the heavy flywheel gave way at last to the engine's steady thump and to the spit and gurgle of exhaust from the stern, he stood and looked at her. She looked at his white hands.

"You'd better get ready to take the wheel," he said.

"Do you think it's light enough?"

"We'll be all right. We'll follow the same course out that we took in. Keep the heading on about 280 magnetic once we get the anchors up. *If* we get the anchors up . . . "

She zipped her foul-weather jacket against inevitable spray. Taking the helm she listened as the exhaust bubbled each time the stern buried in a wave, and turning she saw the ghost of fumes rise, blown away by the wind.

Now Jed stood on the bow with his yellow work gloves and motioned her to pull ahead. There was no yelling, perhaps because the situation had forced Jed to depend on her, or perhaps because the wind was too loud. At each hand signal she pushed the shift lever in and out of gear, working the throttle to make headway against the waves and to keep steerage. Now forward, hard, now neutral, now forward, working the wheel to keep the bow into the sea. All around breakers curled and combed, and behind them thundered on the rocks. They had no windlass. Jed worked frantically at the chain, pulling with all his strength when the rode grew taut, and then gathering hand over hand as the boat began to overtake the first anchor.

This was the most dangerous time for him, with the boat directly over the anchor and the bow rising and falling, sending plumes of spray into the air each time it buried in a wave. If the chain fouled on a rock or coral head he knew he would have to dive into that wild and dangerous maelstrom. He let the cleat take the force of the rising and falling, so that the lifting bow could pull the chain straight up. Once the anchor broke free, he hauled fast, scrambling to keep the flukes from gouging the bow as they rose from the water.

White Shadow danced sideways now toward the rocks, and then rounded up behind the second anchor, the heavy CQR. To keep chain from sliding over the side, Jed lashed the first anchor to the bowrail, then fed the chain, tediously, through the rode hole in the plunging deck. When he stood and arched his back, looking skyward, she knew he was ready to take on the second anchor.

Forward and back, forward and back, she worked the gearshift and the throttle, spinning the wheel from lock to lock to keep the bow into the sea. At last the second anchor broke loose — she could feel the boat alive in the waves and she did not need Jed's frantic hand, lifted away from the chain in an urgent signal, to force the throttle forward, the engine working hard against the waves. If the wind caught the port side of the bow, it would, together with the waves, push them straight toward the sundering rocks.

For a long moment she concentrated only on this, on keeping the bow into the sea, with the propwash building all around the stern, and then she felt the boat crawl ahead, rising and falling, climbing these endless hills, a straight line of movement in the chaos of the waves. Only then did she look down to see that the compass was already on 280 degrees, and she worked the wheel to keep it there.

By the time the depth finder read twelve and then eighteen and then twenty-four feet, Jed had stowed the anchors and chain and scrambled back to the mast to catch his breath. For a long time he stood there, breathing hard and stretching his back, his sandy brown hair blown high by the wind. Then he worked his way hand over hand to the cockpit, released the windward sheet and rolled out half of the genoa jib. It clapped in the breeze. As the wind caught the trimmed jib, *White Shadow* heeled and moved once more like a sailing vessel. The hull threw foam to leeward, driving now, no longer a cork bouncing in the swell. They let the engine run a while to charge the batteries, then shut it down. They sailed south toward Staniel Cay.

For a moment, with the pressure of the wheel's weather helm against her hand, she felt that they were simply sailors again, that it was just the two them and *White Shadow*, the way they had planned. But as she steered before the wind, surfing on waves built by the blustery norther, she thought she saw a rock straight ahead, white in the waves. It seemed pointed, like the peak of the cairn, rising from the sandy bottom. She headed the boat quickly upwind.

"What the hell are you doing?" Jed barked.

"I thought I saw something."

"Saw what?"

"I don't know. A rock or something."

He craned his neck forward and then looked again at the chart that lay on the cockpit seat. "There's nothing out here," he said.

I don't think you want to know, she thought. Because though the cairn was slipping behind them, rooted to its place on the westward-facing cliff, she knew that Jed was about to crash headlong into it. At George Town.

She thought of George Town, of the night she came out of the BaTelCo telephone office where she'd called her aging mother in New York, and had looked up at a string of lights rising into the sky. The lights did not belong to a tower or antenna; they simply rose straight up into the blackness. They seemed attached to nothing. Only after she asked one of the locals on the street did she learn that the lights marked a cable, a cable tethered to a dark blimp above the city. The blimp, said the local man, his eyes clearly visible in the darkness, had something to do with radar and belonged to the DEA. The DEA had always been the enemy for her, and she did not feel differently now. But hadn't the cairn cast its curse on her, spell of blood? She feared that if she didn't break that spell her mind would turn to white shadow and she would no longer think or feel but only drift among these islands with the secret machete and blood on her hands.

She would bring an end to their pirate days.

"What would you like to do once we get to Staniel?" Jed asked, happier now that they were at last underway.

"A good meal," she said. "But I don't want to stay too long. I'd like to go ahead and get to George Town."

"What's in George Town?" he asked.

"Ease the sheet," she said, looking at the compass. "I think we've been pointing too high."

Abraham's Bay

22° 21' N
73° 06' W

DANIEL BERNSTEIN GULPED AIR and bent double on the hinge of his hips. He sank his head beneath the surface, a taste of salt on the stiff rubber of his snorkel. He kicked and struggled toward the bottom — all the things they had taught him to do in the Exumas, in George Town. He saw sand, some turtle grass, a bright green parrotfish, pecking at pebbles. The blue shadow of his boat rose and fell above him with the surge near shore. Water seeped at the edges of his mask, maybe because of his beard.

The first conch shell held only sand, but the second shell when he touched it, moved. He watched his hand reach out in its bright blue glove, water-blurred. He grabbed the shell's spiral and made for the surface.

He burst through, spit out his snorkel, gasped. He had taken his first conch — and none too soon, since Mayaguana marked the eastern boundary of the Bahama Islands where conch still abounded. His gloved hands fumbled with the rubber fins, then he clambered up the rope ladder to his boat. He danced across the deck of his heavy cutter, shivering with the strong east wind, beard dripping, mad Neptune from Brooklyn. Now he could fix his own conch dinner. He had eaten fresh conch in Rum Cay, had watched them clean conch dockside in Nassau. A short notch in the spiral (between rings two and three), a quick cut of the adductor muscle and out slid the slime that made the shell, the main ingredient for conch chowder, conch fritters, conch salad, cracked conch, steamed conch, all delicacies for anyone who no longer kept kosher.

He searched for hammer and chisel, switched on the single sideband to see if anyone was talking about weather. Since he'd pushed off from Rum Cay five days ago he hadn't seen another human being. It took sixteen hours to beat upwind, overnight, from Rum Cay around the lightless Samana Cays southeast to Mayaguana, a remote island 150 miles north of the passage between Cuba and Haiti. With no other boats around, he had rested, read, snorkeled, and made repairs on his boat, *Systole*, replacing, among other things, the corroded wiring on the compass light. On the third day he almost hoisted anchor despite the contrary wind, but as he stood on the foredeck, snubber lines in hand, a northeasterly gust slammed the boat, heeling it over, vibrating the shrouds like bass violins. He had secured the lines and gone below to wait, and already the fourth day at anchor was turning into afternoon.

He was weary of the silence. He wanted to explore nearby Abraham's Bay — the chart showed a small settlement at the bay's east end — but with the wind pushing two-foot chop over thickly scattered coral heads he couldn't convince himself (who would have to be both helmsman and lookout) to risk the trip. He resigned instead to anchor here at Start Bay, a brief indentation on the southern coast exposed to swell, but easy for a single-hander to enter from deep water. As soon as the howling wind dropped below twenty knots, he would resume his eastward journey toward the Dominican Republic by way of Provo, in the Turks and Caicos.

With the chisel between rings two and three he whacked the conch shell with his hammer. Twenty minutes later calcareous shards speckled the cockpit, splintered bone. Conch slime covered several teak planks, and when the chisel slid off the shell he gouged the deck. Still the conch crouched in its chamber. The wind blew Dan's curly hair and beard wild. He jammed his knife into the widening hole and sliced anything he could reach. Out came a glob, orange and rubbery — the mantle, he guessed. Still when he turned the shell and reached his pliers into the smooth horn the conch tightened with an obscene sucking sound. Reaching far in with the pliers, he grabbed the stiff sinewy foot and pulled until it tore loose, throwing him off balance and against the bulkhead. What a thoroughly botched operation. He lifted the shell high in the air, to return it to the sea.

Now a white wooden johnboat appeared around the end of the island, rocking close to where waves folded into ragged coral. At the oars, a man of middle-age pulled hard against the surge. Lean, his dark skin toughened by wind and sun, he strained with a look of resigned fatigue. Dan watched the man, the dip and pull of the oars. In the bow a young boy lay facing aft, his right leg limp on the gunwale. He was staring at an old outboard motor that hung from the transom. Dan called out, happy to see someone moving amid this blank seascape. He saw blood on the boy's leg.

The man slowed his rowing and looked up. "First my young son show how stupid he be, swimmin into th' coral, then th' motor she shut down don't y'know. Won' run a'nother minute." With waves pushing him sideways, he began rowing in earnest again, taking deep breaths.

"I'm a doctor," Dan said, the first time he had pronounced those words in a long while, a form of confession, perhaps, without pride.

The boat had drifted close now — the man could almost reach the cutter's rubrail, but he continued to row, slowly, deliberately, staying in the same place. Dan looked at the leg, at the watery red where coral had scraped away skin. "Here," he said, offering a line. "Let me look at it." The man pulled at the oars until the rope dangled near his shoulder, then he shipped the oars and curled a knot around the boat's center thwart. The boy, in damp white T-shirt and olive shorts, did not move but only watched the sky.

Dan shifted his rope ladder into the rocking boat, then

climbed down, legs flexing with the give and go of the waves. He didn't touch the skin. "That's quite a job you did there," he said. "We'd better wash that out." A shadow passed over the boy's face, but he committed himself to a firm silence, the brief appearance of teeth over his lower lip the only sign that he expected some agony. "I'll get my things," Dan said.

"You sit still," the man told the boy, though he hadn't moved.

Dan brought the water jug he kept near the "go bag" for his life raft, along with soap, hydrogen peroxide, a bactericide, and gauze bandages. Back in the johnboat he poured fresh water over the wound and soaped around it, careful at first not to touch the flayed skin, then gradually moving in. The boy squinted, closed his eyes as hydrogen peroxide hit open flesh.

Dan looked at the blood — not bad, nothing like the bloodied bodies he'd seen during his residency in Miami.

"Stop!" The boy put out his hands.

"Hold still," his father said again, watching, not moving.

"That's all," Dan said. "That's all." He reached for a roll of gauze. The doctor's voice: he couldn't help but hear it, feel it in his throat — second to his nature, as was this determined movement of his hands despite the boy's protests. The father moved now toward the stern and unbridled the motor cover to inspect the wires, the fuel line. Dan finished bandaging the leg, dark red spotting white gauze. He lifted his bag over the lifelines, and with one foot on the rope ladder and the other on the rubrail pulled himself up. The full-keel cutter felt solid after the bounce of the johnboat. When he emerged again from the companionway, he handed down a socket wrench and two spark plugs. "I always keep spares," he said. "See if they'll work."

"Rufus, thank the doctor," the father commanded.

In a prideful but delicate voice the boy said, "Thank you, Mr. . . . Docta." He looked away again at the horizon.

The spark plugs emerged from the outboard with nubs blackened by a dark carbon fur. "Old," the man said and he chucked them into the sea. Dan watched, as the porcelain and metal sank to the sand through clear water. While his father changed the plugs, Rufus braced his leg, as though it might move. Dan sidled forward on his own bow and checked the snubber lines that held the anchor chain. He kneeled to inspect the chafing gear, gray stiff canvas lashed around lines to protect against the bow's abrading pitch and dive. Where the canvas met the bow chock it gleamed shiny black, worn. Dan rotated the canvas, lashed it tight. If the lines chafed through, the boat would likely drift down on the ominous shadow of coral off his stern.

He looked at that dark patch now, and thought about his botched dinner.

With new spark plugs the outboard started on the first crank. The man said nothing but stood in the boat, placing his hands on the cutter's raised caprail like a man overlooking a balcony. Then he began to laugh in time with the outboard's sputter: haw haw haw, haw haw haw. There lay the conch shell, knocked to smithereens, the pitiable creature actually peering out from inside with its tiny frightened eyestalks.

"I had some trouble with that," Dan said.

"Haw haw haw." The man showed white teeth, put one hand forward, pale palm up, while the outboard sputtered on. Dan handed him the mangled conch and watched as he pulled from beneath the thwart a cross between a hammer and a small pick. He whacked the shell once, cutting a gap slightly closer to the second ring of horns. This opened the way into the next chamber down, separated by a thin spiraling wall of shell, and here the man's black hands thrust a knife, slicing the animal's hold, and turning the shell he pried out the soft flesh and offered it on the point of his blade. Dan took it gingerly and climbed down the companionway, tucked it into a plastic container in his refrigerator. When he looked up he flinched to see the man's face in a portlight, peering at this alien craft with its teak tables, bookshelves, and blinking electrical systems. From the stereo wafted, incongruous, Vivaldi's *Four Seasons*.

Dan returned topside to see the man off, but the large hands still gripped the rail, the motor still spitting in neutral. "You fixed th' leg. You fixed th' motor. A good doctor you must be. You come join us for a lobsta dinna. You like lobsta?"

"I like it very much. But I don't think I should leave my boat. Rough sea — and we might not get back before dark."

"We be eatin' a early dinna," the man said with that tinge of high British grace that informs the Bahamian accent.

"That's kind of you," Dan said, hesitating, considering that he did not know this fellow, did not know anything about this island except the guidebook did mention "security problems," whatever that meant, at nearby Horse Pond Bay. Then again he always liked to meet local folk, and besides he was damned sick of rocking, the steady lift and drop dazing him toward stupor. "I'll get my things," he said.

The man looked puzzled — what things would a guest have to get? — but Dan hurried to put on a belt and to fill a knapsack with foulweather jacket, flashlight, and the keys he used to lock the companionway. He also dropped in a miniature can of mace. "All set," he reported. They cast off but had to return because Dan wanted to stow the rope ladder and put out an anchor light in case they got back after dark.

The man watched the movements of the doctor with some interest but gave no sign of what he thought. Dan and the fisherman seemed to move in two separate dimensions, one fast paced and exact, at times almost urgent, the other slow and patient, as though the universe would not likely surprise him.

"How's your leg?" he asked the boy.

"It hurt."

Dan looked at him. "You'll feel better soon." The boy returned his look as if to say that it was only his leg.

When they reached a narrow stretch of white beach the boy jumped out, unconcerned, soaking his bandage in the surf. They struggled to pull the boat well onto the sand before the breaking surge crashed over the transom. Dan leaned his weight into the boat, his sandals digging deep into course sand, and he wondered how they managed it alone. The weight of the boat and of the beach itself felt good against the drift and sway of days at sea. And he had that thought again: here he was, away from his friends and relations, not in exile but wandering as surely as that old archetype, and far. For a year and a half now he had wandered up and down the east coast of the U.S. and then east across the Bahamas. He lifted his knapsack and off he trudged behind his hosts, through the sand and into a landscape as stunted and dry as the semi-deserts of the Middle East.

"I'm Dr. P," the man said as they made their way onto a dry white road.

"My name is Dan."

"Dr. Dan," the man said.

"How did you come by your name, Dr. P?"

Dr. P smiled. "We was out fishin an me I'm wearin a white apron an cuttin up th' fish, blood an guts all over, an one of m'friends he say, You look jus lika doctor. My name is Paul — after the prophet in the Bible — so afta that I become Dr. P."

And, he thought, how did he come by his name? . . . His father worked in the clothing business in Brooklyn and from very early on it was clear that he, Daniel, named not for the lion facer but for a long-deceased uncle, would become, would *be*, a doctor. Yes, he did well in school, little cause for pride or praise, since doing well was simply expected of him. In fact, much of his schoolwork seemed easy, unexacting, compared with his Hebrew studies, and long hours of book work became second nature for him, a soft-spoken boy who loved to read. Not that medical school came easily — he sometimes reeled in disbelief at the initiation rites of internship, endless days on duty, catching cat naps like a refugee. His father, too, had worked hard to put him through medical school, to put his sisters through college and (one of them) through law school. They had helped, working summer jobs, saving gifts they got from relatives in small untouched accounts, but it had been their father who supported them, launched them, who had paid with the price of his life. He never seemed able to repay his aging father and admitted the resentment this caused on both their parts, and now it was too late: he could only be a doctor, a cardiologist, in some way his father's creation, and yet he had repudiated that at age forty-eight, burned out . . . but anyway that was how he got his name, Dr. Dan.

The wind always and immediately lessened on shore, the sun incredibly present, a heavy warm hand laid on his neck and on the crown of his head where curly hair grew thin. He wished he'd remembered to pack a hat, and marveled that his hosts, who appeared unencumbered, had hats and cloth bags, dirty white and no doubt filled with lobster and conch. The road led through low hills where dry underbrush — plants he couldn't name — scrabbled over dust and rock in the relentless sun, almost a waste-land.

He saw no signs of human habitation. Walking to Dr. P's right, he asked one question after another: about Dr. P's fishing methods, what fish he caught, whether or not he sold them, and where. Dr. P answered slowly, politely as they passed a heap of rusted panels that was, once, a Jeep. A brown-spotted dog eyed this stranger with sunglasses and wild hair but did not bark. On the left a house appeared out of barren sand, its walkway marked by conch shells and its front yard devoid of plant life but for a spindly bush flowering by the doorway. They drifted past this house, and past the elderly woman who stepped into the doorway to give a single wave, until they came to a second, identical house, one story, white cinder block, with its duplicate yard of sand.

A woman pushed open the screen door, and Dr. P introduced his wife, Dolores, a middle-aged woman of rich dark skin and high cheekbones and a protected gentle smile. Dr. P said Dolores often cooked for people passing through — sailors, fishermen, the few who ventured here — and after hearing the story of Dr. Dan's help she began preparations for a mid-afternoon dinner of cracked conch, lobster tails, and pigeon peas with rice. For the cracked conch she gathered three fresh eggs from chickens that strutted not only through the yard but through the kitchen, haughty and overweening, as if the humans and not they were underfoot.

"Rum and Coke," Dr. P said, not offering but presenting a filmy plastic glass filled with deep shade. Dr. P was evidently having one himself. They sat outside at a leaning table near the front door on an array of chairs — a straight-backed wooden chair, a blue armchair with stuffing blooming from the arm rests, a cane-bottomed chair (unraveling), and a plastic-webbed aluminum chaise lounge that had perhaps once graced the floor of Sears and Roebuck. Dr. P nodded toward the chaise lounge, but Dan declined, not wanting to lie back, and chose instead the straight cane-bottomed chair, careful not to trust his weight too liberally to the cane. The blue armchair clearly belonged to Dr. P, who leaned back with a regal air, the rum and Coke in his right hand like a mace.

"You have a nice spot here," Dan said.

"It hard to keep the young people on the i-land," Dr. P said. "All our children live in Nassau now, 'cept for one son in Freeport — and Rufus. Rufus, bring the album." Rufus stopped fiddling with a small black radio on the porch railing and hobbled into the house, appearing briefly in the window of what must have been the bedroom, then shouted *I can' fine it.* "In th' dresser, top draw," Dr. P boomed out, lifting his rum and Coke to his lips. In a moment Rufus limped out again to place the album on the table and Dr. P pushed himself up to take a look. "Ah, here my daughter Denise," he exclaimed, as if seeing her picture for the first time. Dan pulled his chair over.

"How many children do you have?" he asked, adding, "She's very pretty." Denise, a teenager in a crisp peach-colored dress, smiled from the cracked pages of the album, her lips glossy.

"Ten," he said.

"Eleven," Rufus said, looking up with dark eyes, a red bandanna now wrapped tight on his head, like memory's tourniquet. The boy seemed even more sullen on land than in the johnboat.

"Ah yeah eleven. I always forgettin Rufus."

"Is Denise the oldest?" he asked.

"No, no. Denise be the . . . fifth chile."

"The sixth," Dolores said, appearing with her hands engulfed in a towel.

"Tyrone is the oldest," Dr. P said in an effort to reestablish his credibility. "He a policeman in Freeport."

"Eleven living children," Dolores said. "Three kept by God."

"Married forty-two years," Dr. P said. "Ten grandchildren with more on th' way."

"Twelve," Dolores said. "Did you forget about Donna's twins?"

"Twelve," Dr. P repeated, a little foggy, as if recalling exactly when the twins had entered the world. "Do you have children, Dr. Dan?"

"No, I'm afraid I don't. I've never been married."

"Never been married," Dolores repeated looking at his face. "He like Leon," she commented to Dr. P. "He never married, our Leon. A prosperous man too, yes Lord, a big man until drink and drugs took him down."

"Leon has children," Dr. P said, staring at the album as though their photographs might be there.

"Not in the church," Dolores said. "Oh look here Leon as a boy. Look a that." All three of them (Rufus looked the other way) stared at a small black-and-white photograph out of which a young, squinting face regarded the future, his hands empty (no baseball bat, no glove, no fishing pole). "And now he a man," she said, as if this were a dire pronouncement, a doom. She walked back toward the kitchen then, joining another woman of about her same age (Thelma, Dolores' sister, Dr. P said). He could hear one of them say, "Now you can't trus' a man." "Only man you can trus' is Jesus," the other said. "Yea, Lord, only man you can trus' is Jesus."

Dan sipped on his rum and Coke, which Dr. P apologized for. "Not very cold," he said. "We cut off th' generator las' night.

Diesel fuel low and th' mailboat she late. Still hadn't lef' port somebody say."

They talked about the mailboat being held up by the wind and looked at the album — Dr. P had some trouble with the names — until Dolores and Thelma brought plates filled with conch, lobster, peas and rice. "Get Dr. Dan a-nutha rum an Coke," Dr. P said.

"That's okay, I'm fine," Dan said but Thelma took his plastic glass anyway and he understood that Dr. P would be insulted if he refused. Rufus sat with his plate on the porch and Dan saw that only the two of them, the two men, would be eating at the table. "This looks . . . " Dan began, but Dr. P was already mumbling, eyes closed, ending with "in Jesus name we pray Amen." Dan started to add "Amen" out of politeness but couldn't bring himself to say it. He muttered only, "Thank you."

The food was spectacular, a testament to Dolores's reputation as a great cook. "A gift from God," she said, when Dan raved about the meal. She had always been a good cook, Dr. P said, even as a girl. And she just got better and better. "Gittin a little tired now," she said. "But I can still cook up some cracked conch. Yea, I can do that." She showed a beautiful smile.

All through the meal and then after, in the waning afternoon, Dr. P drank his rum and Coke, until at last his head began to hang forward, a heavy weight. Even Dan, who had paced himself, showing a half-full glass whenever Dr. P offered, felt both light-headed and heavy, the crystal blue sky lying over him. Part of him wanted to doze, right here in the front yard of this stranger's house, but he kept thinking of his boat, his home, rocking unattended off the reef at Start Bay.

"You know, I really have to get back to my boat, Dr. P. I don't trust it there, riding at anchor."

Dr. P did not seem to hear him. Were his eyes closed or was he looking at his feet?

"Dr. P?"

"He love his drink," Dolores said, taking the empty plastic glass from her husband's hand. "Man's curse."

"I really need to get back to my boat," Dan said, standing, a little unsteady. "I mean this has really been wonderful, but I'm worried about my boat."

"Old Dr. P ain't goin anywhere this night," she said, looking at him. "Maybe Sylvester will take you out. He got a boat with a good motor. Rufus! Rufus! Come here and show the good doctor down to Sylvester's house."

"Thanks," Dan said, slinging his knapsack over his shoulder. "It's been great to meet you. Please tell Dr. P when he wakes up that I very much appreciate his hospitality."

"Yea," Dolores said. "An if you can't fine a ride out to your boat you come on back and stay the night. We can make up a cot for you."

"That's very kind," Dan said, "but I really need to get back to my boat."

"Rufus!" she called again, and at last the boy came dragging around the side of the house. Where had he been? Sleeping?

"Can you find someone to take me back to my boat, Rufus?"

"Take 'im to Sylvester," Dolores said. "He always be takin people in an out Abraham's Bay."

Rufus didn't say anything, but waited for Dan to follow. Dan thanked her again, even shaking her hand, and set out with Rufus to find Sylvester.

An hour later they still had not found Sylvester or anyone else who could take him to his boat. The sun hung low on the horizon, and Dan knew that as soon as it dropped a tropical darkness would fall. It would almost certainly be dark by the time he got back to his boat, and with the high wind and all the coral around he worried that no one would want to take him.

"My motor, she's not workin too good," a man of about thirty was telling them, showing a gold tooth as he faced them in the dirt road. He seemed aggravated, perhaps at having to answer questions. "Go fine Sylvester," he advised.

"Can't fine Sylvester," Rufus said sullenly.

"Probably at the club," the man said, jerking his head toward the waterfront.

"I can't go in th' club," Rufus said, mostly to himself.

"Let 'im go in the club," the man said, indicating Dan.

"Okay," Dan said. "Thanks for your help."

The man barely nodded and continued on his way along the road, heading away from the harbor. Dan too was feeling impatient. "Let's go," he said. "I hope this Sylvester shows up, or else we've got to find someone else to run me out to the boat."

"I could take you," Rufus said.

"I don't know if that's a good idea," Dan said. "Without your dad."

They walked in silence to the waterfront, where the harbor seemed fairly calm close in but grew wilder as one looked south toward the sea.

"In there." Rufus gestured toward a run-down building. Then he turned, and began to walk away.

"Rufus," Dan said. "Where you are going?"

"Home. I tired."

"I guess you are. Does your leg hurt?"

Rufus looked down, remained silent.

"Here. Here's a couple of dollars. Thank you for your help. I'm sure I can find someone here to take me out. Tell your parents I enjoyed meeting them."

Rufus took the dollar bills almost reluctantly and stuck them in his olive shorts. Then he turned again and walked off.

Dan looked along the waterfront at the five or six boats pulled up on the sand, and at the one or two that bobbed on moorings just off the dock. Surely he could find someone here to help him.

As soon as he stepped inside the place, he wondered if he'd made a mistake. The room, while it commanded a pleasant view of the bay through open windows, seemed shut up, shut in. With the low murmur of voices in a back corner, it reminded him of cantinas he had seen in rural Mexico. He walked to the bar, but when no one came over he turned to see the men seated in the corner. They watched him. He shouldered his knapsack and walked toward the corner, where on the men's faces floated a vague hostility.

"Hi. I'm trying to get a ride out to my boat," Dan said. "They told me maybe someone named Sylvester could help me. Or anyone, really. I'd be glad to pay for the service."

The men eyed him, aware that they had the upper hand over this stranger who knew no one here, who apparently had no way to get to his boat, his only connection to the outside world.

They let the silence work on him a while, then one of them spoke. "I know Sylvester," he said. "He don't have a boat."

"He doesn't? That's strange. Dr. P said he did."

Someone laughed. "Dr. P!" he said, as if in contempt.

"Yes," Dan said, "and his wife, Dolores."

No one laughed at Dolores' name.

"What's your name?" one of the men asked.

"Dan," he said. "What's yours?"

The man didn't seem to expect the question in return. He smiled at the corners of his mouth. "My name is Sylvester," he said.

After a moment of quiet, two of the other men began to sputter like outboard motors.

"You're Sylvester. Well, I'm looking for a way back to my boat," Dan said, letting his knapsack slide down his arm into his hand.

"I am the way," Sylvester said. "And the life."

"Sylvester, the preacher," one of the men said.

"I'd be glad to pay you."

"So you said. So you said," Sylvester mused, rubbing his chin. Dan could see that he had a gold tooth, much like that of the other man they had met.

"Do you know Dr. P?" Dan asked.

One of the men pushed his chair back, almost as if in disgust, and wandered toward the bar. "Do I know Dr. P?" Sylvester said. "This is a very small island. How could I not know Dr. P? Dr. P is my friend."

"Well he said you might be able to take me back to my boat."

"Come, sit down. Have a drink."

"No thanks," Dan said. "I already had one."

"Listen, I don't drive my boat for money," Sylvester said. "I do favors for friends. Of course," he said, turning to speak to the man next to him in a vivid red-striped shirt, "I may accept money from friends (the man nodded), but I do it as a favor. For a friend. And my friends drink with me," he said, turning back to Dan.

Refusing to have his eyes caught by the men at the table, Dan looked away, toward the shore, at the boats, at the failing light. He hoped to see someone out there, preparing to cast off perhaps, or working on his outboard, but he saw no one. "Sure," he said at length. "What have you got?"

"Well, since you're buying maybe you should choose. I hear the rum is good here," Sylvester smiled.

"You don't talk like you're from around here," Dan said suddenly.

"How would you know, since you're not 'from around here'?" Sylvester asked. "But you can hear that I have spent time in the United States, eh? In New York, maybe? Is that right?"

"I'm the one with the New York accent," Dan said.

"Yes. That's true."

The man who had gone to the bar returned with a bottle of rum. "Twenty dollars," he said to Dan.

"Twenty dollars? For a bottle of rum?"

"You forget, Mr. . . . Dan, you said? You forget that a bottle of rum must be shipped here from somewhere else. We don't make much of anything on this little island."

Dan considered, then pulled his wallet from his pack. "Here," he said, opening up his wallet. "As you can see I've got enough for one bottle of rum, and that's it."

"Yes, we see," said Sylvester, "but then how will you pay for your ride home?"

Dan felt his eyes shift back and forth uncomfortably. He could tell them that he had more money hidden in his belt. He could tell them he had more money on the boat — which they no doubt guessed anyway. Instead he said only, "Don't worry. If someone gives me a ride, I'll pay them."

"With what?" Sylvester asked, but then he dropped the subject. "Let's sit over here, where we can talk."

"What 'bout some rum?" the man in the red-striped shirt asked.

"Get another bottle," Sylvester said. "I think Dan will find a way to cover his bill." Sylvester smiled again, showing the gold tooth.

Dan frowned, and Sylvester, pulling up another chair near a window said, "I sense (he leaned over to adjust his big toes in his sandals) that you are not a happy person — are you Mr. Dan?"

"I'm a very happy person. I just happen to be very worried about my boat, that's all. It's all I have."

"Ah, I wish I had that much, Mr. Dan. How much did it cost you, this boat?"

"It's not just the money," Dan said, avoiding the question. "It's where I live. It's all the work I put in her. You don't understand — it's my home."

"Your home. And your home doesn't have to be anywhere, does it, Mr. Dan? If things get a little . . . " Sylvester suddenly surveyed the room with mock drama, "tense . . . well, no problem." He raised both hands in the air. "No problem. Mr. Dan, he just moves his home somewhere else."

"What about you, Mr. Sylvester?" Dan set his glass down overly hard, as if nervous. "You were in New York, now you're here. You seem to move around yourself."

Sylvester sipped his rum, and considered this. "Yes, Mr. Dan. You are right. I have been to New York. I have seen some shit in New York.

"Exposure," he continued, with the air of a preacher. "You must have exposure. I've seen the good, the bad, and the obscene." He raised one finger, like a prophet. "On Broadway," he said, "I saw an old woman fallen down in th' street." He spread his arms wide, laying the memory of the old body on the table. "I leaned over to pick her up" (he brought his arms closer together, a large black Pieta) "but my friend said, 'Leave her alone. You don do that shit in New York.'"

Dan watched the arms come back to the table.

"I can do *better* than that," he proclaimed. "On Broadway it came so hot and humid and I wanted to go in the water, but you can't go in that water, Mr. Dan. That water is dark and dirty. I can do *better* than that."

"Sylvester," Dan said. "I don't want to get in your business, but it seems to me that you're the one who's not very happy."

Sylvester narrowed his eyes. "I have seen some shit, Mr. Dan. Did you ever see a man git slit straight up the belly? It's not a pretty sight, Mr. Dan. It's not like sailing on a boat. A man's whole insides live inside his belly, Mr. Dan. And when you slit him that way he just starts to come apart. Did you ever see that, Mr. Dan?"

Dan was quiet for a moment, then he said, "Yes, I've seen that."

"You? You've seen a man's guts all spilling out? I don't think so."

Dan considered for a moment. Then he said. "I've slit people open myself."

Sylvester sat back with a disgusted look on his face. "Mr. Dan. Do you expect me to believe that? No, no, no," he said again, "I don't think so." Then he reached down along his ankle, lifting up his white cotton trousers and pulling from its sheath a long wide blade, which he set on the table. "I don't think you even carry a knife, Mr. Dan."

Dan looked at the knife and then at Sylvester. He did not want to challenge him, eye to eye, but he wanted to see what his eyes looked like. Were they dilated? Blurred? Unfocused? "I don't use a knife when I slit people open," Dan said. "I use a scalpel."

"A scalpel?" Sylvester said in disbelief. And then the smile of understanding came to his face. "You a doctor, right?"

"Yes."

"Dr. Dan. Ho, ho, ho. You had me going, Dr. Dan. Yes you did. So you have slit people up the belly. Yes, I guess you have, Dr. Dan." Sylvester threw the rest of his drink back and fiddled with his knife, shaking his head, as if sharing a good joke with himself. "But you know," Sylvester said after a moment, looking up. "I don't use any an-as-the-sia." He laughed again at that, and the man in the red striped shirt, listening from his place at the bar, guffawed out loud, and repeated, "He don't use no an-as-the-sia . . . "

"No anesthesia," Dan smiled, sipping his drink. "I'm afraid you . . . "

"Yes, you afraid. I can see that. We can all see that."

Dan set his drink down again. "I am afraid of people like you, Sylvester. You are unpredictable. I have seen the results of your work in the ER."

"You have never seen the results of my work, Dr. Dan. And I will tell you," he leaned forward, using his knife as a pointer, "I am afraid of people like you. People hurt so deep they don't even know where they hurt."

"Why do you think that I'm . . . "

"Where is your wife, Dr. Dan? Where are your mother and father? Your brother and sister? Where are your friends? You alone, Dr. Dan. Why? Why are you so alone? Answer me that — and then tell me you don't hurt. Tell me you don't hurt with all that heavy part of the Big Apple in you. All that slitting of bellies. All that lying in the street . . . "

"You wouldn't understand anything about me, even if I told you," Dan said. The sun was going down now, but he didn't feel like fighting it any more. Let it go down. Let the darkness come. Let his boat ride its two anchors. That was the image that came to him now: a boat alone and uncaptained, riding the dark swell.

"I don't think you will tell me very much, Dr. Dan, because I don't think you know how to talk. Your mamma didn't hardly teach you how to talk, did she? Or maybe your ole man wouldn't let you . . . "

"Shut up, Sylvester. You don't know anything about me."

"Ohhhh. Ohhhh. Shut up Sylvester. That is a hostile statement, Dr. Dan. A blade in the belly kind of statement. Do you want to apologize?"

Dan looked out the window again, as if considering. Did Sylvester think he had suffered more than other people? Is that why he took upon himself this right to judge? He thought suddenly about Brooklyn, about his great aunt Ruth from Poland, who came to visit when he was still a boy. She came alone — no one else in her immediate family had survived the camps, only her, alone.

"You are not the only one with problems," Dan said. "My family has suffered too."

"I see," Sylvester said. "But if you care so much about your family why are you not with them now? Why have you left them alone with their 'problems,' as you have so dramatically put it?"

"My parents are both dead, Sylvester. A heart attack and cancer. Both gone."

Sylvester leaned back in his chair. "You have no one," he said.

Dan looked at his iceless drink and felt his throat burn. He had not thought of his Aunt Ruth in many years. At least not so directly. Indirectly he thought of her all the time. Aunt Ruth and all their doomed family.

"Dr. Dan," Sylvester said. "The stubborn man."

Dan spun the glass between his hands, back and forth, back and forth. "The first time I went sailing," he said, "was on the Charles River. I was in medical school. I had never spent any time outdoors — I was a very studious kid." He lifted the glass and drained it. "There was a woman I knew. Melinda. She knew how to sail and she took me out in a Tech Dinghy and let me take the tiller.

"I loved it right away. I never liked being in crowds. I hated the subway, trains, even airplanes. I always hated someone else being in control of where I was going. In the sailboat the city seemed so . . . removed, at a safe distance. We sailed up and down the waterfront at will, no traffic lights, no blaring horns, no crowds, no muggers, no . . . violence. If we wanted we could sail right down the river into the Atlantic Ocean, and just keep going."

"So. I see. That's what you did. You jus kept goin."

"Yes."

"Well. Well," he said again. "I guess that's what we're doin tonight. We just going to keep goin."

"Will you take me to my boat?"

"That depends, Dr. Dan."

"On what?"

"On you."

"—"

"You see, some people that come here are not exactly who they say they be. Take me, for instance. I am not exactly who you thought . . . am I?"

"No," Dan said. "I guess not."

"You are an intelligent man, 'Doctor' Dan. You understand economics. You have visited a few of our quaint little islands. You have seen our 'industry' and our 'economic development.'"

"What do you mean?"

"I mean we don't have any. What we have, Dr. Dan, is a 'tourist economy.' Do you know what that means? It means we have to bow and scrape to whoever decides to grace us with their presence. Bow and scrape."

"You have a service economy. That's all. So do a lot of other people."

"We need alternate means of income," Sylvester went on. "And that's where the problem lies. Some people don't want us to have alternate means of income, Dr. Dan. They want to keep us in what you call a 'service economy.' I call it a 'servant economy.' I don't like being a servant, Dr. Dan."

"Well, if you think I'm . . . "

"I don't think anything," Sylvester said, leaning forward. "That is a big mistake, to think something. I don't think, I find out. Once I find out, I know. And then I don't have to think, do I?"

"I can tell you right now that the only thing I'm interested in is sailing south. I didn't even plan to stop here."

"Oh really? Then why are you here now, in our little club?"

"I was just looking for a ride back to my boat."

"But why aren't you on your boat? Why are you on the island? If you wanted to come on the island, why didn't you come up to the dock in your dinghy like anyone else would do? Why did you sneak around the back way?"

"My dinghy is still lashed down on deck. And I only came ashore to have dinner with Dr. P and his wife."

"Dr. P! You traveled all the way from New York to our little island here to dine with the world-famous Dr. P, who hardly has a pot to pee in. Why am I having trouble with this, Dr. Dan? Why do we suddenly seem to have all these doctors around here, who may not even be doctors at all?" Sylvester stood up, tall in his white trousers, and now he seemed genuinely agitated, as though he were honestly confused and no longer playing a role.

Dan shifted in his chair and wondered if he too should stand, if it were time for him to try to leave, no matter where he went. Of course leaving would be hard, even if Sylvester did not try to keep him. The island would be dark, the only lights kept alive by diesel generators, and those would be shut down soon to conserve fuel. He did not know the roads or the terrain. Still, he could navigate by the stars . . .

"While you're thinking, I'm going to hit the bathroom," Dan said suddenly, standing.

"Leave your pack here," Sylvester said, just as Dan was slinging it over his shoulder.

"No. I can't do that."

"What's in that pack, Dr. Dan? Your gun?"

"No. I don't have a gun. My personal belongings."

"Leave the pack, Dan."

"I'll tell you what. I'll leave the bathroom door open. You can watch me if you want." Dan started toward the bathroom, not looking at Sylvester but listening with the whole right side of his body for the sound of approaching footsteps or any other signal of intent. He heard nothing.

When he went into the men's room he heard Sylvester's voice: "Leave it open."

He did. He unzipped his beige canvas shorts and pulled down his underwear and sat on the john with the pack at his feet. He did not take anything from the pack or even open it, but as he pretended to strain on the toilet, he fumbled with his belt, as if absentmindedly, not looking at it, but feeling with his fingers for the secret compartment and his extra money. From time to time he glanced into the room, where Sylvester was talking in a low voice with the man in the red stripes and another man with a tattered tan shirt unbuttoned to his waist. They looked his way, making sure he hadn't moved.

After he'd gotten a twenty dollar bill from the belt, he stood up and flushed the toilet. The water in the bowl barely stirred, though he heard a steady drip from the pipe under the sink. He lifted the pack and walked into the room again.

"Listen, here's the twenty for the other bottle. I've got to push on now."

"Well, Dr. Dan foun twenty more dolla in the can," Sylvester said, apparently regaining his island accent.

No one seemed to want to take it, so he placed it on the counter and took a step toward the door.

"Wait," Sylvester said. "Where you goin?"

"Dolores said she could put me up for the night. I think I'll head back there til morning."

"What do you think of the United States?" Sylvester asked, one finger raised, as if to make a point.

"Look, I've got to go," Dan said.

"What's your rush? I mean Dolores ain't goin to take you to your boat. And this island ain't goin nowhere. I just want to know what you think."

"The United States has its problems, like any country," he said. "But in most places it's a beautiful country. The cities have real problems — as you know."

"And why do the cities have such problems, Dr. Dan?"

"Is this a test?"

"Honest question, Dr. Dan."

"Poverty. Racism."

"Ra-ci-sm," Sylvester said. "Where does that come from, this racism?"

"I don't know. You can find different kinds of racism all over the world."

"You don't find it here, now do you, Dr. Dan?"

Dan looked around. "I don't know," he said.

"No. You don't know." Sylvester had taken a few steps forward and now stood between Dan and the door. "You want poor people jus to behave, right, Dr. Dan? To stay in their shacks. You don't want poor people to have dreams."

"Of course I want people to have dreams. Why wouldn't I?"

"Because that might break up your little world, that you have made so nice for yourself, with your stocks and your bonds."

Dan looked at him. It was true that his stocks and bonds were largely supporting him now, the principal set aside against his old age.

"If I have stocks and bonds what should I do?" he asked. "Give them away?"

"Jesus gave away his worldly things."

"Sure. But let's say I gave them to you. Would you then give them away yourself? It wouldn't be any better for you to keep them, would it?

"Each one of us must pass the test," Sylvester said. His eyes had gotten that blurry, fluid look to them again.

"What test?"

"If you don't know, then I pity you."

"Look, one thing I can tell you is I don't need your pity, and I don't want it. We just don't see the world the same, you and I, and that's all there is to it. That's just the way it is."

Sylvester had stopped looking at him even before he finished speaking. He looked now out the glassless window at waves gone invisible in the dusk, perhaps listening to their incessant whisper against the shore. Dan, too, looked out the window and thought of his boat riding untended at anchor. He felt a painful surge of longing.

"For in much wisdom is much grief: and he that increaseth knowledge increaseth sorrow."

"What? Is that the Old Testament?" Dan asked.

"That which is far off and exceeding deep, who can find it out?" Sylvester said again.

"Ecclesiastes, right?"

"Not bad, for a Jew," Sylvester said.

"How do you know I'm a Jew? Besides, what do you mean, for a Jew? Jews wrote the Bible, you . . . "

"God wrote the Bible," Sylvester said, looking at him directly now.

"Then Jews took dictation," Dan said. "At any rate, it was their handwriting."

Sylvester kept looking at him. "Daniel," he said. "In the lion's den."

Dan looked around. He felt again how alone he was here, and remembered all the stories he had heard of boats found adrift or at anchor with no one on board, no sign of where their owners had gone, only the stench of foul play — why else would someone abandon their boat, their floating home, with all their worldly possessions?

Sylvester went on. "Do you remember the story of Daniel in the lion's den, Dr. Dan?"

"Yes. His faith protected him. Like the story with Abraham and Isaac. It was a test of faith."

"A test," Sylvester said, knowingly, as if they had come full circle and he had made his point.

Dan looked around again, and saw that in the far corner of the room the man with the tan shirt (and, he noticed now, a red scarf or bandanna knotted around his left biceps) was doing a line with a rolled-up dollar bill. No question that the man knew that Dan could see him. Did they mean in some way to implicate him? "I'm not sure I know what you mean," he said.

"How many children did your momma have?" Sylvester went on. "Dan was Jacob's fifth son. His mother's name was Bilhah. What was your mother's name."

"Let's keep my mother out of this," Dan said.

"Ohhhhh," Sylvester said. He seemed to feel that he'd hit a nerve. For a long moment he looked at Dan in silence. And then he shifted his eyes to the other side of the room, where both men now stood bent over the table.

"My mother's name was Natalie," Dan said. "She died of cancer this past year."

Sylvester looked at him again. "Bilhah has died," he said, a kind of pronouncement. "Daniel's faith is shaken."

"What? Listen, Sylvester, I have really enjoyed speaking with you here, but . . . "

"I'm sorry about your mother," Sylvester said. "I'm sorry about your faith. That it is shaken."

"There's nothing wrong with my faith."

"Isn't there?"

Dan put his hand to his forehead involuntarily and began to rub it back and forth, something he used to do in medical school when he struggled to memorize a difficult piece of anatomy.

"Don't tell me about faith," he said. "Don't even talk about it unless you are qualified."

"Qualified?"

"Yes, qualified. By grief."

"Oh!" Sylvester said, as if struck. "'Qualified by grief.' Now we are getting somewhere, Daniel. Now I think I am beginning to hear you, way off in that fog you're sailing in. Do you believe man is made in God's image?"

"No, not exactly."

"What do you mean, 'Not exactly,' Dr. Dan?"

"I don't know. I guess I think that God has many forms."

"Many forms. Well you believe in the Garden of Eden, right? When God took the side of man and made woman, to be his mate?"

"No. No, I definitely don't believe it happened quite that way."

"Then let me ask you this. You believe that Jesus Christ is the son of God and sits on the right hand, in judgment."

Dan looked up, but his eyes felt tired. "No," he said. "You know I don't believe that."

Sylvester pursed his lips, like a lawyer on the verge of closing his case. "No of course not," Sylvester said. "You are a Jew." Sylvester said. "Practically a heathen."

Dan felt a rising discomfort. "Look, Sylvester, my grandfather told me it was best to avoid two subjects in any conversation — politics and religion. I guess I . . . "

"The killers of Christ."

"Listen, Sylvester, Jesus was a Jew himself. The Romans were the ones with all the power. They crucified plenty of people. If Jesus was killed, the Romans must have been behind it. Nothing happened in their empire without their control."

Sylvester watched him as he spoke, as if he were less interested in the words than in the way Dan moved his mouth, the way his jaw was shaped, the way his beard covered his face. Then he began to nod, very slowly, almost imperceptibly, as if understanding something he had struggled with for a long time. "Now everything comes together. Now everything is clear."

Sylvester eyed him with one eyebrow raised, not raised exactly, but cocked, as if it were kept there, straining, through an act of will. "You are saying to me that you are un-re-deemable."

Dan shifted his weight, feeling an old anger. He said he didn't look at the world that way.

"It don't matter what way you look at the world," Sylvester said, taking on his island accent again. "It matter the way the world look at you."

It occurred to him that Sylvester was stoned solid. Or was it simply a twist of mind? He couldn't be sure.

"Daniel. Dr. Daniel. Are you surprised to find the lions still here, so far along in your travels?"

"Surprised to find you? Yes, I guess I am. You certainly seem to know your scripture."

"If I told you, theological studies . . . at NYU . . . would you believe me, Dr. Dan? Would that surprise you? Would that fit with your expectation of me — of us — here in this little settlement by Abraham's Bay?"

The man with the bandanna and the man with the red-striped shirt seemed to stand more erect now, looking at him.

No, he did not believe any of this. Hadn't this conversation gone on long enough? Was Sylvester pushing it toward some conclusion he would just as soon not reach? He looked down at Sylvester's big toes.

"God be with you and protect you, Sylvester," Dan said, improvising. Then he pushed by and headed for the door. As soon as he got past Sylvester, who stood a good three inches above Dan's five foot ten, he swung the pack in front of him and stuck his hand inside, feeling for the can of mace. If Sylvester tried to stop him, he would get a face full.

But he heard nothing. Felt nothing. Dan kept walking, not looking back, not giving anyone a reason to engage him, to call to him. At first their mouths seemed sealed, then he heard

Sylvester's voice raised one last time, saying, "Be not righteous over much; neither make thyself over wise: why shouldst thou destroy thyself?"

Why, indeed.

The road, white coral sand, caught the moonlight and made an easy path. He followed it straight back across the island, toward where he thought Dr. P's house stood, but along the way the road forked three times, and each time he felt uncertain about the direction. After the third fork he found himself climbing and descending a series of ridges covered with scrub. He had seen such ridges on many of the Bahamian islands — usually iguana lived there in round holes dug in the sand, claw prints leading in and out. He didn't fear iguana, but he didn't relish the idea of walking among those dark holes in sandals with his toes sticking out. He pulled his flashlight from the pack and held it in his right hand, but refrained from turning it on, a signal of his whereabouts.

After walking for another hour, Dan realized that he was completely turned around — he could hardly believe that the island was large enough for him to be this lost. Tired, drunk, hungover, he left the road and sat down in the sand, risking the flashlight — shining red through the closed fingers of his left hand — to make certain he wasn't sitting on anything unpleasant.

From the pack he pulled his yellow foul weather jacket and lay it across his chest. Falling back, exhausted, with his head on the pack, he stared at cumulus clouds racing across stars that glittered white. A strong wind still blew from the east and scrub brush shook around him. With the echo of Sylvester's voice in his head, he recited his own favorite lines from Ecclesiastes: "The wind goeth toward the south and turneth about unto the north; it whirleth about continually, and the wind returneth again according to his circuits." Slowly the stars sank into the dark well of the sky.

He could hear the words his mother had once spoken, not

long before she died: "Sailing around on a boat. It's just not what you expect from a nice Jewish boy."

He listened to her voice in the wind.

He was playing on the rug, in their apartment, in Brooklyn. Great Aunt Ruth was talking to his parents while he pushed a toy train, his hands the hands of a giant, the hands of God. The edge of the rug made a high cliff, with the wooden planks of the floor a gulf far below, and the train ran perilously close to the edge. Aunt Ruth — everyone called her Mrs. Kupper — was telling his parents stories of trains, stories which he was not meant to hear as he played on the rug, but he understood even then that these were not stories but reports, reports of people packed into trains until they could not breathe and then taken away to . . . where? Places with foreign-sounding names he did not recognize. Perhaps his parents had looked anxiously to see if he could hear, to see if he was still caught up in his own train. Or perhaps they did not even think of him then, playing silently in the corner, their minds fixed on unspeakable images of cruelty and despair. He did not fully understand those stories, those reports from the frail Mrs. Kupper, who seemed to tremble as she spoke, but the train in his hand took a more sinister shape. When it crashed into the valley below it carried millions into the void.

———

Just before dawn, after navigating by the stars toward the island's southwest corner, Dan came at last over the final dry ridge and there she lay, apparently untouched, the small cutter-rigged sloop that had brought him hundreds of miles to here. The battery-powered anchor light had grown dim. Carefully, over sharp oolitic limestone that could cut the soles of shoes, he picked his way toward water. There was no beach here, the waves hitting rock, but the water, though stirred, stayed clear enough for him to see an open stretch of sand in the gathering light, and with his pack on his back he jumped into the sea. He knew that a thin reef separated the shore from deep water, and he swam with his head high, trying to see the most likely place to pass through, the best place to avoid the breakers and the sharp elkhorn coral. If only he had his snorkel, he could dive down and scout a passage. For a long while he treaded water, moving left and then right, but the reef seemed unbroken and he feared he would have to scramble over coral to get to the boat, a grim prospect, since he knew he would run the risk of cutting himself, as Rufus had.

When he drifted far to the right, farther than he wanted, he saw the water change color. He started to swim for the darker blue, but then he remembered the current. He was already downstream from his boat. If unable to swim against the westbound tide, he would not only not reach his boat, but he could be swept clear past the end of the island. He remembered how the current had thrown him off course as he rounded not only this island but also Rum Cay, when his boat must have been doing six knots on a close reach. He hated to think of what chance a swimmer would have against that same current. He fought his way back toward shore until he could stand. The waves lifted and lowered him, a great surge working toward the island's end. He slogged against it in his sandals, one foot after the other, his progress slow, and with each slop of the incoming swell he thought he heard a voice, calling. You. Unbeliever.

At last he worked his way upstream, shivering in the strong east wind, and he dove once again toward the reef. He wanted above all else to reach his boat, to climb aboard and be . . . home. He saw to his left the waves change their pattern. This could mean smooth coral — brain coral perhaps, just below the surface — or it could mean a break in the reef. He wished again for his mask and, even more, his fins — he swam so slowly without them — and taking a deep breath he lunged for the smooth space in the breakers. He strained to see through the stirred-up water. Sure enough, a large bulbous brain sat there, ominous, as if contemplating his death. Already he had to struggle to keep from being swept west, but to the right of the big yellow brain the water cleared and he swam for that spot, wondering and wondering, what kind of world was this and why was he in it? He, a physician, a cardiologist, a Jew, swimming for all he was worth in the midst of sharp coral, the waves lifting him like a new kind of gravity that attracted and repelled, attracted and repelled, undecided whether or not to hold him on earth. A wall of elkhorn appeared on his right, and he had to hold himself off. If he were to die here, would he have been wrong? Wrong not in the ways that Sylvester thought him wrong, not in the ways his parents thought him wrong, but wrong . . . before God?

He tried not to touch the coral, found it difficult to kick without fear of scraping his legs. Then he saw that he might be free, was almost free, and doing a kind of underwater elementary backstroke he pulled himself clumsily, ponderously away toward open water. He broke the surface, and the boat moved toward him. With a sense of joy not felt since he first bought the sloop, he swam wildly until he reached the hull and realized he could not climb aboard.

When underway, he often trailed a line — something to grab in case he fell overboard. But at anchor he used the rope ladder, the one he'd stowed to discourage anyone from climbing aboard. In fact everything about the boat seemed tucked up and sealed, unassailable. He grabbed at the rubrail's long strip of teak capped with bronze. His wet hands slipped from the rail. Almost an arm's length above the rubrail rose the deck, unattainable. He began to tire in the current, and wondered if he might die here after all. He kicked toward the stern and watched the self-steering gear plunge up and down in the swell. When the canoe stern dipped into a trough, he timed his reach, grabbed a bracket with first one hand, then the other. He held the frame for the steering gear and rode it up and down, exhausted. At last he grabbed a lifeline stanchion on the taffrail, his feet hooked around the steering gear. For a long moment he stayed there, a sea monkey clinging to the extreme end of his boat. When he'd gathered his strength again, he pulled himself to the taffrail, fumbled to free his foot, then pushed against the steering gear. He'd lost his sandals and the teeth of the steering gear poked his puffy feet.

He shoved his knapsack aboard, squeezed his shoulders beneath the lifelines, fell headfirst into the cockpit. Over him the heavy tiller twitched in its harness. The sun now rose on the horizon and the sky deepened, an immaculate blue. It seemed he could hear the speech of the sea, tapped out through quick jerks of the tiller.

"Go and get it," a voice called on shore and he sat up to see three men, Sylvester and his friends, standing on the dry ridge looking at his boat. Another man, farther down the ridge, was just disappearing, going to get something, a motor-driven skiff most likely. Dan did not wait to start his own engine but rose to his feet and scrambled forward, hunched low, as if he expected someone to shoot. The men called out, but he could not understand them in the wind. Grabbing the handle, he began to pump at the windlass, timing his movements to the rise and fall of the hull, and the bow inched forward, following the chain toward the first anchor. He hated pulling the boat closer toward shore when all he wanted was to get away from land, but he had no choice. Even if he were willing to cut free the anchors, that would take quite some time with a hack saw, since his rode was solid proof-coil chain.

His real worry was this: if one of the anchors hung up on coral — as it had done on Conception Island — he didn't think he would have time, or strength, to dive overboard and work it free.

The first anchor came up spilling pure sand, but when the boat moved over the second anchor, the chain slammed in its chocks with each passing wave, the anchor unmoving. Dan kept tension on it and finally he felt that imperceptible easing, that sense of release, as the boat let go of land. At once, he feared that he'd made a mistake not turning on the engine, the coral reef only fifteen yards off his bow, but the wind was strong out of the east, still some twenty-five knots, and with every rise and fall of the waves, he felt the hull sliding away west with wind and current. Jamming the anchor onto the bowsprit, he hustled to the cockpit and rolled out a scrap of the genoa jib, throwing the helm over hard. The inky black coral patch slid by his port quarter.

With the blustery wind, the boat veered steadily from the reef. The men were yelling again, and this time he raised his hand to them, not in farewell or in salute, but as a sign — of strength perhaps. He would have to raise the mainsail soon to make way upwind against the waves, but for now he let out more of the genoa and tied it off, sheeting it in until he was almost on a close reach, heading south-southeast. Then he slid the lines for the steering gear into their jam cleats, using another set of lines to adjust the vane so its blade sliced straight into the buffeting breeze. Wummp, a shot of spray rose high and fell like heavy rain across the cabintop. He eased the sheet and pivoted the vane, the boat now sailing due south on a beam reach, the island dead astern. The men had already begun to shrink, and the set of ridges near Start Bay dissolved, one into the other.

He was free again, free and alone and escaped. He stood for a long while at the stern and watched the island shrink, the boat's bow parting the sea. No one knew where he was or where he was going. He was wandering again, belonging to nowhere but his boat. All morning Mayaguana slipped astern. After he'd made a tuna sandwich on the last bread he'd bought in Rum Cay, he climbed back up to see that the island was gone.

His lungs swelled with salt air. Over the stale bread he almost sang out: "All the rivers run into the sea; yet the sea is not full; unto the place from whence the rivers come, thither they return again."

He had returned.

Leaving for Samaná

THE LIGHTS OF PUERTA PLATA came across the water to where Akeel stood in the cockpit. He leaned against the lifelines and worked his chin back and forth, left and right. In a week Akeel Wilson would celebrate his eleventh birthday. His father said they could have cake. His father lay below in the cramped cabin, curled on the main berth, asleep. He was supposed to be in bed too, in the V-berth, but he couldn't close his eyes. He kept thinking about his mother, who he could hardly remember. Everyone said he looked like her, that he was dark like her. He thought too about what Ramon had told him, that he and his father were soon to leave for a place called Samaná. Ramon's father was the boss of the dock, and so what he said was probably true, but when he thought about this he could hardly swallow. He didn't want to go back in the ocean again.

He looked at the shore lights and thought of the dark-haired woman who had rubbed his head today, teasing him. His father liked the women in Puerto Plata. To him they were all strangers, the ones that looked old and heavy, and the ones who looked young and bored. Sometimes they were nice to him, but always he shied away, circling behind his father, anxious to get free, to go home.

Home was the boat now, secured by a long line to a dock piling. In the dinghy they could shuttle back and forth along the line and keep the boat well away from rats on the dock. No, he didn't always feel safe here, but the boat had become familiar, and he returned to it faithfully. He feared that something terrible might happen if he didn't check back to this base, their mildewed sanctuary on the water.

When his father first spoke about the boat, it sounded like an adventure. The bus ride thrilled him as they clicked off states down to Nyack, New Jersey, and once they moved aboard he said he liked the boat more than the dirty apartments of Chicago. He felt like a pirate. And on a night like this, with warm wind in his curly hair and lights blinking on shore, he felt like a pirate still, moving through strange places where people did not speak his language.

Out of the east the wind blew and blew, another message he could not understand. More than once he heard his father curse this east wind, which would not change direction but always came from where they wanted to go. Where his father wanted to go — because he did not want to go anywhere. He had made three friends at the dock, Luis, Ramon, and Juan. They could speak some English, especially Ramon, and they let him run with them across the street to the park. There waves erupted in white foam against Hispaniola's north shore. One day Ramon threw a stone and hit him in the leg, and he cried so hard that they gathered around him and spoke in low murmuring Spanish. Perhaps even though his father had the smallest boat in the harbor, a dirty white sloop with leaky decks, they still worried that there could be trouble. That had been his lucky day, because he found a ten-dollar bill near the marina, American money, probably dropped by people on one of the sailboats, and he had stuffed it in his pocket before anyone could see. Even now he reached his hand into his khaki shorts to feel that it was still there.

But today they had made him cry again, because they told him that tomorrow he was going to Samaná. He tasted salt and vinegar at the corners of his mouth. He looked at the city lights once more and then lay down in the cockpit on the damp cushions. He did not mean to fall asleep, but when he opened his eyes the sun was coming up, and he sneaked down past his father, who snorted and snored below.

That day, when they headed toward town to buy meat (canned beef from Argentina), his father let him run with Ramon and Luis as long as he promised not to go far. His father sauntered off down the street and he watched until the tall thin figure with dirty blonde hair had gone. Ramon looked at him then with a level gaze and said, "Adios."

"Adios? I'm not going anywhere," he said.

"Si. You are goin to Samaná," Ramon said. "Hoy dia."

"We're not going any place. My father is just buying some canned meat."

"He es gettin ready for the trip," Ramon said. Luis, who could not speak very much English, just looked at him.

"We're not going anywhere," he said again, and in his throat he could feel the rawness.

Ramon picked up a small rock and hurled it into the harbor where it disappeared with a dark plunk. Then he turned and walked away, Luis following. "Adios," he said again.

Akeel wandered along the docks, looking at the sailboats. After a while his throat felt better. The tourist dock, they called it, but his father had told him it was really an old commercial dock — now semi-abandoned. Rusty iron re-bar, exposed, surrendered to the sea's salt. He passed wide around dangling electric wires, sinister snakes. He looked at the mountains, toward the white likeness of Isabel de Torres, the sad patron saint of whatever happened here.

He walked off the docks and into the parking lot, circling with his head down, hoping someone had dropped more money. As he circled, he could see the fat guard at the entrance watching him. The guard carried a gun, an automatic carbine, which he held casually in the crook of his arm. Every now and then he reached up with his free hand to rub black stubble on his face. Akeel kept circling, kicking up dust with his shoes, the lot a vast and featureless desert. The sun felt heavy on the back of his neck. When he saw his father walking past the guard, a knapsack over one shoulder, he ran to meet him.

"We're not going to Samaná today, are we, Dad? We're not going are we?"

"We won't go until tomorrow," his father said, irritated.

"Tomorrow!"

"You heard me," he said.

"I don't want to go to Samaná — ever." He followed his father to the end of the pier and stood with his arms hanging down, his body limp. His father climbed into the dinghy below, but he did not follow. When those pale blue eyes looked up, he could see his father's patience grow thin. Like the guard, his father showed dark stubble on his face, and sometimes he looked like the homeless men in Chicago, men they had known well.

"You didn't want to come here either, remember?" his father said. "You wanted to stay in Provo. Now look. You've made some friends here and you had a good time."

"I don't want to leave my friends," he cried.

"You'll make new friends in SAMANÁ," his father said, his voice rising.

"I don't want to go to Samaná."

"Get down in this boat," his father said, dropping an oar as he gestured with one hand, the blade banging against the floorboards. The boy took an involuntary step back.

"I'm warning you," his father said. "If you don't get down here in this dinghy . . . "

Perhaps because of the anger in his father's voice, he began to back away, and his father started to curse, holding the dinghy to the dock and yelling. His legs turned and he began stumbling and then running back down the dock.

Other people on their boats, preparing to have drinks or a late lunch, saw the boy with dirty curls run by and saw his father bang his knee as he scrambled up the dock's rotting makeshift ladder.

The boy ran onto the dirt lot. He wanted it to be the first night again, when they had finally come in off the sea, and it was like coming home for good.

His father caught him as he neared the park. He felt the hard clamp of his father's hand around his arm, fingers rigid and tight, like anchor rope when it went hard in a big wind. Immediately he felt himself swing on the pivot of his father's grasp, trees along the shore gliding away left, wild carousel. "You stop when I tell you!" his father yelled in his ear.

He tried to look at the wind-blown trees — they seemed to wave all boats away from the shore — but his father grabbed his chin and spun his head around.

"I'm sorry, Papa," he said. "I was afraid."

"You better be afraid," his father yelled, "or I'm gonna knock the shit outta you!" He felt two hands on him now, shaking him. His face: he felt it begin to collapse in on itself. "You better not cry!" his father screamed. "I swear I'll smack you!"

He looked down. He saw his father's shoes, not boat shoes like the other men wore, but black sneakers, without socks, the same shoes he had worn in Chicago on the concrete and asphalt streets. He knew his father did not have money to buy new shoes. "I'll be good," he said. "I'll be good." He did not know exactly what that meant — probably it meant that he would go to Samaná, that he would leave his friends. He felt them vanishing already, boys he had hardly known, who had taunted him, and now he would leave them as he had left everything, in Chicago, in Florida, in the Bahamas, and now here. Soon he would leave Samaná too, and go on and on. His life had became nothing more or less than leaving, ever since his mother had begun the leave-taking that morning when she was not in the bed and his father had spent the night alone.

His father began to drag him by the arm back across the lot, and he said, "I'll come, I'll come," but his father would not let go and kept pulling him toward the boat.

"We could go to Dominican Joe's," he said. "And have

lunch." He knew his father liked Dominican Joe's, and he hoped this might break the evil spell of his anger.

Instead, his father wheeled around and leaned into his face. "Oh yeah? What are we supposed to do for money? Do you think they're going to feed us for free?"

"I have some money," he said, and then felt afraid: money was too powerful a thing for him to have, especially without telling his father — it now seemed like a dark secret he never should have kept.

"What? What are you talking about?"

He pulled the ten dollar bill out of his pocket and held it out to his father. "I found it this morning," he lied. "I was going to give it to you."

"Where? Where did you find it?"

"On the ground. Near the marina. I was going to give it to you, honest."

"You didn't take this off the boat, didya? If you took this off the boat . . . "

"Dad! I would never take it off the boat! I would never take it off the boat! I found it on the ground . . . near the marina. Dad!"

"All right. All right. You found it on the ground. Near the marina." His father looked at the bill for some time, as if to convince himself not only that it had not come from the boat but that it was real and not some pretend money his son had found.

"We could eat lunch," he said again. "At Dominican Joe's."

His father's pale blue eyes changed now, quickly, abruptly, the taut painter of his anger parted. He seemed almost serene, as if remembering a fond moment, now focused on some place that was not here in the flat blue light of Hispaniola.

"Can we . . . "

"All right. All right," he said again. For a moment longer his father stood looking at the ten dollar bill, then he put it in his pocket. "Let's go eat lunch," he said. "But not at Dominican Joe's. I know another place."

The downtown cantina was quiet, not like at night when people crowded around the bar. His father walked directly to a bar stool and sat down. "Com'on, Akeel," his father said. He didn't usually sit at the bar, but this time his father helped him up on the stool and he let his feet dangle, using the bar to swing himself left and right, right and left. "Settle down," his father said. He looked at his father, who appeared neither serene nor angry now, but expectant — not impatient, but determined, as he sat waiting for someone to serve them. He knew people liked that about his father: he did not stay angry long. In fact, he thought, maybe it would be better if he stayed angry longer — but he never did. The anger always bled away from his face, leaving a placid gaze. It was almost, at times, as if his father did not mind giving in on the small daily battles, saving his energy for a larger war ahead. He wondered what that war was, and whether his father would ever fight it.

"Buenos," a man said. He turned to see the bartender coming toward them with a woman who might be his sister — they both had dark eyebrows and dark eyes, with pupils as black as the ebony shells he found on the beach at Conception Island.

"Buenos," his father said. The man had already gone around behind the bar, and the woman, perhaps recognizing his father, walked up and stood close to the bar stool, so close her breasts brushed against his father's arm.

"Que tal?" she smiled.

"Nada mas," his father said. During the last two weeks he had learned a few words.

Akeel ordered a Coke while his father and his woman friend drank tequila, straight from small tumblers, and after a while he got down from the stool and walked with his glass to the far wall to look at the pictures there. Some were drawings and some were photographs and with some it was hard to tell. The men in the pictures were probably famous, but he did not know them. He looked at their faces and tried to think of who they were. He had seen lots of photographs before, but after being on the boat for so many months, things looked different. He stared at a picture of a woman and thought about what it must have been like at the moment the camera clicked, how she must have felt, with the photographer standing over her. He wondered if she knew how her blouse looked, unbuttoned halfway down — like the woman at the bar — with the rounded tops of her breasts full and exposed. He wondered if his mother ever looked like that. He had seen only a few pictures of her, one that his father kept in his wallet, and another that he remembered from his grandmother's apartment, on the dark sideboard near the door. After his grandmother died all the furniture was sold or given away, and he didn't know what had happened to the photograph. He hadn't really thought about it until now.

He looked at the picture of the woman and pretended it was his mother. The woman's hair was not as black as his mother's, but that didn't matter.

"How are you?" his mother asked.

"Oh," he said, "I'm okay."

"Do you have any friends?"

"I had some friends here in Puerto Plata," he said, "but they weren't like best friends. We're going to Samaná tomorrow. Dad says I will make some new friends there."

"Oh."

"At first I didn't want to go to Samaná, but . . . "

He was getting tired of talking to his mother and didn't know what else to say. Then a roach appeared on the frame, looking over his mother's shoulder. "Git!" he said. "Git!" He took his straw and poked at the roach, which lit out across the wall in the open. He tried to stab it as it ran, jabbing his straw all along the wall, hitting some of the pictures as he went.

"Hey! Hey!" his father said. "What th' hell are you doing!"

"I saw a roach," he said.

"Impo-sí-ble!" the woman said, looking with mock horror at the bartender, who shrugged his shoulders.

"Well just settle down," his father said. His voice had taken on a different quality now, sluggish and sloppy. The woman laughed and ran her fingers through her hair.

After a while he got another Coke and began moving his neck back and forth. He leaned his head all the way to the right as far as it would go, and then he leaned it to the left. Each time he tried to make it go farther, but he could feel something like elastic or rubber bands pulling at the opposite side. He began wagging his head back and forth faster and faster and faster until he felt a little sick. The room seemed shallow, losing its weight and depth.

He asked his father if they could go now, but his father was speaking to the woman, who was practically sitting in his lap. "Cuánto dinero?" his father said. The woman leaned over and put her lips to his father's ear and whispered something. "Mañana," he said. "Dinero mañana." She leveled at him a long questioning look. "No," she said. "Ahora." She had beautiful white teeth.

"I can get it to you mañana," his father said.

"El no tiene dinero," the bartender said, rubbing a glass and holding it to the light. "El no tiene dinero."

The woman said something to the bartender very fast, a kind of question, and the bartender answered her in the same quick speech. He could not tell what they were saying. The smooth olive skin of her face took on a look of disgust, and she began to move back down the bar.

"Mañana," his father said, as if this were the only word he could say in his favor, but she moved to the last revolving stool, nearest the door. His father slid from his stool and walked toward her. His walking had changed, like his speech. "Mañana," he said again. He reached out to touch her shoulder, took hold of her blouse. She jerked away, and her blouse came loose from her slacks, a tan breast sliding free as several buttons popped off, one button bouncing on the bar.

"Eh! Eh!" the bartender was saying as he lurched toward his father, grabbing his shirt the same way that his father had grabbed the woman's shirt and pulling him against the bar. Akeel didn't know what to do and looked over at the picture of his mother on the wall, to see if she might help.

"Don't!" he yelled. "Don't do that!" He ran to his father and grabbed him around the waist.

The woman began to yell at them all. She had pulled away and gestured at her blouse, where the buttons had popped. Her voice was loud, and it seemed she might soon do something truly horrible and violent. "Come on, Dad," he pleaded. "Let's go!" But the bartender still had a handful of his father's shirt, twisting it, so that the material bunched tight against his father's neck. The bartender was speaking to his father in low, threatening tones, which he couldn't hear over the scolding voice of the woman. He looked up at his father, who looked bewildered and unable to understand. His father seemed in a trance, not grasping where he was or what had happened. Akeel looked at the woman, her pretty face now twisted in anger. He looked at the bartender's expression, cold and menacing, like that of a snake.

Holding to his father's belt, he began to cry. The woman stopped yelling then and looked at him. Her eyes glared red, not from crying but from something else. Slowly the bartender let go his father's shirt and put both his hands on the bar. "Dinero," the bartender said. "Para la camisa. Para la tequila." His father looked at him but did not understand. "Dinero," the man said again, "money," and finally his father reached into his pocket and pulled out the ten dollar bill. It looked crumpled and old, worse than it had looked when he pulled it from the puddle near the marina. It seemed to have shrunk in size, and he wondered if it were not good money after all. The bartender reached out and took it before his father could even offer. "Es todo?" the bartender said, but his father only stared vacantly at the ten-dollar bill, as though he had meant to give it to someone else.

"Go! Go!" the bartender said, flicking his hands at them. "Boracho!" he said.

The woman picked the button from the bar and turned it over in her hand before sticking it into her tight slacks. She leaned her head back and shook her hair free. He pushed against his father's hip, and finally it moved. They drifted past the woman, his father still pleading with his pale and vacant blue eyes. His father had become the sad observer of his own life again, and they made their way toward the door, shoulder against boney hip in an awkward dance, father and son.

It took a long time to get to the marina. His father kept stopping, the energy going out of him so that he simply slowed and slowed until he ceased moving altogether. He stood on the side of the road, looking down at his black sneakers. "We're almost back to the boat," Akeel said, and now the boat seemed like home again. He wanted only to be there, with the dinghy tied to the stern and water all around so no one could reach them. He didn't care whether they went to Samaná or anywhere else. He only wanted to be on the boat, lying in the V-berth with his comic books and his army men, at anchor, so the boat would lie still and not toss his things around.

Suddenly his father leaned over the curb and began to puke. He kept out of the way but held his father's leg: he was afraid the tall thin body might lean too far and fall. Late afternoon had overtaken them — the light had that thin and delicate quality of the tropics before night suddenly drops its canopy of stars. He knew that they should get back to the boat before the light left, but they couldn't go anywhere until his father finished. He saw the fragile dilapidated hillside shacks, white and orange and turquoise, turn lovely as they rose in the distance toward the crest of the mountain. As the sun sank, light clung to the shacks and to the peak where Isabel de Torres stared blindly over them toward the sea. He pulled at the heavy leg, but his father doubled over again, coughing in pain. "I love you, Dad," he said.

Overhead a frigate bird made its way along the coast, heading east, against the trade wind, toward Samaná.

Isabel

THE CANADIAN BOATS had already hoisted anchor. One white mainsail after another climbed its mast, wind whipped. Diesel engines coughed smoke as a half-dozen sloops pointed their bows into the swell and plunged east along the north shore of the Dominican Republic. The sun sailed in the opposite direction, its blazing masthead going down over the western horizon.

They planned to motorsail all night, taking advantage of katabatic winds that dropped down the mountainsides. It was a good plan, except now the anchor chain hardened at the bow and would not budge. Jonathan Burke, forty-one years old, with close-cropped beard, thin and a bit out of shape, signaled to his wife to cut the throttle. Without a windlass he had to hoist the chain by hand and feed it through the hawse hole. He waited for the rise and fall of the bow to jerk the anchor free, but the chain just slammed in the chock. Stuck.

He watched the other sailboats leave this small bay at Sosua. The word had gone around in Puerta Plata that a group of Canadians planned to push off for Samaná, and he and Isabel had decided to go with them. They didn't often see things the same way lately, but they agreed that it was best not to sail these waters alone. Now the other boats pulled away and he prickled at this separation from the pack.

"Caught!" he called to Isabel, waving his flat hand back and forth. She put the engine in neutral and stared at him with dark questioning eyes. He clambered back to the companionway and barked that he was getting his snorkel.

She asked what they were stuck on.

"Hell if I know," he said.

He hated going overboard at dusk, the very time when sharks began their crepuscular hunt. Soon visibility would vanish from these reef-strewn waters, and he had no underwater light. Without time to deploy the dinghy, he pulled the rubbery mask over his beard, grabbed his fins, and jumped overboard. Cold seawater rushed to his armpits, his crotch. Drifting in a deadman's float, he pulled on his fins, forcing ghostly white feet into stiff rubber. He blew on the snorkel to clear salt water, took several breaths, then dove.

The heavy Bruce anchor lay almost twenty feet down. He had no trouble following the chain's arc to the anchor, but once there he ran out of air. He jiggled the fouled chain, then headed up.

He broke the surface gasping, had trouble getting his breath.

"You have to pace yourself." Isabel stood on the bow, brushing curls from her face.

He squeezed the chain, angry. He didn't need her lectures. It was true. He had rushed. Even with the light going, he forced himself to wait for his breath. And not for the first time he asked himself what the hell he was doing out here. He was a creative writing teacher, a man who lived a life of the imagination. He had no reason to be hanging to this chain as it plunged in cold waves. This broad embayment, where they'd anchored for the afternoon, wasn't even a real harbor. And now, shark hour.

"Okay," he whispered to the chain. He took several measured breaths and dove. He pulled himself down using the chain and got there faster this time. He could see the lone piece of brain coral and the links wrapped around it. The coral's surface showed canyons of curved channels. He tried pulling the chain. Looped beneath the coral, it wouldn't move.

When he broke the surface a second time he focused on measuring his breath.

"What's up?" Isabel asked. Her face was framed by wild curls, as she rose and fell on the bow.

"Wrapped around brain coral." He felt bad about the coral, and this added to his anger. Hoisting himself on the chain he scanned the waves for fins. "You have to pull forward slightly," he said, "to ease the chain. Only slightly. Or you'll pull my arm off. Understand? Say you understand."

Isabel brushed a shock of curls from her face and said, "Got it."

He said something into the snorkel's plastic, but it sounded more like humming.

White smoke raced from the stern and he felt the bow slog into the wind. The reefed main was loose and slatting. He dove again. The light had dimmed — he was out of time. He pulled hand-over-hand down to the gray anchor, barely visible, and prayed no moray eel waited on the coral's underside. He saw the chain slacken as the hull's shadow drifted overhead. Gray steel links around the edge of the coral started to fold. At last he unwrapped the chain counterclockwise and out of air he made for the surface. If the anchor had been any deeper, he thought, or more tightly wrapped, he couldn't have freed it.

"The ladder," he sputtered, but Isabel had already thought of this and was dropping it near the stern. He handed up his fins and scrambled onboard, making straight for the bow before the anchor could foul again. He shouted for her to alternate forward and neutral, to hold position. Not taking time to put on his gloves, he pulled the chain and dropped it clattering on the deck. He would stow it later. At last he felt the bite of the anchor itself and kept tension as the bow plunged. When the flukes broke free he hauled with all his strength. Over his shoulder he shouted, "Get your course!" Off the starboard bow a slate gray fin sliced the water, and he said, "Jesus, Joseph, and Mary."

He dragged the anchor over its roller and fed the chain into the locker, arms aching.

Balancing back along the deck, he fell into the cockpit and collapsed against the coaming.

Isabel looked at him. He was shivering.

He pulled binoculars from their holder and looked for the Canadian boats, far ahead. "I'm glad we got out of there," he said. "No place to spend the night. Especially if the wind gets any north in it."

"Isn't it gorgeous?" Isabel said. He looked at her, dark hair wild and wind-blown. In the west the sky blazed with the sun's last light. To the east the shoreline, jagged and steep, arced toward the great cape of Francés Viejo. Her delicate right hand held the wheel, her left the coaming. Her face glowed with excitement.

He made his way below. In the pitching cabin he turned on the red night lights for the knot meter and depth finder and the red chart table light. The numbers of the GPS already glowed green. On the chart he slid parallel rules along the rugged coast, from Sosua to the first cape, then the second, then the third. All upwind. It was going to be a long night.

He climbed halfway up the companionway. "Our course is about 104 degrees true, but we'll just have to motor-tack on and off soundings." This was their strategy: to motor-tack offshore until they lost the shelter of the capes and the katabatic winds, and then to tack back toward shore until the depth finder sounded the bottom. Then they would motor-tack offshore again. With the throbbing engine, the main pulled in tight, and the aid of nocturnal winds, they could make their way against the contrary current and prevailing easterlies of Hispaniola's north shore, the so-called Thorny Path.

He asked if she was still okay with taking the first watch.

She said she was great. She could use a little coffee.

He took a final look around at the deepening darkness then dropped down the companionway. With a flick of the spark-gun he lit the propane stove and stood watching the blue-and-yellow flame play against the pot. Once the coffee began to steam, he held a thermos over the galley sink and poured with care as the boat plunged. When he reappeared in the cockpit she reached for the thermos and puckered her full lips. He gave her a peck on the mouth and said he was beat. He would relieve her in three hours.

―――

After Jonathan disappeared below, Isabel locked the wheel and poured coffee into the stainless steel cup. Steam flew away. The wind felt soft on her skin and carried the fragrance of Hispaniola. She slung the binoculars around her neck, lifted them to watch the flicker of white stern lights ahead. When the Canadians tacked she would see their green starboard running lights, a clear signal they'd altered course. Sighting about 110 degrees off the binnacle's lighted compass, she searched for that other white light, the beacon on Cabo Francés Viejo, but so far nothing.

Now the stars brightened in earnest, the big dipper straight ahead. She wished Jonathan could see this, share this moment with her, but of course they had to do this in shifts. And with no autopilot (only a windvane, which they wouldn't use so close along the coast) they had to hand steer. Still, she wished he could sit with her in the cockpit, as they did on their night sails in the Chesapeake Bay, especially when they were younger. Before that episode at Fallon. Or had he started to change before then? She couldn't be sure.

Out of habit she checked the depth finder but it showed only two aphasic hyphens, the bottom of the Atlantic far beyond its reach. Though infamous for rocks and currents, the Dominican Republic's shore was steep-to, and boats quickly found deep water. That meant they also quickly found shallow water, she realized, but on the off-shore tack there was little to fear. Farther out, the chart showed there was much to fear. To the north, a good distance away, lay the Silver Banks, and east of that, the Navidad Banks, endless miles of reef, hidden by shadowy corrugations of waves. In the dark, and perhaps even in the light, those dangers would remain largely invisible until it was too late.

What a night! The sloop arced over each wave like a dolphin and sent spray flying to the lee. The diesel engine kept the boat moving forward and allowed it to point high, but the real power through the waves came from the main, even with its single reef. Discounting the low throb beneath her feet, she felt the boat sailing on her lines, sailing close-hauled, and she thrilled at finding the slot.

———

In the sea berth, tucked between pillows on one side and the stretched canvas of the leecloth on the other, Jonathan Burke tried not to dream. His mind gave way to the diesel's pounding heart and the rush of water in his ear. He tried not to think what he always thought, that he had tried to live a life of the imagination, and had failed. He could feel himself collapse, his head heavy with too much dreaming.

He was staggering at the front of the room, telling his students to be quiet. They joked and jeered, ignoring him. He had no voice, and his mouth opened and closed without sound. Then Rachel rose with a question. Her long dark hair and dark eyes. Her clothes, over-large and loose, fell from her thin body. He waved her away, a bad trance, but she kept staring, powerful eyes shining into bad places. And as in so many dreams, he reached out, waking the moment he touched her.

The cabin was not completely dark. The GPS and radio lit the chart table, dimly, with their green glowing numbers. He pressed the button on his cheap wristwatch, but though the dial lit with pale white light, his eyes, blurred with sleep, could not read it. He lay for a moment longer, lulled by the incessant rising and falling, even if tired of it.

He slithered out of the sea berth feet first and stumbled forward to pee. Just as he stepped through the head's narrow doorway the boat fell into a trough and he slammed forward into the bulkhead. He put his hand to his forehead. I'll have a nice knot there, he thought, like the time that nun whacked me with a ruler.

The boat lurched again, throwing his right shoulder into the doorjamb. Sharp pain. Hit me again, he thought. Punish me. He thought again that this sailing trip was Isabel's idea, to break free, but he was not free. He was paying penance. He was in purgatory, or worse. He held on in the dark, abiding his torture, one of the damned.

When he finally climbed the companionway with more hot coffee, he saw that the stars had wheeled west. Canopus sank near the sea. "Everything okay?" he called. Isabel, her curly hair tucked beneath the hood of her windbreaker, said "Fine." She had that soft voice that came at night underway. In no hurry, she lifted the binoculars slowly to scan the shoreline to the south. In the last three hours she had, remarkably, caught all but one of the Canadian boats, no doubt a trick of the currents, and he could see the white transom light of the lone boat ahead of them, about a mile or two off.

Jonathan took the wheel and listened while she updated him on their position. Then he wished her a good rest. She stood behind him for a while, kneaded his shoulders. He reached for the binoculars, to look for landmarks along the coast. Waves continued to come at them as only waves can, mountains that melted away. Isabel kissed him on the cheek then disappeared below.

He locked the wheel long enough to transfer fuel from a fifteen-gallon bladder tank in the cockpit locker. He'd jury-rigged a hose through a petcock to the main aluminum tank low in the hull, and so far the contraption worked.

This jack-legged fuel system was only one of many make-do things on the boat. Glancing around, he could think of a hundred connections — electrical and mechanical — that he'd clamped, taped, tacked, coiled, bound, and screwed. Each could pop loose without warning, spilling water or diesel fuel or propane or ending a vital electrical link between an antenna or a transducer and the radio, the GPS, the depth finder. He lived in constant fear of what would go wrong.

All night they traded the helm, but during the day they sat together in the cockpit, silent, and sailed across the melancholy Bahía Escocesa. According to the guidebook, a troubled woman haunted this wide bay, and at night one could hear her weep. It did not say why. With the wind at a decent angle, they cut the engine and sailed close hauled for hours, but the Canadian boats hugged the shore and made better time toward Puerto Escondido. As evening approached, Jonathan started the engine again and headed straight for high rocks guarding the hidden port.

By the time they neared the harbor's narrow cut, they'd almost caught the Canadian boats again, and they could see each one make its sharp turn toward a fjord sliced into steep rock. They neared the cut, side by side, Isabel at the wheel, the boat sliding closer to sheer gray cliffs. In a north wind, the fjord wild with breakers, a boat could not enter here. In a steady east wind like today, the harbor offered shelter, protected by verdant mountains that rose to a height of some three thousand feet as the land lifted from the shore.

Already, so fast, daylight was fading, and once in the secluded harbor Isabel steered among the other boats while he went forward to lower the anchor. On his signal she backed down until the rode went taut. She killed the diesel, then joined him on the foredeck. They sat, backs against the cabin, looking landward. She squeezed his hand. Along the narrow sand beach stood small thatched shacks backed by palm trees. Palm fronds waved in balmy air. "This could be the South Pacific," Isabel said, leaning against his arm. "One could lie among the palms and forget about everything."

Jonathan said, "Maybe. The guidebook says you're not supposed to go ashore."

The sun slid behind a rocky promontory. They went below then to heat a bowl of canned chicken soup and munched on crackers they'd bought in Puerta Plata. They also listened to the VHF radio — they wanted to hear what the Canadian boats were saying. When he carried the bowls to the sink and started to wash them, she followed, reached her arms around him from behind. "It's so beautiful here," she said. When he turned she caught his face in her hands and put her lips against his. At that moment the radio crackled and one of the Canadian boats called out to the others.

"Hey," he said, holding her off, "let's see what the Canadians are up to."

"I don't care what the Canadians are up to," Isabel said. "I want to know what's up with you."

"I just want to hear the plan, that's all," he said. "I expect they'll pull anchor around midnight. Just hang on."

Isabel lifted her black sweatshirt over her head and shook out her curls. Then she walked to the forward cabin and swung the door shut.

At the edges of his mouth he licked salt.

The Canadians all agreed that in order to approach Samaná in broad daylight they would leave around midnight. All except one woman named Nancy Watkins. Jonathan and Isabel had met her briefly in Puerta Plata. A stocky, graying woman, she had sailed a Freedom catboat with her teenaged son all the way from Toronto, through the locks and down the coast.

"It took us so long to get here," she complained. "It's seems stupid to leave so quickly."

"But we can't go ashore here," another boat, *Sundowner*, said. "It isn't allowed."

"Oh, who cares, really?" Nancy Watkins said, sounding tired and exasperated.

"It isn't allowed," the man said again. "You're liable to run into trouble with the authorities."

Other boats spoke up, and in the end, despite her arguments, they all agreed that it was a beautiful place but they had no choice but to haul anchor again at midnight. They could not stay. Then, as an afterthought, *Sundowner* said, "*Dream Cloud*, you there?"

Jonathan reached over and pulled the mike from its metal clip. "We're here."

"How about you? Coming with us?"

"We considered selling the boat, but we decided against it. We'll leave with you."

He had meant this to be funny, but the voice in the speaker just said, "Right."

He sat on the berth in the main cabin and set his wristwatch for 11:50. Then he leaned back and rested his eyes and a little later, without thinking, he buried his face in a pillow.

Midnight. Boat engines coughed, their stertorous rattle like that of old trucks. Each time he turned the key his chest tightened as if to lift the high-compression cylinders through an act of volition. And each time, remarkably, *Dream Cloud*'s old diesel turned over, grumbled and started to run. With the engine turning the alternator, all systems were go: the batteries charging, the electronics and running lights switched on, the radio ready for transmitting without fear of draining the batteries. He hauled the chain and this time it came aboard freely. The bow fell off the wind. Once more they were underway.

He stayed forward to secure the anchor, and Isabel took the wheel. She said little but her eyes took in everything, the parade of white stern lights, the ceiling of stars, the vertical rock walls lit by a half moon. She did not look at him.

As soon as they rounded the dark headland, ocean swells lifted the hull, but it was not bad, nothing like leaving Big Sand Key, off the Turks Channel, where waves piled up on the Caicos Bank. Here the sea had less bulk, waves capping gently in the breeze, white crests softer and less threatening. He remembered that they were in the lee of Cabo Cabrón, and that this technique, first used as far as he knew by Columbus, of ghosting close inshore under protection of the great capes — Isabela, Macoris, Francés Viejo, Cabrón — worked wonderfully well. Of course Columbus had stayed too close inshore and had lost the *Santa Maria* in a grounding.

He took the wheel while Isabel went below to check the chart again. He could see her face, scarlet in the glow of the red chart light. Then she switched off the light and left him in darkness. He looked toward the blackness that lay before the bow. The Thorny Path.

"Cape Cabrón," he said when, hours later, she stepped up through the companionway in her bright yellow slicker. She had overslept and looked surprised to see the predawn light. She peered over the blue canvas dodger, steadying herself with both hands. There lay the dark headland, rising some 400 feet out of the sea, and beyond that, the suggestion of Cabo Samaná, only a shadow but slowly taking shape.

Isabel came toward him to take the wheel, which he surrendered. He went below to check the bilge. At times, wallowing among the waves, *Dream Cloud* felt sluggish, and when he lifted the board over the bilge's deep well he expected seawater, sloshing, drowning the batteries, steadily filling the boat. The sea could enter in so many places — around the spinning propeller shaft, where a steady drip slipped past the packing gland, around the half-dozen through-hull fittings (where he had installed the new knot meter, the new depth finder, the enlarged cockpit scuppers), and by way of the ground plate, where the heads of two large bronze bolts showed signs of electrolysis, turning as pink as coral. He feared that one day the ground plate would simply fall off, leaving two neat quarter-inch holes, where water would gush.

He lifted the floorboard and clicked his flashlight. The water lay low in the bilge's dark and oily cellar. He felt his muscles relax: the skin of the hull with all its holes still held.

When he climbed into the cockpit again, the world had changed. The predawn sky, adorned with colossal, rainless clouds, had taken on the air of a giant cathedral. Light streamed from the stained glass of the horizon. Isabel had tacked away from shore, away from Cape Cabrón, but now well off to starboard Cabo Samaná began to grow in height and mass, plunging out into the eternal east wind and rolling seas. Like the prow, he thought, of Hispaniola itself, the second largest of the Greater Antilles, a ship of stone forever eastbound for Africa.

As they tacked again, he saw that the small fleet of Canadian boats had dispersed, no longer motor sailing purposely forward, but all beating in different configurations into a congenial wind. They had all day to get to the small harbor in Samaná Bay, and no one was rushing. With the boats scattering far and wide, so many bandannas in the breeze, he felt alone before this single promontory jutting from the east end of the island. The small sloop made its way against the wind, slipping past the white-foamed rocks as frigate birds circled high overhead. It seemed to him, as the gray details of boulders came clear, that they were rounding Cape Horn, at the very end of the world.

More than that, he saw that all the events of his life had placed him here, rounding this high cape in the luminous dawn, and he had to ask himself, wasn't it worth it? And then for no reason he thought of that line from St. Augustine. *Into Carthage I came burning.*

No one enjoys the light, the laughter, the smells of a crowded restaurant more than those who have just come from off the sea. Jonathan and Isabel looked around with amused astonishment. A tall Englishman, blonde hair brushed back over his ears, lounged against the bar, which he occasionally slapped to make his point. The bartender watched with what seemed mock intensity, while others continued to talk among themselves, center of a clamorous universe. At the round tables they heard not only Spanish but English, French, and German and a language they could not name — Norwegian perhaps. And all the faces seemed bright, bronzed, infused with Dominican energy.

Between the tables, dipping and sweeping more like a hostess than a waitress, a young Dominican girl greeted everyone, including him, showing a sweet smile. Though incongruous on one so young, she wore a pink strapless dress cut low, perhaps made for an older sister. After every dip and stretch she had to hoist it up with her free hand to keep the glossy material over her slight breasts. Jonathan ordered the local beer and let the light and music of the place flow over him. Isabel looked lovely across the table, her dark eyes drifting over the scene, her hand around a glass of wine that gleamed ruby red. She had changed her sweatshirt and slicker for dangling earrings and a violet blouse, scooped, showing tan skin.

He ordered fish — grouper, the special of the night — and fresh vegetables (something they had had so little of, not only at sea but also in the Bahamas). When his meal came he looked at it for a long moment, not wanting to end this anticipation, steam rising from the boiled potatoes and the fish, something waiting to happen, as before a summer rain. Now the young girl appeared and poured into his glass the remaining beer, pure amber. Her hands were delicate. Compared with her, all others in the bar, men and women alike, seemed old, bound by gravity, tied to the trivial. She, with long dark hair and slender arms, appeared to Jonathan to step from another race, another time.

He drank the beer with relish, washing the salt-lined walls of his throat, and it passed right through him. He stood, the ground moving gently as it did after days at sea, and told Isabel he'd be right back. She looked at him, the hint of a question at the corners of her eyes.

"Everything satisfactory, I assume."

The accent, so bluntly American, startled him, as did the face he turned to see, of a middle-aged, balding but very "present" man, who seemed at once clever and solicitous. "Wonderful," he said. "Is this your restaurant?"

"It is indeed. I'm glad you're enjoying yourself. Name's Morgan," he said, presenting a carefully manicured hand.

"A pleasure to meet you, Mr. Morgan. I was just . . . "

"Not Mr. Just Morgan. Please."

"Certainly. Morgan. I was just on my way to the men's room. Am I heading in the right direction?"

"Yes you are. Right back there. Past the . . . women's room." As Jonathan navigated through the tables, Morgan leaned over to converse with Isabel.

In the men's room the familiar posture of leaning over a urinal, rare in these months of sailing, brought back his past life. Those years of commuting into Philadelphia from the suburbs, the too-busy monotony of the workweek melting into the undirected haziness of week-ends. Was it that languor that had in some way led to the unfortunate event at the school? He shuddered. Even here, with so much water in between.

He twisted the four-bladed knob, but the pipe only bled a brown and sluggish dribble. Over the sink, held to the wall by a rusted thumb tack, a clipping torn from some tourist booklet informed him that Columbus had arrived at Samaná Bay on November 22, 1493. He claimed to have seen mermaids.

Leaving the soiled men's room he walked past the unmarked door he assumed was the women's room and listened to the sound of a woman there — was she moaning? calling? singing? The sound did not resemble speech. It did not, in fact, resemble a woman, though now he heard another sound, what he could only think to call a titter, of another woman perhaps, a young woman. He must have carried his curiosity with him to the table, because his wife asked, as he sat down, "Anything wrong?"

"Wrong? No. No, not at all. Bathroom's a little on the dingy side," he said serenely.

She gazed at him with a penetrating look, as though she had finally begun to see that no matter how long they stayed together, she would never understand him.

———

The next day they dinghied in from their chosen anchorage well out in the harbor, tying their old inflatable among a tangle of others at the main dock. They decided to split up to take care of their chores. He was to find out about diesel and ice. She would look into the possibility of taking a tour into the mountains, and perhaps even catching a bus to Santo Domingo.

Diesel fuel apparently posed no problem and could be had right on the dock, as long as the electricity was running. Ice, on the other hand, was a major problem, because every time the electricity faltered, the ice melted, and so most stores didn't want to deal with it. He decided to walk to the edge of town, to Morgan's place, which seemed to have plenty of ice, and where he could also grab something for lunch — something of a splurge, since they'd just eaten out the night before, but he figured what the hell.

A young man in a flowered shirt led him to a table and he wrestled with the menu, half Spanish, half English, looking up occasionally to see if the girl from the night before might be there again. Sure enough, she came from the back, looking much the same as he remembered her, though now she wore casual clothes, khaki shorts and a white T-shirt. "Buenos dias," he said. "Buenas," she answered, but not so gaily as the night before.

He ordered chicken soup and fresh bread and sat fiddling with the spoon until it came. All through their trip he'd encountered moments such as this, sitting in a restaurant or leaning against a wall in the middle of the day, feeling, well, useless, and thinking about what everyone would be doing back home in the middle of the week, teaching, working, keeping up with their schedules. At these times he felt uncertain about his decision to take this leave of absence without pay, each day taking its toll on their meager savings, without leading him toward the next phase of his life. He couldn't think what that would be, this next phase of his life. Sometimes it seemed he could hardly think of anything other than what could go wrong, what had gone wrong.

The young girl appeared again, with a hanging basket dripping red blossoms. She watered it with a short green hose and then tried to hang it near the entrance, stretching high on her toes, her body straining to reach a hook that eluded her. He started to get up, to see if he could help, but hesitated. Then the man named Morgan appeared from the back with an amused smile. He said something to the girl through his grin, and putting his hands just below her rib cage lifted her high enough to reach the hook. He held her there a moment, even after she had released the hanging basket, and she brought her hands down to his wrists as if to push them away, saying, "Basta."

He relaxed his grip then and she slid down to the floor, but he did not move his hands away, so that the T-shirt gathered in his palms as she slipped down, baring her stomach, and for a moment he kept his hands on her, with the cloth gathered there, long enough for her to make a quick hissing sound, then he let go and the T-shirt fell.

She turned on her bare heels and walked briskly through the door to the back, while Morgan, who seemed now to recognize him, sauntered toward the table. "Mind if I sit down?"

He said nothing but did not object, looking with some curiosity at this man with thinning hair and a bronze complexion, a man who, he guessed, may have been plump in the United States but here had managed a certain trimness.

"So how long have you lived here, in Samaná?"

Morgan did not answer but pulled a silver case from his breast pocket and withdrew a cigar-colored cigarette. "Mind?" he asked. Then he lit it and placed the match carefully in the ashtray. Beneath his open shirt a gold chain glinted. He thought for a moment that Morgan may not have heard.

"You would like to ask me a few questions," the bronze man said. "I'll tell you what. I will answer your questions if you will answer mine. Fair enough? It will be a kind of trade."

"What questions?" he asked.

"Oh, I don't know. The same kind of questions you ask me, I suppose."

The young man with the flowered shirt brought the soup and placed it in front of him, along with a small loaf of bread on a white plate. The bread looked fresh and hot. "All right," he said. "I was just wondering how long you'd been in Samaná."

"Five years," Morgan said. "Before that I was in Santo Domingo for several years, but I would rather not talk about that evil city."

"Did you have a restaurant there?"

Morgan smiled at him and then took a long drag on the dark

cigarette, the end heating to red. "My turn," he breathed. "Why did you leave the United States?"

He brought the soup to his lips. It was hot, like the bread. "You say that as if I was forced to leave the country," he joked.

"Do I?" Morgan said.

He met the man's eyes then, and saw that they were hazel, almost a touch of copper. "My wife and I planned this trip for a long time."

"Well," he said, "that's not exactly an answer to my question."

"Okay," he said. "I needed to get away."

"I gathered that from your wife," Morgan said. "What I was asking was *why*."

Morgan continued to smile. He seemed to enjoy this kind of conversation.

"Don't worry, I'm not a fugitive. Just some personal trouble."

"Some trouble," Morgan said. "Yes we all have some trouble. But life has its compensations, doesn't it?"

Did Morgan mean to imply something in particular? He continued to eat his soup and didn't take it up.

"Any more questions?" Morgan said, tapping his cigarette.

"Not really." Then the young girl came out and started to wrap utensils into red cloth napkins. She focused on her work and did not seem to notice them. A wisp of brown hair fell forward across her cheek.

Morgan twisted his cigarette in the ashtray, the bright parrots on his shirt shrugging their shoulders as he moved. "Isabela," he said abruptly. The young girl looked up from the utensils. He beckoned with his hand, and she came toward the table. "Come here," he said and she moved next to him. "You are wondering how old she is. Is that your next question?"

"Sure," he said. Trying to smile at her, as if to reassure her. "How old are you?"

"Cuántos años?" Morgan said.

"Quince," she said, very quietly, looking down as if to hide her smile.

"Muy joven," Morgan said. "Muy guapa. Muy bonita."

"Yes," he said. "All right if I take the bread with me? How much for the soup and the bread?"

"Is that the question you want to ask me?" Morgan said. He reached up and put his hand around the girl's waist. "One hundred dollars," he said.

He laughed suddenly, a kind of hiccup. "Expensive soup," he said.

"The best you'll ever have. Take my word for it."

He stood up and took the bread, leaving an American ten dollar bill on the table. "I think that's enough questions," he said.

"Come again," Morgan smiled, still sitting with his arm around the young girl's waist. "I would like to hear more about your trip. And here — a little prize for the question game." He held out a stumpy cigarette, twisted at both ends. Though uncertain why, Jonathan took it.

"Where have you been?" Isabel asked when he finally returned to the dock. "I'm about to starve."

"Sorry," he said. "Ice is hard to come by here. We'll have to get it later."

"Well let's eat something. I can't wait any longer."

He looked toward the restaurant across the street. "How about Samaná Sam's?"

"Fine," she said, "just so long as it's fast."

That night, sitting in their cockpit, they watched as a dinghy from one of the Canadian boats headed straight toward them. The white-bearded captain, Louis, came alongside, killing the engine at the last minute and grabbing the rubrail. "Ahoy, *Dream Cloud*," he said, though they were sitting right there. He asked if they would join him for a *sundowner*. They looked at each other. "Well . . . " he started to say, but Isabel answered that they'd love to. "We'll head over in about ten minutes, how's that?" she said.

Louis said that would be super and thumped on the hull, as if testing it. "Scandinavian boat, isn't it?" Yes, they said. "Pretty," he said. Then he added, "I'm an Alberg man myself," and yanked at the cord, the small Yamaha engine roaring to life. He aimed the hard-bottomed dinghy toward his sloop, an orange-hulled, racy-looking boat with a swept-back dodger. Isabel said it didn't look anything like an Alberg.

A short while later they climbed into their own dinghy and started, after a few pulls, the four-horsepower Johnson. Their soft dinghy moved more slowly than the hard-bottom boats, but they didn't have far to go, and before long they pulled alongside, realizing as they secured the dinghy's painter how much higher this boat's freeboard was. In fact, every boat they'd visited since setting out some five months before had been bigger than theirs: longer, deeper, wider. Though they never thought of their boat as large, on the northern Chesapeake Bay where they most often sailed, the boat felt stout. Once on the ocean, it shrank.

"Hey, *Dream Cloud*. Come on aboard." Louis helped them up and handed each a rum drink made with a sweet fruit punch. "Have you met my wife, Elaine?"

Elaine held out a dainty hand made rough from several months of weather and rope burn. Her eyes looked clear, even if circled with fatigue.

"Wasn't Puerto Plata awful?" she said, offering them each a cushion with a blue compass rose stitched on the front. "There were rats!"

"Oh, I liked it there," Isabel said. "It was a great place to reprovision. Very cheap."

"Exactly!" Louis said. "The best place in the Caribbean for reprovisioning." It seemed that Louis and Elaine had already discussed this.

Jonathan settled back against the high coaming and sipped his drink. Other people's boats. They always looked in great shape and didn't reveal their leaky through-hulls, failing alternators, wood rot beneath the cockpit. It was all surface aboard someone else's boat, and he could relax as he never could on his own. That was the complaint he heard most often since they'd set out: the endless maintenance, the constant struggle to stay ahead of the next disaster. He looked across the water as twilight settled on the town. In the center of the harbor an elaborate foot bridge led to a small island surrounded by some two dozen boats at anchor. *Dream Cloud* swung gracefully from her chain, and from here Jonathan could see no blemishes.

"Excuse me?"

"We were just talking about why we decided to go to sea," Elaine said. "Louis was facing a possible bankruptcy trial," she went on gaily. "How about you? What convinced you to take this trip?"

"Just a glutton for punishment, I guess."

"Jonathan did have a bit of a run-in with his school administration," Isabel said.

"Sounds juicy. Tell us all about it. Was anyone killed?"

"No, it was nothing really," Jonathan said.

"Where do you teach, Jonathan?"

"The Fallon Day School," he said. "In Philadelphia."

"It's a really good private school," Isabel said. "He teaches English and creative writing."

"Oh, how nice," Elaine said. "Did you have an argument with your principal, then?"

"Yes, I guess I did," Jonathan said. "We didn't see eye to eye on the curriculum."

"Oh," Elaine said. "I see." She seemed disappointed in the story.

Isabel lowered her rum drink and looked at Jonathan. "Well," she said, "it wasn't quite as simple as that."

"I'm sure they don't want to be bored with details about my job," he said. "So tell me, Louis, how you got here. Did you cross the banks from Miami?"

After they returned to the small sloop and secured the dinghy, Isabel, who'd drunk a few rum punches, became sullen. "Why didn't you tell them about that asshole Dr. Bevin?" she said. "It would do you good to get it off your chest."

"That whole thing's my business, Isabel," he said. "If it's all right with you I'd just as soon leave it behind."

"You're never going to come to terms with it if you don't even talk about it," she said. "I mean you were completely innocent. It's their problem, not yours." She swayed slightly as she hung onto the boom. He wished she would lower her voice.

"Let's drop it," he said.

"Maybe I don't want to drop it. Maybe I want to hear you talk about it for once."

"Well you can talk about it yourself. I'm going to bed." He climbed down the companionway and yanked the damp T-shirt over his head as if shedding his own skin.

He collapsed into the berth and at once feigned sleep, listening to Isabel move around the cabin in lurches, spinning with the weight of the over-proof rum. At last she climbed into the forward berth and shut off the cabin light, leaving him to stare at a sepulcher-darkness.

A sad panic came over him, as though the child in him had suddenly awakened somewhere horrible — a Spanish dungeon reserved for the faithless — and he wondered: How did I come to be in this place?

He loved sailing (at least he had loved it as a boy), and he felt at ease with the notion of living on a sailboat, but what was he doing, really? Was he actually trying to escape — from himself? What about the writing he said he would do? That dream of syllables, of words filling page after page?

I want to hear you talk about it, she had said. But, God, hadn't they talked about it, and talked and talked? The truth was (the truth!) that no one knew but he what had happened, not only during the "incident," but before, during and after. In his mind. In his heart. He still felt (at least most of him did) that the "incident" had been innocent enough. And now, lying in this narrow berth, dark as his soul's grave, he saw it all again, the thin, thin light that came into the classroom, blocked and caught by the veiled dust that always hung in empty schoolrooms. Everyone was gone except those teachers and students who stayed behind for extracurricular activities, and in this room, he, alone, and Rachel. Rachel, dark, beautiful, and brilliant, who would edit this term's collection of mediocre and youthful poetry, the anthology he pulled together every year. Seventeen years old, with long and unruly hair, clothes unruly as well, holes in the knees of her jeans, her shirttail half out. He must have assumed at some (presumably weak) place behind his navel, where the Chinese place the chi, that she herself had an unruly spirit.

No, this was to make too much of it. And to sell himself too short. He had taught many students and had developed a professional manner that allowed him to befriend them without coming too close, to gain their trust but still demand their respect. Then why had he, that day when she did not wear jeans but a miniskirt, red plaid, why had he reached out and placed his hand on her knee? Later, before the principal and her parents, he would say he was simply making a point and had reached out thoughtlessly, punctuating his thought with his finger. And she had misinterpreted it. He regretted any misunderstanding this had caused . . .

Her parents, her stiff and defending father, her mother, worried and wounded, clutching her purse as if prepared to strike him with it, and he drawing on all his persuasive skills to get past this moment in his life, past this one small impropriety, this misjudgment — this *innocent* misjudgment, he had called it.

But how innocent, that was the question lodged not only in their eyes, but in his own heart. Even now, lying in the berth, he could call up at least a half dozen young students who had exchanged glances with him, young women moving into the prime of their beauty, flashing their pert smiles and cutting their eyes. He had never touched any of them, but looking through the lens of the "incident," he lost confidence. If the opportunity had presented itself — and isn't that what had been presented to him, in that classroom with the thin light, an opportunity, and hadn't he taken advantage of it?

Or had he simply reached out to touch her, as he said? He tried to think. He relived the moment (again), listening to her speak, watching the wooden earrings she wore that day, a collection of varnished triangles, as they hung from her ear and banged against the gentle curve of her neck, earrings (he thought) that belonged on a much older woman. He saw how her lips moved, closing softly over her teeth. He saw how her youthful lids, free of wrinkles, slid down over the almond clarity of her eyes. He saw how, from the unremarkable cloth of her skirt, her uncovered legs bent at the knee with the fluid curve of a swan's neck. He reached out.

There. At that moment. What could he find in his mind? What had he intended? What signal of peptides had raced between head and hand? If she had not stood and looked at him, and left the room —

No use. The truth lay in his hand, in sinew and tendon and bone. His mind did not have access to that information. And so no matter how many times he struggled to think of it, he came up empty, a man unsure of whether he had been wronged or whether he had, like a lucky criminal, escaped the consequence of his crime.

You were completely innocent, Isabel had said. But he was not — could he ever be? — sure.

For seven days they swayed at anchor in the palm-ringed harbor of Samaná. Isabel bought a whole bag of mangos from a woman on the street, and as she ate them juice ran from the corners of her mouth. They wiped sea salt from the stainless steel fittings and the mahogany cabin. He ran the engine to charge the batteries and then changed the oil, ferrying the used oil in a plastic jug to the dock where he hoped it would be recycled. For much of the time they reclined in the sunny cockpit and read. He read about Hispaniola, making long notes in his journal. His ball point pen slid across humid paper, as he tried to capture the history of this place.

The native peoples were Tainos, and they called this island Quisqueya. Quisqueya. What did that mean? The Spanish renamed it Hispaniola, Columbus establishing Navidad on the north shore, then, a little farther east, on a cove, the settlement of Isabela. The area proved swampy, and disease claimed many of his men. The Spaniards enslaved the Tainos, taking the women for concubines and often working the men until they dropped. After fifteen years of subjugation, the native population fell from an estimated one million or more to some 50,000. He read that by 1517, only 11,000 of the original inhabitants remained. In 1518 small pox reduced the natives further to some 3,000. These Spanish Christians, who at first viewed the Tainos as an inexhaustible supply of free labor and love slaves, had virtually wiped them out in less than a single generation.

The native Tainos used tobacco and other narcotics to get high, he read, and that night after Isabel had fallen asleep, he sat in the cockpit alone and smoked the joint Morgan had given him. He also sipped a rum and Coke to cut a gnawing anxiety. Overhead stars swirled like Taino dancers, and some glided to earth and landed in the palm trees that ringed the hillsides around the harbor. The east wind blew, and the naked palms swayed their hips and waved their arms over their heads. He heard the groans of a terrible kind of love as conquistadors took the native women in the hills. The wind took up those moaning cries and played them off all the shrouds of boats in the harbor. *Dream Cloud* moaned far into the night, even after his eyes closed, and the stars stopped their dance.

The next day, squinting in bright sunlight, Jonathan read how the Buccaneers — named for their fire-cured rawhide — settled on the North Shore of Hispaniola and plundered passing ships. These Buccaneers ultimately governed the Island of Tortuga, off the coast of Haiti, and one buccaneer turned wealthy pirate eventually became the governor of Jamaica. His name was Henry Morgan.

"What the Europeans did to these people," he said to Isabel, who sat on the opposite side of the cockpit, reading her Jane Austen novel. "Even the privateers we read so much about in our history books."

Isabel looked up. "Sometimes when you trim your beard a certain way, I think you look like a privateer," she said.

———

And so on the eighth day he walked out of town in his stiff boat shoes, kicking up dust, recalling one particular sentence he had read: "The offspring of Spanish men and native women had given rise to a handsome race, some of spectacular beauty." Two young boys standing by the road watched with clear liquid eyes, and one called out, *Hay-sus*, probably because of his beard. When he arrived at Morgan's he saw neither Morgan nor Isabela, nor even the young man who had waited on him before, but only one older man with a well-trimmed mustache who showed him to a table, and he began to doubt his first appraisal of this place. Then he saw the girl, not wearing the low-slung dress of the first night or the T-shirt of the second day, but only shorts and a tank top with something in Spanish written across the front.

"Is Mr. . . . is Morgan here?" he asked the mustached man.

"Si, Señor. Un momento."

Morgan appeared in a white shirt, a cigar rising out of the pocket, shrouded in cellophane. From his left ear hung a round ring. Morgan did not seem particularly glad to see him.

"Back from Puerto Rico already?" he said.

"No. I don't think we're going to Puerto Rico."

"Oh. I thought you were."

He realized that the mustached man was hovering near the next table, and that he had not ordered anything. He didn't think that he would. "I have another question for you," he said.

Morgan raised an eyebrow and collapsed back into a cane chair, reaching instinctively for his cigar. He peeled away the cellophane.

"Another question."

"Yes. It's about Isabela."

Morgan looked up. He stared at Jonathan with hazel eyes that appeared now as pale as amber. "Is-a-bela," he said. He let his tongue move over all the syllables.

"I think I'd like to see her."

"To see her," Morgan said.

"Yes," he said again. "To see her."

"Well it just so happens that she is here."

"I know."

"And," Morgan said, "what if your wife should come by? What should I tell her?"

The jungle cat, playing with its prey. "Don't tell her anything."

"Hmmmmm," Morgan said. He sat back in his chair, examining his cigar, moving his fingers up and down the brown tobacco leaf.

"Well? Can I see her?"

"Still one-hundred dollars," Morgan said. "A bargain at any price."

He reached into his pocket and felt for his folding money — two wads of bills he had put there this morning, standing at the chart table drawer, furtively removing the cash from its envelope in the old engine manual, where he kept it hidden, moving quickly, before Isabel came back from the V-berth. He pulled out ten ten-dollar bills and handed them to Morgan.

"Do you know the name of the oldest street in the oldest city in the so-called New World?" Morgan asked with a wry smile. "Calle las Damas." His smile vanished as he added, "First door on your left."

Jonathan got up and stepped away from the table, a hollow feeling in his head and stomach, as if he'd been drinking. He did not look at Morgan — he did not want to meet his eyes — but walked straight toward the back, disciplining himself not to make, in the midst of his uneasiness, some clever or obscene remark. The back of the place looked familiar — he recalled that first day, when they'd just arrived in the small Dominican town, when he had walked to the men's room. Only now he was knocking on the door of the other room, the *women's room*, feeling less like a teacher than a teenager, as if this were the first time he had knocked on a woman's door.

"Sí?" An old crone stood in the doorway and regarded him. He thought that she might prevent him from entering.

"Isabela," he said.

She looked at him still, and then he heard Morgan yell from somewhere near the bar: "Maria. O-kay. Es bueno . . . "

The woman pulled the door back then, without emotion, not welcoming him, not resenting him, simply allowing him. With her graying hair pulled back in a bun, she looked almost prim, though tired. Before him light bounced from white-washed walls. At the rear of the room the walls turned right, making a small dark hallway that followed the western wall of the building. He tried to picture the shape and size of the structure as they came into another room, two cots pressed against the wall among a confusion of cosmetic jars, hair brushes, and hand mirrors. Above the cots a mirror, frameless, captured his bearded reflection as he passed. He looked away. The woman named Maria walked on without a word and he followed. Turning right, past a toilet splotched with brown, they came to a dead end with two doorways covered by cloth. Through one of them, past a curtain white but no longer clean, he saw someone, either a woman or a man, corpulent, with folds of flesh above the hips, lying face down on a cot.

"Isabela," the woman said.

He turned to see the woman holding a curtain to the next room, where sunlight ignited a constellation of dust particles. He watched the tiny flecks drift through the doorway, and then he pressed a five-dollar bill, wet with perspiration, to the old woman's palm and stepped into the room. The young girl sat on the cot, a half-dozen magazines spread around her, most of them, it seemed, in English. Her shirt said, "A Dios." After the old woman left, he straightened out the curtain so it would cover the doorway completely, then leaned against the wall opposite the cot and looked at her.

"Do you speak English?" he said.

She shrugged her shoulders. He saw how young she was, like the children he saw daily in town, the ones with no shoes, the ones who said they were in school but who every morning greeted him as he came ashore to eat breakfast or to search once again for ice. And yet not like them: in some way . . . what? More savvy? Or simply more beautiful, one of God's masterworks, just as one orchid among a thousand will have petals more perfect.

"No puedo hablar Español bastante bien," he said.

She looked at him still, almost smiling. "Que lastima," she said. Her eyes were amber, not unlike Morgan's, full of light, the eyes of a young conquistador.

For a long moment he leaned against the wall, needed its support. He felt his own sweat. Air drifted through an open window. He looked down at his dilapidated boat shoes and at loose threads that hung from his olive green shorts. He felt out of place, overdressed, perhaps because of his knit shirt, navy blue, with its rolled collar, more suited for a golf course than for . . . here.

"Su nombre es Isabela," he said.

"Me llamo Isabela," she corrected him.

"Sí."

"Como te llamas?" she asked.

"Juan," he said.

"Como no," she said, not believing him.

"Sí," he said. "Es verdad."

She nodded, still not believing him — and not caring — and leaned over to move the heap of magazines, gathering them into a loose pile, these faces with heavy made-up, a bright collage that she shuffled together and dropped on the cement floor beside the cot.

"There is something I want to say. About something that happened to me," he said. "I may have done something wrong."

"No entiendo," she said.

"It may not seem like such a terrible thing to you." He felt the tip of his tongue run along the dry surface of his upper lip. "But . . . I was unable to sleep."

"No entiendo," she said again.

He looked out through soiled white curtains to the tangled courtyard where a few customers now ate, hidden from view by a trellis overgrown with bougainvillea. At the center of a dusty clearing off to the right a chicken pecked, while species of plants unknown to him, their roots in search of water, baked in tropical sunlight.

"You see," he said, "I haven't been able to make love to my wife since then." Rubbing his forehead, he tried to think more clearly. How could he be so thirsty? "I was always the innocent one," he said, smiling wryly. "The good husband. El bueno. Understand?"

"No entiendo," she said.

"And in one moment I was no longer the good man. Her parents looked at me with such awful suspicion. Everybody did."

He walked over and sat on the edge of the bed. She moved her bare legs to make room. He saw how the bottoms of her feet had already become rough. "My father left when I was seven," he went on. "I never met the woman he ran away with, but I saw her picture once. She was very young. Very pretty. Like you. I became 'the man of the house' then, the one who never let anybody down."

"Basta," she said. She slipped down lower in the bed and placed her fingers over her bare thighs in a gesture most likely taught her by someone. Morgan maybe.

He noticed on the windowsill a ceramic cup, off-white, with a broken handle and an abstract sun on the front, red-orange. He felt a sudden sympathy for the hands that shaped that clay.

"Muy hermoso," he said gesturing toward the *taso*.

"Sí."

"Sometimes, in my country, when we can't speak to each other, we pay someone to listen to us. Where I come from we pay for everything. Even talking." He laughed abruptly, and this startled her. She watched him with dark eyes, her lips showing the hint of an uncertain smile. As if to settle him, she reached out and touched the bottom of his unraveling shorts. Electricity — the voltage of another's hand — ran to his brain, where it found negative ground. With her fingers among the loosening threads, he reached his own hand into his shorts and pulled out the second wad. She looked at it, clearly uncomfortable with all those folded bills.

"Para Morgan," she said in her child's voice. "Solamente para Morgan."

"No," he said. "Para tu. Here. Put this here." He took the beige shorts from the floor where they lay next to the pile of magazines and put the money in one of the pockets.

She watched him, frightened, as if the money were dangerous. "Cuánto dinero?" she asked.

"One hundred dollars," he said. "Ciento American. Para tu. Para su familia."

She seemed uncertain, then as if moving in a gesture known to women, and only to women, for ten thousand years, she began to lift the tank top over her head. He reached out quickly and took her wrist. "Esto no es . . . You don't need to do this. Ever. Entiendes?" For a long moment they remained like this, her stomach and chest bare, her skin bronze. He felt taken by the very color of her — then she relaxed and lowered her arm.

"No," he said, "I am not innocent." Then he pushed himself from the bed and left.

That afternoon, when he returned to the boat, Isabel told him the Canadian boats were leaving. "They're headed for Boqueron," she said. "Across the Mona Passage."

"You know we can't go with them."

"I know," she said.

"We're out of time and we're out of money."

"I know."

"And Fallon Day School is the only job I've got right now."

"I know," she said. Her eyes glistened in the sunlight. "It's just that I don't want to go back."

"No," he said. "Neither do I."

The Canadian boats waited for sundown, for the wind to drop. Jonathan and Isabel were just finishing dinner when they heard the familiar voice. "*Dream Cloud. Dream Cloud,*" the radio said. "This is *Sundowner.*"

"Channel 10, *Sundowner,*" he said.

"Sure you don't want to come with us?" the voice crackled from the charcoal gray box.

"Wish we could," he said. "I'm afraid we have to head home."

"Roger. Well smooth sailing. We'll drink a rum for you in Boqueron."

"Yes," Jonathan said. "Good luck."

"Thanks. You too. Over and out."

Over.

And out.

They sat in the cockpit and watched as the Canadians crawled over the decks of their boats. He saw running lights, red and green, come alive and shadowy anchors break water. He heard the clank of chain on deck and the low rumble of diesel engines as the boats ghosted away from their anchorages. He saw Isabel standing in the cockpit with the binoculars, watching the boats weave their way through the harbor without them. He ducked below and switched on the main engine battery and then came back to the cockpit to turn the key. The diesel lumbered and then started, as it always did, one more miracle.

"We have to charge the batteries," he said.

Truth was he felt dead in the water, with the other boats underway, prepared for sea, while they remained tied to the bottom. He also wanted the radio, to listen in on the Canadian boats as they decided how close to cut the coral reefs heading east.

The hills of Samaná folded toward the mountains of the interior, where, he'd heard, soldiers on horseback rode into villages and swooped up young women, taking them to Puerta Plata for the amusement of the troops. Was that true? He didn't know. The dark mountains held their secrets.

He felt better with the engine running, as if they might actually hoist anchor, but Isabel sat in the cockpit with the binoculars in her lap, her eyes liquid stars. He looked at her, at her long dark lashes and full lips. She looked regal, with her high cheekbones and sculpted nose. He wondered why he hadn't thought of this before, that her name was the same as the first cape they'd sighted as they approached Hispaniola: Cabo Isabela. Was it possible that she had not only Russian but Italian or Spanish blood? After all, there were theories that Columbus himself had been part Jewish; perhaps Isabel's forebears had traveled through Genoa or Cadiz. And yet it had been that other Isabela and her husband Ferdinand, the Catholic monarchy, who expelled the Jews. He looked at her again. No, she was her own royalty, with her own strength, which never failed to surprise him. Whether crossing coral reefs or setting out in the dead of night, she never appeared to have second thoughts. Though raised in Philadelphia, she seemed at ease with the sea. Between the two of them, she was the sailor.

She had also weathered Jonathan's struggles to leave behind his Catholic upbringing, not to mention what had happened at Fallon. But there was no reason to be remembering that now, not here beneath the stars of Samaná, dancing again.

He moved to put his arm around her but she did not want his comforting. She seemed a child of the sea, and he could hardly hold her. For a long time they sat watching the eastern horizon, at first watching the tiny white stern lights and then simply the horizon itself, the dark east.

Isabel stood and handed him the binoculars.

"I'll see you in bed," she said.

"Yes," he said, taking hold of her arm. "You will."

She looked at him and her arm slipped away.

"If you're lucky," she said.

Then she climbed down the companionway.

Souvenir's Last Passage

O NLY A FOOT FROM HER FACE phosphorus ignited the dark sea surface, white light. Nan Gray, trim and athletic for her sixty-four years, clung to the lifelines and watched as if forced. She loved the way this white magic boiled past the lee rail, but she had thrust her head out not to watch the water but because she was about to get sick again.

At the stern the windvane dipped to the left and kept the boat plowing through the waves.

There, it came, and went, angry hand at her gut. What anger was this? And why tonight, after weeks aboard, as they worked the boat north along the Lesser Antilles? Then serenity, quiet at the center of anxiety's ring, the peace of the recently nauseated.

The ring of anxiety was vague, but also had one specific cause — the person she loved most was losing his mind. Even in her fatigued state, riding these relentless seas between Barbuda and St. Barts, she could recall with absolute clarity (and the same gripping of the stomach) the first time she glimpsed what was now becoming his future. She and Bill were walking across the yard of a friend's house on the York River. "I saw Fran last week," Bill had said. "She's got to have a hysterectomy." The news might have come as a shock, except that he had pronounced this exact sentence not twenty minutes before. She recalled how the muscles in her legs had frozen, a stabbing chill down her back. She'd almost stumbled. Bill must have thought the news had blindsided her.

Everyone repeats now and then. Everyone has lapses. But deep intuition and more than three decades of marriage told her this repetition was like nothing he had uttered before. A bright and quick-witted man, a scholar, he knew exactly what he said and when he said it. That he would appear so completely unaware that he had just said this same sentence twice, to the same person, during the same walk along the river, frightened her. As the weeks and months passed, her premonition proved true. His memory was washing away. And because memory — more than she had ever understood — forms the frame for personality, for consciousness, he was losing nothing less than himself.

Despite the warm east wind, a chill came and she trembled. This blasted seasickness was taking its toll. She felt foggy.

Though hours away from St. Barts, she pictured the rocks and reefs the chart showed around the island. She needed to get to the navigation table, with its perpetual demand for exactitude, but felt unwilling to go below. In ten minutes her midnight watch would end and it would be Bill's turn. Would he remember? Would he know why his wristwatch beeped?

She rubbed her hands against her face and felt the roughness of her aging fingers: was this last passage a foolish, romantic mistake? It had been Bill's fervent, no, desperate, wish, once he began to understand what was happening to him. "Take one last sail with me, Nan," he implored. "I'm up to it. I know I am. And even if I weren't, you can handle the boat as well as I can. Maybe better. Please. It will be the last passage for us."

No, she had said. There will be plenty more passages. Plenty more.

A wave sloshed against the side of the bow and came washing back, licking her face. Since they'd put out from Venezuela, where the boat had spent hurricane season, she'd learned all too well that this would indeed be their last passage, and wondered now that she'd let him talk her into it. "He will begin to make irrational choices," the doctor told her, describing the long torturous path toward oblivion on which he had embarked. "Oh," she said, "we've always made those." The bald doctor had looked at her over his reading glasses, without humor.

"Hey," he said, and she wheeled around, wide eyed. He was standing in the cockpit, his thin gray hair matted by sleep. "It's my turn."

She nodded and smiled. She twisted back toward the sea, her eyes stinging, as if to watch the phosphorus one last time.

"You didn't think I would miss my watch, did you?"

"No, dear. Of course not. I just haven't been feeling that well."

"Throwing sea pizzas? Why don't you take a break."

"I haven't gotten a fix," she said weakly.

"Don't worry about it. I'll take a look. Go on, get some rest."

"Thanks, Bill. I think I will. Call me if you need me." In her exhaustion her voice sounded child-like. She didn't even visit the head, though she knew she would regret this later, when her bladder wakened her. For now all she could do was peel off the damp foul weather jacket and slide into the sea berth, full of hope that once she settled in she would sleep and would not get sick again.

She lay in a twilight world of rushing water, wondering whether or not she had fallen asleep, stumbling vaguely from one dream to another. Informing those dreams was the endless, recurring, indomitable hope that Bill was getting better, that the medicine was working, that his memory had improved today, that his up-beat speech and behavior were not superficial, that he really had gotten control of this disease, and was licking it. That he was re-creating himself.

"Nan. Nan. Get up."

No, she thought or said. No, it simply could not be. They had agreed on three-hour watches, a compromise between two and four. Three hours could not possibly have passed so quickly. She moaned aloud.

"Shush," he said, for no apparent reason.

"Is it my watch already?" she whined, her face in the pillow.

"Not yet," he said.

She opened her eyes. If it were not yet her watch, what was he doing?

"Is there something wrong?"

"I think so," he said. "I'm not sure."

She felt weary tears shoot toward her eyes. What was he thinking now? Last week, on the way to Antigua, he had turned the boat around, somehow convinced that he was supposed to find the reciprocal. But he had been fine for much of the time — what was it now?

"Bill?"

He had gone. She cursed and crawled from behind the lee cloth. A lurching wave knocked her off balance, and she fell headlong against the quarter berth. Bracing both knees against the berth she thrust her arms into the stiff damp cloth of her foul weather jacket, then leaned over the chart table to see whether or not Bill had gotten a fix. He had. A neat X lay halfway between Barbuda and St. Barts, only slightly off their rhumb line. She looked at her watch. He had charted the fix only a half hour ago. Now where was he?

Nan climbed the companionway, nervous that she could see Bill nowhere, then she felt his bony hand draw her into the well of the cockpit. "What in the hell? . . . "

"Hush. Don't say anything."

"Bill. Oh, Bill. Listen, everything is all right. Just let me . . . "

He held her, gripping her arm above the elbow, the bones of his fingers firm through the crinkling foul weather gear. "We're being followed," he said.

"Followed?" This struck her as ridiculous, and she felt a sudden angry laugh rise in her throat. She was sick. She was tired. She was not exactly a spring chicken, and damn it all, it wasn't even her watch yet.

"They don't have any lights."

"What?"

"No running lights. I saw them through the binoculars when I was doing my usual 360. I don't want them to know how many of us there are, or anything about us. I'm sure they've been looking through their binoculars too."

"Let me see," she said.

"Just stay low," he whispered. "All we need is for them to see an elderly woman and her senile husband. We're an easy target, my dear."

She took the binoculars from around his neck. "Where are they?" she asked.

"Off the port quarter. Stay down."

The port side dipped with the wind, making it difficult to stay out of sight. She crawled along the cockpit seat, then raised her head just enough to lift the binoculars over the weather cloths. Nothing. Nothing. Bingo. There was a boat, black shadow, lightless, parallel to their course and probably closing. She couldn't tell what kind of boat it was, a motorboat of some kind, a fishing boat perhaps, except where were its lights?

She remembered reading of pirates off Barbuda.

"You're right," she said, when she'd slumped back into the cockpit floor. "A boat with no lights."

"He's been getting closer ever since I saw him. That's why I called you."

"Now I wish we had a gun."

"You and me both. Tell you what. I'll get the flare gun and you make a call on the VHF. No, wait. They'll be listening. No offense, but it would be better for them to hear a man. You get the flare gun and I'll make the call."

"Where's the flare gun?"

"Under the sea berth. At least that's where I saw it last. I think. I'm not sure."

With the windvane pointing the boat toward St. Barts, they scurried below. There she held her fingers over the front of her flashlight, to dull its glare. She could hear Bill on the radio as she lay on her belly, rummaging in the storage space beneath the sea berth.

"Hello all stations. Hello all stations. This is the yacht . . . " He stopped.

"*Souvenir*," she said out loud.

"Damn," he said. "This is the yacht *Souvenir*," he said, then stopped again. "I don't know what to say." He did not say this to her, by way of asking advice. He said it to the bulkhead, by way of admitting defeat. His mind had failed him, and in the dim red light of the instrument panel, she could see him clenching his fist.

She got up and stood beside him. "Try this," she said, as if making a suggestion. "This is the yacht *Souvenir* at 17 degrees, 45 minutes North, 62 degrees, 25 minutes West. We are being pursued by an unlit vessel. Please stand by to render possible assistance."

"I don't know," he said. "That sounds pretty vague."

"We may not have much time," she rasped. "If they board us, we at least want people to know our last position. How else can anyone help us?"

"How can anyone help us anyway?"

She looked at him.

"Go ahead," she said. "Give our position."

"This is yacht."

"*Souvenir.*"

"*Souvenir.* Our position is."

"17 degrees, 45 minutes North."

"17 degrees, 45 minutes North."

"62 degrees, 25 minutes West."

"62 degrees, 25 minutes West."

"We are being pursued by an unlighted vessel."

"We seem to be pursued by an unlighted vessel. Anyone with information please call at . . . what's our phone number?"

"We don't have a phone number. This is a radio. Did you take your hand off the transmit button? Take your hand off the button."

"I wish we had a weapon," he said.

"Let me look for the flare gun again," she said.

"Oh, the flare gun. Good thinking."

"It was your idea," she said, as she dove back to the berth.

Just as she thrust her hand into the locker the boat lurched, a sickening shudder. Every movement and sound signifies in a boat at sea, and there is no sound worse than that of unexpected contact. They were alongside.

"Hurry!" Bill called. Had someone stepped aboard?

She aimed the flashlight at the brilliant mess. There it was in the back, an orange plastic cylinder. She grabbed it. The lid wouldn't budge. Were those footsteps on the deck, or the jib block banging?

Bill stared with a bewildered look, a look she had not seen on his face until now, of confusion, of fear. A look she knew would begin to take away . . . everything. Perhaps it would be best to let the pirates board, to let them do their worst — because what could be worse than this?

"Are we sinking?" Bill asked, puzzled.

"No. No, we're not sinking. Only there is a boat following us."

"Are they friendly?"

"We don't know yet," she said, her voice catching.

The lid came off. Inside was a flare gun, still wrapped in plastic, with three cartridges. She jammed one flare into the barrel; the other two she dropped into the pocket of her foul weather gear. Clicking the barrel back in place, she headed for the companionway. Bill grabbed her. "Where are you going?" he asked.

"I have to see what they're up to," she said, trying to pull his hand away.

"Let me take the gun," he said.

"No, I don't think that would be a good idea."

"Why not?"

"I just don't."

"Who's the skipper of this vessel?" he asked. Now she felt his eyes go hard in the dark.

"Let me get by," she said.

"You're trying to take control," he said. "You're trying to control me."

"Bill, this is not the time to argue."

"Who's arguing?" he said. "I'm not." He spoke as if he were addressing a stranger, his voice blank.

She felt another sickening bang as the nameless boat bounced against their hull. Before she could think, Bill turned and bolted up the companionway, as though the shock of the contact beckoned him. She followed. He was facing the black boat, which had dropped back slightly, clearly visible in the moonlight. As far as she could tell, no one had boarded, but to make certain she peered forward over the dodger.

Bill faced away from her, toward the black boat, yelled something lost to the wind. *Souvenir* plunged through the waves, pursuing her rhumb line to St. Barts. No one on the other boat said anything that she could hear; nor did she see anyone clearly, only a shadowy figure at the stern. She held the flare gun straight up in case it should go off, her elbow bent, the gun behind her head.

Bill pointed toward the other boat and then gestured away, signaling them to stand off. She did not think they could see him, until a shot rang out and Bill spun and dropped to the cockpit floor. Her first thought was: The worst has happened. The very thing she'd read about in sailing magazines and worried about all these years. She had feared this moment, but not expected it, not really. Now strangers had invaded from whatever world they inhabited out there to arrive here, in the fabric of her real life. Cocking the flare gun with her thumb, she leveled the barrel toward the spot where the shadowy figure stood and squeezed the trigger. White fire shot from her hand. The flash smacked directly into the black boat, then fell into the water, where it bubbled furiously. She spilled the empty shell to the cockpit floor and grabbed a second flare from her pocket. She loaded fast and aimed. She knew they would shoot at her now, though crouching behind the weather cloths she would be difficult to see. She aimed farther aft this time and as the black boat dipped into a trough she squeezed the trigger and once more flashed her white fire. This time the flare landed in the cockpit, where it sputtered and spun angrily.

Now she could see the shadow in the cockpit become a man, brilliantly lit, with the flare at his feet. A second man emerged from the cuddy where he'd been steering. He ducked back inside and reappeared with a fire extinguisher. Already dark smoke billowed from the cockpit, evidence that more than the flare was burning. The black boat veered toward them now, and the first man jumped back toward the wheel to avoid a collision. At the same moment, she felt a jab in her ribs and spun around to see Bill with blood spreading from the wound in his shoulder. His right arm dangled uselessly, but in his left hand he gripped the red plastic jug they used to hold gasoline for the dinghy's outboard motor.

"Take the top off first," he said, catching his breath. Though they hadn't discussed this for many years, since their first trip alone in the islands, she knew exactly what he meant. Twisting the top off and yanking the metal chain out of the opening, she pulled herself up to the lifelines. As the black boat banged against them once more, she tossed the squat jug end over end into the wide cockpit. The man had extinguished the fire from the flare, with only a little smoke rising from charred wood. Now he set down the fire extinguisher and headed for the rifle leaning against the cuddy cabin, the rifle that had shot Bill. The first man was still at the wheel, trying to keep the two boats close but not colliding as they rose and fell in the waves. With the flare gun in her left hand, Nan fumbled for the third flare in her pocket and then jammed it into the barrel. The man grabbed the rifle and slid the bolt back and then forward. Her nausea returned as she watched the man drop to one knee as if he'd had military training. He aimed the barrel toward her.

She did not fire at the man, but at the back of the cockpit, where the gas can had rolled. The flare exploded from her hand, bounced inside the cockpit, and then lit up the night. She saw the man's face quite clearly, and heard the bullet whistle past her head. The aft end of the black boat rushed into flame. With no more flares, she collapsed behind the weather cloths and stared at the burning boat.

Some of the gasoline, she thought, would drip into the bilge, taking volatile fumes as it went — and this could cause an explosion, possibly blow the main fuel tanks. They had talked about this long ago. She and Bill.

She turned to see his face lit by orange fire. He was holding his shoulder, his fingers red. His eyes looked almost blank, but the corners of his mouth twisted in a weak smirk. "Give 'em hell," he said.

She turned toward the black boat. It drifted astern, on fire, dipping up and down with the waves. *Souvenir* kept plunging ahead, as before.

For several minutes they watched the glow fall astern. Evidently the men had found another extinguisher. Already the glimmer was fading, and it seemed that there would be no explosion. The flare gun dangled from her wrist as she climbed down the companionway to get the first aid kit. She found it in their "grab bag," kept near the companionway in case they had to abandon ship. She climbed back into the cockpit and slid next to Bill, who lay against the coaming. Had the bullet passed through, or was it lodged inside him somewhere? If it was lodged in his shoulder, was there anything she could do about it?

"End of story," he said.

She met his gaze. He was looking straight at her now, very focused. "You're going to be all right, Bill," she said, but she had begun to tremble, and so the words did not come as strongly as she'd hoped.

She tried to pull away his foul weather jacket, but he yelled in pain, so she found scissors in the first aid kit and began to snip the jacket from the wound. Then she cut his T-shirt, exposing the hole in his shoulder. She knew little about such things, but the bullet seemed to have made a rather neat entry. What happened on the inside, she could not say. She poured hydrogen peroxide on a piece of gauze and wiped all around the wound, trying to sanitize the area as much as possible.

"Oh, man," Bill rasped. "Oh, man."

"You'll be okay," she told him again. "This may hurt some." She took a wad of sterile gauze and pushed it right into the wound, to try to stop the bleeding.

"Whoa," Bill cried. "Whoa."

She held the gauze in place as he squirmed and then she began to wrap more gauze around the shoulder, continuing until she reached the strip of cardboard at the end. She didn't know what else to do.

"Let's go below," she said, taking his good arm.

They looked downwind as they stood, for the other boat. With the fire out and no running lights, it would be hard to spot in the endless waves. Perhaps the black boat would leave them alone now. Perhaps they had run out of extinguishers. They wouldn't know she'd spent her white fire.

The companionway was too narrow for them to go together, so she went first, then helped him down. They banged their way arm in arm past the chart table to the sea berth, where he stumbled in and lay on his back. "Just lie still," she said. "Just lie still."

"Let's go home now," Bill said, not bothering to open his eyes. "I'm tired."

"Yes," she said. "We'll go home now. Try to sleep."

At the moment home was Gustavia, where she hoped they would understand her high school French. When they got a little closer she would try to call on the VHF, but now no one would likely hear her except the black boat — and she didn't want them to hear anything.

How much farther was it? She pulled herself to the chart table and wrote down the bright green numbers from the GPS display. Then she carefully measured out the latitude and longitude, placing a neat X on the chart. She walked the silver compasses to the chart's edge. About twenty-eight miles out, she figured.

Bill's breathing came heavy but regular. She needed to look around and climbed to the cockpit with the binoculars. As she hunched toward the wheel she kicked an empty flare shell. It thunked and rolled across the fiberglass cockpit. Crouched low behind the weather cloths, she brought the binoculars to her eyes. In the peaks of dark waves she searched for the black boat. One after another, black shapes dissolved into oblivion as wave after wave formed and then moved on. After a while she grew dizzy from looking.

In the east the sky gave the very first hint that she would see another day. She checked the compass heading, still right on the money, and then leaned back against the coaming, watching for the dawn. *Souvenir* surged ahead. Whether or not Bill survived the gun-shot wound, she knew she would soon have to learn to live without him. For the first time since her early twenties, when they had been married in the university chapel in Charlottesville, so very long ago, she felt that she could.

Anchorage

17° 00' N
88° 06' W

IN EARLY AFTERNOON, HENRY CLAY, seventy years old, white-haired and wiry, threaded his way through the Belize reef. He knew he was in the shallows and watched the sandy bottom slide by in ten feet of water. Clouds of shadow ghosted across the white sand, dark brothers of the cumulus that drifted overhead.

The mainsail billowed, waves slapped the heeling hull, but the shore of the nearest island seemed unmoving, arrested in time. A cloud in the white sand became a thick bed of turtle grass, risen to touch the keel. He thought, *I'm aground.*

Even after two years of single-handing, his first instinct was to call his wife, Millie, his sailing partner, his life partner. But of course she was no longer here to help him. He looked at his wrinkled hands.

With a curse, he worked forward, brought down the main and furled it. He trimmed the big jib tight, hoping it might pull the bow around, toward deeper water. Back in the cockpit he started the engine, pulled the gear lever into reverse. Propwash bubbled alongside. He stood on the toerail, grabbed the starboard shrouds, and rocked back and forth. In. Out. In. Out. Sometimes this rocking moved the keel enough to break free. This time, though, nothing.

He took a deep breath. Sea salt. He looked across the broad expanse of water and low-lying islands. *Madrigal* had worked her way inside the barrier reef, so she was protected from the big swell. Safe from the seas and yet somehow lost. The reef stretched nearly a hundred miles both north and south.

He put the engine in neutral, and the propwash died. He would have to cant the boat. Kneeling at the bow, he untied the anchor and paid out a length of chain until the flukes brushed the water's surface. Then he climbed into the dinghy, brought it around to the bow. Once he'd wrestled the anchor onto the plywood floorboards, he reached over and hit the button for the windlass and paid out more chain.

Steel links spilled into the dinghy, metal cataract, and he thought how the anchor had become his albatross — not when it was down (the big Bruce had never slipped, never failed him in a dark wind among breaking reefs) but at times like this when he had to man-handle its weight. Aware that the anchor had become too much for him, he'd spent a lot for this electric windlass, but even during routine anchorings he still had to wrestle the anchor off and on its roller. Often it would come up backward and he had to lean over and twirl it around, careful not to send his back into spasms.

If the electric windlass packed up, he'd have to haul by hand all the weight of chain and stock. He didn't know how long he could.

With a pile of chain aboard the dinghy, he rowed toward deeper water, heavy links slipping over the side faster than he wanted. Soon he was pulling a long line of chain, a tough job in a rubber boat with short oars. When he got as far as he could from the boat, he wrestled the anchor overboard with a splash. Then he rowed back, upwind.

Once aboard he put the engine in reverse and throttled up. Again water roiled around the stern. He walked to the bow and punched the windlass button with his foot. The heavy motor whirred and dragged chain over the bow roller until the links grew taut. He clipped the main halyard to one of the links and then eased off until the chain went slack again. He tightened the halyard with the windlass, and soon a length of chain rose clear

of the water, angled up toward the masthead, pulled by the halyard. He hated to put this load on the rig, but he thought it was-
n't worse than full sail in a big wind.

The boat heeled. Water crept toward the starboard toerail.
For a long moment the boat leaned, going nowhere, the weight of
the eight-ton boat pulling hard on the halyard. He hung sus-
pended on a line — not hooked to heaven, but to earth, to sea, to
time. Something slipped. The keel canted and the engine drove the
boat astern. He scrambled to the wheel and throttled back. The
rig creaked with the strain. He slid the gearshift to neutral and
hustled forward again, to ease the halyard.

That's when the pressure came to his chest. Not a pain but a
weight, a heavy hand pressing on his breastbone. He thought he
knew what hand it was. The boat drifted backward, leaning right
as if someone had grabbed its ear.

He took a nitroglycerin capsule from his breast pocket and
popped it in his mouth.

He forced his breath, tried to move more slowly. One hand
on his chest, he hit the windlass button, paying out halyard, easing the strain, the mast righting itself. With the tension off the halyard, he could rest. Catch his breath. He put two fingers on his
left wrist and felt the miraculous lub-dub that kept him alive. Still
pumping.

He wanted to lie down, but he couldn't leave the boat like
this, with the halyard hanked to the anchor chain.

Once again he wrapped the chain around the windlass and
hauled it in. When the halyard shackle came across the roller, he
detached it and walked it back to the mast. He rested. For now
he just clipped the halyard to the whiskerpole ring, snugged it up,
and cleated it off.

The boat swung to anchor in deeper water, but he knew it
could drift back on the bar, and he'd be right where he started.
After arguing with himself, and pausing once more to catch his
breath, he hit the windlass and pulled the anchor all the way in
until it struck the roller. The boat drifted toward shore. He

scooted back to the wheel and with an eye on his depth sounder he threaded a channel between the small islands and then circled until he felt comfortable with the swinging room. He lowered the anchor back to the sandy bottom.

With the engine shut down, he hunched over the binnacle. No sound but the quiet wash of waves against the shore and that whisper the islands made in the wind. He went below, exhausted.

———

Bong, bong, bong, bong. The main halyard drummed against the aluminum mast without pause. Henry thought to let the noise be, to isolate it in a far corner of his mind as he slept, but the tinny reverberations escaped, rippled through his cerebrum. At length he rose and pulled himself up the companionway. All around the world glowed with what light remains just after the sun goes down.

He stood looking at the light. How could it be that he was seventy years old? He felt he'd lived life up close, concentrating hard on the delicate and tedious detail of it, and when he finally remembered to look up, seven decades had gone by. Seven decades, it turned out, was not a long time.

He unlaced the halyard from its cleat and led it forward to a lifeline, away from the mast. His hands held long memories of cleats and line. Since his earliest days sailing on the Chesapeake Bay, when his father had taught him to tie his first clove hitch, he had felt at home on boats.

Along the shore twilight fixed the mangrove trees, making their dark photograph. He had come a long way to find this necklace of small islands strung along the world's second largest barrier reef, here off the coast of Belize. He had followed a larger ring of islands all around the Caribbean, the dream that he and his wife had nurtured through a lifetime of work. She had helped with all the hard preparations for this journey, but after sailing through rough weather from Beaufort, North Carolina, to the Virgin Islands, she fell unconscious in the cockpit just as they neared St. Thomas. Perhaps two weeks at sea had been too much for her. Or maybe the stroke would have taken her anyway. He would never know. He called ahead for help and then single-handed into the harbor at Charlotte Amalie. By the time they got her to the hospital she was gone.

She would have loved it here. The air carried that soft touch of the tropics, laced with the tang of the sea. Stars appeared, and thinking not only of the tropics but of his life, he felt he had misjudged the speed of the dark.

Before the light left altogether, he checked the anchor one last time. At the bow chock he inspected the chaffing cloth, old canvas that kept the snubber line from rubbing. The lashing had come loose so he bent down to tighten it. When he stood up he felt that pressure in his chest again. I haven't even done anything, he thought. Only tightened some lines.

He wondered what he should do. He considered leaving his boat in a marina somewhere and returning to Richmond, to have Dr. Kay check his heart again. But he also knew that the word would likely come that he had no business out here, alone off these nameless islands, with the sun down and Canopus beginning his nightly carnival in the southern sky. But I do, he thought. I do have business here.

He had to finish what he and Millie had set out to do. To sail the full circle of the sea called the Caribbean.

Down below, the air of the cutter felt close, even with the ports opened. Despite this warmth, he lit both kerosene lamps and watched their light spread a yellow veil on the berths, on the wide teak table, on the mahogany paneling of the bulkhead. The color of home. He placed the match in the sink, lowered the side of the sea berth, and climbed in. Throw cushions took the familiar shape of his body, and the hull rocked slightly. Was this death's cradle?

He did not close his eyes but looked at the overhead, at the dark woodwork of the cabin, at the bright souls of the lanterns. No wonder the Israelites spoke of fire in the burning bush. The fire lived, moving, consuming itself, at once working away from extinction and toward it. He felt the final fire in himself. He did nothing to stoke that flame or douse it. This burning in the cerebral cortex lay beyond his powers to control. He was merely the wood, the wick.

But the fire. Images rose of the fire that had been his life. A slow burning fire, without many flare-ups, his time as salesman and then company executive. A life in the suburbs and in the automobile, with only those moments on the water clearly distinguished from the rest. That and the watercolors he had tried to paint, mostly of the Chesapeake. A good life, shared with his wife. And with his three children as well, until their own lives had caught them up, absorbing them in the same delicate and tedious detail. Now they wanted him to stay with them. They wanted him in a room, out of harm's way, in a nursing home eventually, safe from everything except age and death. And if you were not safe from that, how safe could you be?

He had no desire to disintegrate in their midst like an old armchair, a candidate for the trash heap except for sentimental attachments. *Now listen to you*, Millie would have said. *You are describing yourself as a chair. Does that make any sense?*

"Where are you, Millie?" he said. A cold thrill passed through him, as though he had spoken aloud in a movie theater. But there was no one to hear him, so he spoke again. "Where are you, Millie? Are you here? Can you see me? Can you hear me? Are you waiting for me?" And then, as if he had established contact, "The kids are fine, Millie. Really. I know you were worried about Susan the most, but she is fine. Susan and Billy and Brenda. All fine. No tragedies. No car accidents or leukemia or alcoholism. All fine. All well. All but me, Millie. I am not well."

Now he was talking to himself. He pursed his lips. Was he really that bad off? The light in the lantern flickered and he watched as though it were the display of an EKG. Fear had entered the cabin and passed its electric current through everything, cushions, berth, and bulkhead. He wanted to get on the radio and call someone, but he had only a VHF system and who would be there to hear him? It would not reach Dangriga, the nearest town. Another boat perhaps. He pushed himself out of the berth and walked to the nav station. The radio sat silent and dark and he reached over and clicked the dial, orange numbers jumping to the screen. This new light pleased him, and he switched on the auxiliary battery to make certain the light would stay bright.

Selecting the scanner, he watched the numbers cycle with incredible speed, and hoped for a voice. The display stopped and the broken static of a far-off conversation filled the cabin; then the numbers roamed once more, finding nothing. He manually returned to the channel where the voices had been and listened for some moments to jagged static and shards of words . . . yesterday . . . don't think so . . . not if I can . . . What were they speaking about? Where were they? He gave up after a while and scanned again, ending on channel 16, where boats would most likely hail one another. After a long silence, during which he ate a peanut butter sandwich, he returned to the chart table and took the microphone from its clip. He wanted very much to call his children, and his grandchildren. For a moment he felt confused, as if this might actually be possible. He wanted to call Millie.

"Testing, testing," he said aloud, checking his own voice, to be certain it would not crack or squeak, then he pushed the button on the side of the mike and with the transmit light screaming bright red he spoke into the airwaves: "Radio check. Radio check. This is the yacht *Madrigal*. Does anyone read me?"

A long silence. Nothing. Not likely, here in this dark stretch of reef. Again. "Radio check. Radio check. This is the yacht *Madrigal*. Does anyone read me?"

"I read you, *Madrigal*," a voice came, startling. "Loud and clear."

He felt his pulse jump. He held the microphone nervously and tried to remember radio protocol. "Would you switch and answer on channel 10?" he said.

"Switching channel 10," the voice came again. It struck him more clearly that this was a woman's voice.

He fumbled to channel 10, waited a moment, then spoke again: "This is the yacht *Madrigal*, do you read me?"

"This is *Evening Star*, *Madrigal*. I hear you fine. Over."

"Glad to hear it, *Evening Star*. I've been having some trouble with my radio," he lied.

"Your voice is a little faint, but I can hear you fine."

He realized that he had no air in his chest and took a deep breath. "I'm anchored on the Belize reef," he said. "Just north of Dangriga."

"Roger. We're on the reef also. We just sailed in from Glover's atoll today. Over."

He wanted to ask her exact position — he wanted very much to know where she was — but realized that she would probably not want to broadcast it. He also wanted to know if she were alone, but that too was a bad question, and it was not likely in any event. "My name is Henry," he said without thinking. "Henry Clay, like in the history books."

"My name is Millie, Henry. Nice to meet you."

His heart tripped in his chest. He struggled to say, "Hi, Millie."

He held the black microphone in his hand and looked at it carefully. Was he really holding it? Or was he still lying in the berth, having this dream?

"Well, my husband's telling me we'd better conserve battery power," the voice said.

I'm having a heart attack, he wanted to say. Come and find me. Show me who you are, Millie.

"Roger," he said. "Let me just give you my position, in case I have more radio trouble." He read off the latitude and longitude he'd marked on the chart.

"Roger," she repeated. "Are you having any other trouble?"

No, Millie. Don't worry. I'm okay. The kids too. Everyone's

fine. Only I miss you, Millie. I get very lonely. And I think I may be dying. "No, Millie. I'm fine."

"We'll be standing by channel 16," she said after a pause. He could tell she had heard something in his voice. He could hear her concern for an old man on the other end of the radio waves.

"It was nice to talk to you, Millie," he said. Adding with whatever authority he could muster: "This is the yacht *Madrigal* returning to 16. Over and out."

"*Evening Star*," she said, "back to 16." He immediately hit the button that called up channel 16 and sat listening to the silence. She would be listening as well, she and her husband. He tried to imagine their boat — he wished he had asked her what kind of boat they had. He tried to listen through the silence to the sound of her being there. He could hear nothing, but listened nevertheless. Listened to her listening. Millie.

The cutter tugged quietly at its anchor. With the wind he felt the faraway world pass overhead, all commerce and compromise, all exchange and surrender. As if to catch a sun already set, clouds rose out of the east to ride the trade wind.

The Wild Child

TED JENKINS EMERGED from the narrow hatch in the port cockpit seat, scowling as he scraped his elbow. The red plastic funnel slipped from his left hand. He heard it bounce down into the engine well. He thought to let the damn thing just stay there, but he would have to search for it later anyway, and with his luck it would get caught on the propeller shaft. Cursing, he slid back into the hold, into that shaded underworld where he spent so many hours working on the engine. He spotted the red funnel lying (sure enough) against the propeller shaft, where every three or four seconds a drop of water gathered and dripped from the packing gland. He would have to tighten the stuffing box again.

He sat staring at the engine. He had just replaced the oil that kept disappearing from the transmission. Exactly where the oil went was anybody's guess. Most likely a seal had failed, but after weeks of searching he could not find the leak. Perhaps, as another sailor had suggested, the oil was migrating back into the engine, but if that seal were bad, why wouldn't the oil run downhill into the transmission, rather than uphill, into the engine?

What a world, where oil could run uphill.

A bead of sweat cascaded down the center of his bare chest. It was a good engine, a Volvo diesel, but now twenty years old and clearly in need of an overhaul, it seemed to wait stolidly, like an ox, for its next burden. His blue eyes moved over the metal: the oil filter, the fuel filter, the thermostat, the water pump, the fuel feeder pump — he had replaced them all. If something went really wrong — the main fuel pump, the crank shaft, the pistons — he would be out of his depth and would need a professional mechanic, a real service shop. But here in Belize City — or anywhere in this part of Central America — he wasn't certain where to get help. Then again, looking at his transmission, he realized that help was exactly what he needed. He snatched the funnel and squeezed out the hatch again, back into hot sunlight.

As soon as he emerged, two things assaulted his senses: the pungent smell of vinegar and sea death that wafted from a bucket full of conch shells being "cleaned" by his daughter, and the sight of Karen herself, face down on the cabintop in the sun, her feet toward him, her bare buttocks tan and gleaming in the light. She had this bathing suit made for her "special" in Florida before she came down to join him, but since the "suit" consisted mainly of a single string between twin cheeks, he hated to think how much she must have paid per square inch for the thing.

Karen had been with him for almost six weeks now and would soon head back to the States, though she had no clear plan. Sometimes she spoke of working for a cruise ship line, but she had done little to learn anything about it. He turned away from her and watched the wind generator prop spinning in the breeze. That first windy winter in the Bahamas the wind generator had kept their batteries up enough to run the refrigerator, but since then he'd stopped using the refrigerator, and his batteries were failing one by one. The electrical system — in fact the whole boat — was, after three years at sea, wearing out.

"When're we going to town?"

He turned to see Karen raised on one elbow, twisted and watching him through the reflecting plastic of her curved sunglasses.

"Whenever you want," he said.

"What?"

"I said whenever you want."

"Do you want me to fix some lunch first, or should we eat in town?"

"Whatever you want," he said.

She looked at him a moment longer and then dropped back on her stomach. Her skin was smooth, oiled teak. While he had, with each passing month, become leaner, more wiry, reduced to sun-darkened sinew, these past few weeks had done nothing to change the melon-like fullness of his daughter's twenty-year-old body. Her tan had deepened and her hair now had blonde streaks from the sun — that was all.

Twenty years old. Though he would just as soon not think about time, nor keep track of the stations of his life, Karen was for him clock and calendar, and today, her birthday, he could in no way pretend not to know it. Twenty years: time rose in the pit of his stomach, and he resolved not to think of it. Then Karen would squeeze past him in the companionway, on the deck, in the galley, and the tide of his tissue and bone would rise again quickly, until the gauge read twenty. He knew the gauge would not stop there, but would climb on and on until it reached his current age of forty-seven, and then would continue until the end.

He thought he might have a drink before lunch.

"How about beans and rice?" Karen was on her feet now, leaning against the boom.

"Sure." He stuck the funnel in the cockpit locker beside the extra oil. He did this, as he did so many things on the boat, without thinking — the cockpit, the cabin, the sails, everything now an extension of himself. He could find anything in the dark, even in a heavy sea, and at one point or another he'd had to.

It was in the Rio Dulce, in Guatemala, that they had begun eating beans and rice, where the locals ate this same dish day after day. Actually, he had begun eating peas and rice in the Bahamas, where pigeon peas served as a staple, but the beans and rice of the Rio Dulce had more Latino kick, and he preferred it to almost anything else these days, except at times he found himself craving a juicy American hamburger, with melted cheese, a discomforting desire since he told everyone that except for seafood he did not eat meat.

Karen handed up bowls of beans and rice, the bottoms of the bowls hot on her hands. They rarely ate at the settee any more — beneath it the life raft and old outboard motor left little room for their feet. They took their meals in the tropic breeze, out in the cockpit where the bimini shaded the sun. She was reading a book by John D. MacDonald called *A Flash of Green*, and as she read she lifted the spoon toward her lips with a vague absence. He pulled the book he was now reading — a thriller by Elmore Leonard — from behind the dodger. He did not look up but turned the pages and tried to remember where he'd left off. At every point it seemed that he had read that part before, perhaps he had read this book before. The boat stepped sideways in a puff of wind, a gentle, comfortable motion. *Last Chance*, a heavy cutter, moved slowly, solid as a house. And this was his house now, his home. He looked at Karen and tried to connect the tan nearly naked woman with the small gap-toothed girl who had played on the living room rug in Boston, when he was still young, and Anita still alive.

She looked at him as he ate his beans and rice and read. How wiry he had become, brown and hard. Life had whittled him down, removing all the soft and vulnerable parts, leaving only this essence of himself, this core. He reminded her of the letter opener she'd bought in Guatemala City on one of their earlier excursions, a hard dark splinter of wood with a thin head carved at the top. She'd tried to get along with him this time, but she couldn't be sure if he really wanted her around. He didn't look at her very much, didn't look her in the eye, only sometimes he seemed to watch her when she faced the other way. She focused on her novel again, about a developer destroying a wetland, and then after a while she let the book slip across her chest and fell sound asleep. Water and wind.

Ted washed the bowls in the sink, using the saltwater pump as always. To kill off any microbes that may have found their way from city sewers he poured in a capful of bleach. At sea, or along the reef, he didn't think twice about the purity of seawater, for washing dishes at least, even though all manner of creatures lived in it — it was clean. Here, he wasn't so sure.

He dried the dishes and put them away. In the cockpit, she lay sleeping. She looked like her mother — different, but alike, in that haunting family way that leads to sudden recognitions: yes, that must be your sister, your mother, your daughter. He wondered whether Anita's spirit had entered her daughter from beyond the pale, to make her lips part just so, to relax her dark brown eyebrows into that familiar expression of quizzical content. But no, this was Karen, all of her, lying face-up on the cockpit seat, her bare legs bent and sprawled as if someone had thrown her there.

"Hey, time to get up. You want to get into town before the shops close, right?"

She said yes, but did not open her eyes. She lay there, waiting for her mind to come back, then sat bolt upright and put her bare feet on the cockpit sole. (In this, too, she resembled her mother, who moved fast from sleep to busy herself in the waking world.) After a moment Karen was stashing her book behind the dodger, tying on the piece of cloth she called her "butt wrap," and sticking her money and other gear into a black belted bag she called her fanny pack. Everything about her seemed to involve her butt, her fanny.

He untied the line to the not-so-well-inflated dinghy and pushed away. He moved so deliberately now. She had noticed this the first time she saw him cleaning fish he'd caught: he stared right at the fish and moved his knife back and forth across the scales as though every ounce of his attention were fixed there. Maybe it was.

They both turned to look at *Last Chance* as they sped away. A Union 36, riding high at anchor, with daring bowsprit and sweeping sheer, a cutter designed by a dreamer.

At the King George Hotel, they squeezed in among a bevy of other dinghies, struggled to climb the high wooden dock clearly built for larger vessels. Two overnight dive boats sat moored to the end of the pier like small ocean liners. He felt weary. Fatigue struck him whenever they entered a port crowded with tourists and all those who service them. He loved the small fishing villages and harbors he'd visited all around the Caribbean, including Placencia in Belize and the cays along the Belize reef, but being "in town" tired him.

For two hours he followed Karen into the few shops they could find, watched her slipping clothes on and off, then his patience ran thin. She saw him shift his weight from sandaled foot to foot, earth grown hard. "Want me to run you back to the boat?" she asked.

"I don't know. What are you going to do?"

"I'm gonna poke around some. It's my birthday, remember? Maybe I can find someplace to dance."

"By yourself?"

"Don't worry," she smiled. "I make friends easy."

"I don't know if that's a good idea."

She looked at him, but he was looking off across the harbor, back toward the boat. A white visor shaded his eyes but left the top of his head exposed to the sun. His close-cropped beard, once blond, was turning as white as the visor.

"Let's face it," she said, "I've been making my own decisions for a long time."

He set his jaw. "You've made some bad ones," he said.

She started to rise in defense of herself, but thought better of it. "Okay, so I've been making my own *bad* decisions for a long time."

He had to admit that. He had lost control of her before she was sixteen. When she got married at eighteen he thought that her place in his life had changed for good, that someone else would worry about her from then on, but now, less than two years later, she and her tattooed husband had split — and here she was again.

"Don't stay out late," he said. "I mean it."

Last Chance moved with the wake of a passing boat, some kind of fishing boat he guessed, the cutter's mast top dancing gracefully among Caribbean stars. He liked being on the boat alone. Dark harbor waves heaved and sighed and made their way toward the shore. He had read that the sea was not humanity's natural home, that humankind passed through as aliens, temporary guests, but for him this wash of water had become terra cognita. He was not looking forward to living without it.

Searching for something different on the bookshelves, he pulled down an old hardcover book he had gotten from his father many years before, a book about shipwrecks and castaways. He sat down in the cockpit and as the faint twelve-volt light glowed from the dodger, he read about Daniel Foss of Maryland, ship-wrecked in 1809 somewhere in the Pacific. Foss lived for five years on a barren island, eating seals. Alone. Alone. He looked up at the cockpit light — he had gotten the idea for this light in the Exumas, from a boat called *Moonshadow*, a Morgan 41, which always seemed to have a light burning in the cockpit. It made sense — like a porch light. He could read from it (just barely) and it gave him a sense of security.

After a while he left Daniel Foss stranded on a rocky island, and throwing back the rest of his after-dinner rum went amid-ships to relieve himself before bed. Looking at the lights of the city, he thought back on all the anchorages he'd found with this small sailboat, all around the island chain, across South America and then Central America. Cities like Charlotte Amalie in the Virgins and Castries in St. Lucia; and small towns like Samaná in the Dominican Republic and Placencia here in Belize. And count-less empty anchorages behind small sometimes uninhabited cays, in the Bahamas and along the Belize reef. It was the cities he liked least.

He tried to read a while longer but kept drifting off and climbed down to the bunk by the settee. He slept here now, beside the wide teak table, and let Karen have the V-berth. He knew she'd be home late. She always was. He felt that old anger rise in him, that old loss of control. He reminded himself of the truth that she had gone out of his control long ago. Even the family therapist (the third one) had suggested at last that the best thing was to "give her space." And that he had done. She came and went at will now, and of course had been on her own for several years, and married . . . Still, he did not like to think of her in town alone and regretted that he had let her take the dinghy. Yes, he should have kept the dinghy; then he could have driven in now to see if he could find her.

To see if he could find her. He thought back on all the times, in the greater Boston area, he had tried to find her, those desperate telephone calls, those awkward discussions with other parents. "Sorry to bother you, Ms. Wilkins, but this is Ted Jenkins. Have you by any chance seen Karen this evening? . . . " He wondered if it would have been different had she been a boy. A son. Would he have taken him (her) fishing? Would they have "bonded" in some way? Or did every parent feel like this, that the true coming together has not happened yet, because in some way it was true that they had not come together, and he wondered if this feeling of being disconnected from her would follow him to the grave.

When he awoke again it was 2 o'clock, and he got up to see if the dinghy was back, pulling at its painter. The wind had picked up and the cutter rose and fell gently with the swell, the salt air lifting his hair like a hand. The space behind the stern was empty. He got his binoculars and scanned the dock area and the harbor, including other anchored boats. He saw no sign of her.

~~

Karen had danced with almost all of them. She felt the electricity of this night in a country far from home, far from memories of her mother's death. She did not think of why she was here, or what it would mean, or how she would feel about it, only once she fantasized about telling her friend Steven about this, about her adventure, but when she would see him again she could not say, and since he had let her cat die when she had gone on her Rocky Mountain trip (locking Jo-Jo in the car and forgetting about him), she didn't really want to speak to him anyway. She had no real motivation for staying so late and dancing so hard other than it was her birthday. That and the energy that beat in her bones.

The men, day laborers it seemed of every hue and creed, did not perhaps understand this energy, but they responded to it, appreciated it, were grateful for it. One after another, with their cotton shirts open and their hard dark bodies glistening with sweat, they danced with her, their eyes bloodshot, as if they lacked sleep, but their bodies very much alive, full of sun and sea and the rain forest that crowded the mountains above them.

She did not think of what she must look like to them, at least she did not think long about this, only that she was a foreigner, and young, and beautiful, but to them the sun had turned her hair a color they'd never seen, and though her skin had turned dark, her green eyes and sun-bleached hair had a light beyond sunlight. As the night wore on, this light confounded them, and the alcohol that they drank eroded what barriers prevented them from asking, What light is this? And how can I have it?

The first arm that wrapped around her she welcomed as a sign of acceptance — she let the arm remain for a while before spinning away, maintaining her autonomy, believing that she could maintain it. The next arm seemed to her more annoying, then more menacing. She began to see that she might lose the space that allowed her to whirl free among the other dancers, to turn around and around with that energy she had, that mysterious electricity that had caused her mother, long before she died, to label her a "wild child."

"Come to my house," the man named Miguel (if she remembered right) said to her. He smiled as he said this and kept smiling after. She tried to figure if he were her friend, if he were in fact trying to help her, to steer her away from danger even, or perhaps not, perhaps he had seen the light in her and was now wanting it, wanting to take it for himself. She couldn't be sure.

"I guess I'd better get back to my boat," she said. "My father will be looking for me."

"He won't look for you," the man said.

"What do you mean he won't look for me? You don't know my father."

"He won't look for you," he said again, still smiling. This infuriated her.

"I'm leaving," she said simply.

And now the man let his smile fade. She sensed a situation. She could see his mind race, as he pushed the damp hair from his forehead with a flat hand, trying to think of his next move. She did not give him time to think, but looked for the fanny pack she'd taken off so she could dance — as soon as she found it she would head for the door. But the pack was no longer draped over the chair in the corner where she'd left it.

"Where's my fanny pack?" she asked the man named Miguel, but he simply looked around as if to assure her that it was not there. Miguel's advance had already begun to lose its importance, because several other men were also standing around her, holding their glasses of beer or rum, each of them watching her, in some way connected, perhaps by the bond of simply being men, standing in a circle around a young woman. She felt her voice rising: where was her fanny pack? But this, too, drew her tighter into the circle, and she could see that her anger amused them, perhaps even excited them, and she knew enough not to flounder. "Oh forget it," she said. "I'll come back for it tomorrow."

She took several deliberate steps toward the door, but no matter what route she chose, a man stood in her way. She looked for the bartender. Where was he? The whole bar had the look of a place that had closed down. When had that happened? How late was it anyway? How long had she been here? Was she really that drunk? Why were there no other women? She aimed for the man who seemed the least threatening and moved quickly toward the door.

"Hey," he said. "Where you *goin?*"

She ignored him, but now the men had shifted and instead of one man several stood between her and the door. She could see that the door had once been painted red. For the first time she felt that she might lose control of the situation. "I thought you people in Belize were supposed to be nice," she said. A man with stubble on his cheeks smiled very, very broadly, showing he still had many of his teeth. "We are not from Be-lee-say," he said, as if this were the clue to the joke. "Please," she said, "I have to go." She didn't like the sound of her voice. Not at all. She heard a kind of surrender in her tone, a hint of pleading. The sound of a victim. No, she did not like that at all. "Listen," she said. "Get the fuck out of my way or I'm callin the cops."

Perhaps it was her language, or the idea that she could so easily get hold of the police, but something struck the men as very funny. Almost in unison they burst out laughing, and several of them elbowed each other, sharing the joy of the moment. She wished then that she could be part of that circle. She would laugh from her gut, and slap the man next to her and take another long swig of *ron*.

Instead she was the one in the middle, with no power. She pushed her way through the men toward the door. For a moment she thought they would let her leave — to avoid a scene perhaps — but the last man took hold of her arm just above the elbow, and even when she tried to shake him off, he simply would not let go.

"Hey," the first man said again. "Where you *goin?*"

She tugged her arm, but his fingers had found muscle and tendon. She could see more clearly the sweat on his neck. Her words, victim's words, had not worked, and this so enraged her that she kneed him in the groin, and when he bent forward she kicked again as hard as she could. Now she had a shot at the door. Her hand grabbed the latch and she could see quite plainly the peeling red paint, but someone grabbed the back of her shirt. She tried to pull away and then wheeled around, prepared to kick again, when someone else grabbed her hair. This she found more difficult to fight. Now the muscles in her neck strained toward the right, where her hair was taking her. The rest of her body could do little more than trail behind, struggling but ineffective, her feet wanting to kick but instead stumbling across the wooden floor in a sideways dance.

When they started to lift her onto a table, she kicked someone again, only this time a hard, incredibly hard, fist struck her on the inside of her right thigh, cramping the muscle with a pain that became a numbness, crude anesthetic, so she could hardly move her leg. Now her shirt was torn up over her head and she knew this was it. They could see her now, all of her, the tanned places and the pale, and there was no way to stop them. As much as a part of herself refused to accept it, and though she continued to thrash her arms, her legs, her head as much as she could, she understood that she had been beaten. Tears of rage slipped from the corners of her eyes, rage, rage. She spat at them. She hated to have them win.

———

Alone in the cockpit with another rum, unable to sleep, and staring at the dimly lit docks as if to will himself there, Ted Jenkins sat thinking of when he'd met his wife, Anita. The first thing she'd told him was that he was not a well person. He had laughed.

"You look like you forgot how to breathe," she said.

He remembered: The band in the fraternity house basement was playing a Rolling Stones song, "Nineteenth Nervous Breakdown." It seemed not only appropriate but arranged, as if the song, the moment, the buzz in his head were choreographed to occur at precisely the same instant, in harmony with the moving lips of this young woman with the long straight almost Indian hair who now stood directly in front of him, so directly that it seemed a challenge. He knew immediately that he would have to turn and leave or she would change his life.

He stayed.

"Breathing is very important," she had said, her deep brown eyes on him. He heard only a trace of her Costa Rican accent. "You must be aware of how the air enters the nostrils and finds its way down into the lungs." People seemed to speak this way at that party. That crazy party — he couldn't even remember how he got there. Following her lead he drew in a deep breath of air but then coughed, bringing his hand to his chest as if in pain. He couldn't remember now whether the smoke that rose from his fingers came from a tobacco cigarette or that other kind he'd learned to smoke.

"Wow," she said. "You're not well."

They had started dating then, he resisting her long, drawn-out and ceaseless monologues and she aiming her spiritual artillery at him, as though to drive him from his besieged malarial city. Miraculously, he discovered times, usually late at night, when she would suddenly stop talking, and a door would open and he would walk out of himself and straight into a midnight that was her territory, for him a rare and exultant exploration. His hands confirmed then what he surely sensed from the beginning, that she had, rising from her remarkably smooth skin, an unspoiled passion, a physical fire.

He remembered the never-dark of the cheap student apartment where she lived, with the street lamp outside the window, and inside the perpetual disarray that was her life. They spoke little of their past, his in New England, hers in Central America. And not at all of the future — how could they when, with their mantras and their books about Buddhism, they were trying so hard to be present? Then Karen came. Not Karen, at first, of course, but only a missed period, a realization, a medical test, a night of walking around Harvard Square, as if the crowds of people there might help protect them from the responsibility of becoming . . . parents, adults, themselves.

They lived together above the loud streets then, in Boston, in Brookline, over a kind of drugstore which called itself, for some reason, a "spa," while he struggled to finish his belated course work at Boston U. Sipping his rum, he realized that during those early years they had achieved a remarkable and unexpected happiness. They (he and Anita) had recognized that sense of joy at intervals, standing over Karen's crib, staring at the small body that had become the center of a new solar system, the stuffed animals and mobiles and jangling things like brilliant and colorful planets meant to orbit around these small hands and feet, perpetual motion. At intervals, yes, because for much of the time he'd lost himself in a flurry of demands and pressures, at first in graduate school and then as a new civil engineer in a company supported by municipal contracts, and finally as a major partner in the firm.

That had all begun twenty years ago. Twenty years ago tonight Karen had come into their lives. And for the past five years Anita had not been with them to count the time. Ironically, though he had been the one to smoke when they first met, a habit he gave up immediately because of her, she had been diagnosed with lung cancer before she turned forty. A rare form, they said. And in less than six weeks she was dead. So fast, so fast, with so little time to say good-bye.

He looked at his watch. 3:30. The boat hung from two anchors, buried deep in harbor mud. It would take forever to get them up, a mess of muddy chain. He would swim ashore.

The water was not cold, but it nevertheless chilled him. They never swam at night because of the sharks — he thought of the sharks they had seen while snorkeling on the reef, nurse sharks mostly, and even motoring across the banks he had seen one from his perch in the rigging, whipping its tail from side to side as it shimmied through the water. In one hand he held high a plastic bag with clothes, sandals, wallet, glasses, and this impeded his swimming. After a while he put the end of the bag in his teeth and swam a determined breast stroke, his eyes, blurred without his glasses, sweeping the surface of the waves in search of fins breaking water.

⁓

T.C. Burgess did not have much patience with tourists. It was not that he did not like them. He liked them okay. But so many of them seemed like spoiled children. At the least inconvenience they whined and complained and began to cast blame in every direction, like those lawn sprinklers he had seen advertised on television once (the television that droned on and on now in the lounge of the King George Hotel, to keep the tourists occupied).

And many of them seemed so soft — in fact many of them were soft, with little paunches that puffed over their belts like dinner rolls, all puffy and spongy. Even their faces looked soft, as if your fingers would sink into the bags beneath their eyes and into the pudginess of their cheeks. Only their young women were beautiful, he would give them that. That kind of softness belonged to another category, something he could not think about for long without some physical uneasiness, and so he preferred not to think about it at all.

He leaned back in the wooden chair, its springs complaining as he put his feet on the desk. T.C. Burgess was not soft. His skin clung to him like a leather glove. He had always been thin and at thirty-nine was thin still, and wiry. He could still climb a coconut palm with his bare hands and feet, a machete in his mouth. Whenever possible he went without shoes, and his dark rawhide feet looked like shoes themselves, or else like the paws of some ebony animal. When he wanted to he could move fast, like the jaguars that lived in the Cockscomb Basin, but most of the time he did not rush — waiting for the well-timed lunge.

The night shift didn't bother him. He came alive at night. The only problem was that much of the trouble happened at night, and some of the trouble was bad, especially now that these damn gangs had started up. Might as well be L.A., he thought.

The telephone startled him — it always startled him, even when he expected it, steeled to its ring. "Burgess," he said. It was the front desk. "Missing person," the sergeant was saying. "Young woman. Or else her old man has lost it."

"Who is it?"

"A tourist. Off a boat."

A tourist. Oh man. "Where is he?"

"King George Hotel. I think he's already looked around some."

He looked at his watch. 4:30. "Tell him I'll be there in fifteen minutes."

"I'll tell you one thing," the sergeant said. "He's wired."

"Stoned?"

"Don't think so."

Burgess hung up the phone and put on his shoes. Tourists made him nervous — he wasn't sure why. You just never knew who they were, really, what attachments they had, what past. It was as if each of them dragged a long invisible cord leading back to wherever it was they came from, and this made them unpredictable, like electricity.

When he arrived at the hotel he knew immediately that Ted Jenkins was the man in question. He looked not only off a boat but out of the sea itself, as if he had just emerged. "Lieutenant Burgess," he said sticking his hand out American style.

"Ted Jenkins. My daughter's missing, lieutenant. I know something is wrong."

"How old is she?"

"Twenty."

"Twenty. Um. Has she ever done this kind of thing before?"

"No. Never." He knew if he said, "All the time," the police would lose interest.

T.C. Burgess stood looking at him. He knew that the policeman was figuring: a twenty-year-old woman (not exactly a child), and this man who was her father . . . what was it about him that he did not trust. Ted stood wondering whether there was something, in his own voice, in the way he tried to match the policeman's gaze, in the very air itself, that called up those nights in the Boston suburbs, or in the heart of town, when he searched and searched for her. Could this man named Burgess sense this?

"When did she disappear?"

"Earlier tonight. She was supposed to be home around . . . midnight."

"And when was the last time you saw her?"

"Around dinner time, I guess."

"Was she with anyone?"

"No."

"Where was she going?"

"She said she might go . . . dancing."

Burgess drew his lips together, considering this. "Come with me," he said. Ted followed the lieutenant up a shallow set of stairs to the bar, with chairs turned upside down. He stuck a cup of water in the microwave and set the timer for two minutes. "I'm afraid all they got is instant," he said.

"She could be in trouble," Ted said, looking at him through glasses still fogged with moisture. The policeman appeared indistinct, dark angel.

"I need more information." Burgess stood waiting on the microwave.

"The information is that my daughter is missing," Ted said harshly. "And," he searched for the words, "she is very . . . beautiful."

The way the American said this impressed him, as if the word "beautiful" were a code word. He looked at him — there was nothing soft about this tourist, that was for sure. "You've been at sea for a while, haven't you?" he asked. "You're pretty well baked."

"Three years," Ted said.

The microwave bleeped. "Look, if you're not going to do anything but drink coffee I'm going to go look for her myself."

Burgess shook his head, hunting along the counter for the sugar container. "Sit down," he said. "I'm going to look for her.

And I imagine I will find her. I know this town pretty damn good, mon." This last was said with an unusually thick Caribbean accent, as if for effect. He thought maybe Burgess was toying with him.

"Then what in the hell are you waiting for?"

"Sit down," he said again, dropping back onto a bar stool. "You see, there are so many things I don' know about your daughter. Has she been with you all along? Or did she just arrive? Has she traveled in Central America before, or is she, as you say in America, just off the boat?"

"You've lived in America yourself," Ted said.

"Long Beach, California. You wouldn't know it to look at me, but once I was a promising young musician." Burgess smiled at him, but only for an instant. "You see," he went on, "I don't even know your daughter's name."

"Her name is Karen," he said, and then added for no apparent reason: "It's her birthday."

T.C. Burgess listened to everything the American told him. She had green eyes and tawny skin. Her mother was Costa Rican. And with every question, he began to understand that this young woman, this Karen, was, what did they call it, a wild child. Going off alone. And if she was as "beautiful" as her father said, well then . . .

You have told me enough," he said at last. "You can go back to your boat if you like."

"I'm not going anywhere," he said.

"Suit yourself. I don't think they will mind if you stay here." He indicated the empty bar. "Tell them I let you in."

"Wait. Why don't I go with you?"

"No. This is police work."

"Then when will I hear from you?"

"Soon. In an hour or two."

———

She had found that her struggling did no good whatsoever, in fact made things worse, so she determined to lie still, to separate mind from body. She forced her thoughts to far away places, other times, other men. At first they let her go, content with her body alone, but one of them, who had waited so long for his turn, grew impatient with her lifelessness and shook her by the chin. "Ey! Are you asleepin?" She lay as if dead. The other men laughed and this made him angry. He took the cigar from his mouth and pushed the lighted end against her hip. She screamed and writhed beneath him, trying to pound him with her fists. "Ay!" he cried. "Mucho mejor!"

Sometime before dawn the room grew thinner, the voices farther away and then everything darker and darker, until not even the sharp pain on her hip, her thigh, was enough to bring her back.

"She gone," one man said. "Let her go," another said. "We had enough."

"I ain't had enough," Miguel said. The other men looked at him.

"What you thinkin, Miguelito?"

"We take her back to camp. That would give us somethin to play with, eh?"

"You look for trouble, Miguel."

"And when we tired of her, she can shine my boot." He raised a dusty boot to make his point.

"She American, Miguel. Peligroso."

"You think I give a sheit what she is? They can come get her if they want, and they can have my machete." He walked over to the wall and lifted his machete and held it to the light. Old and rusted, it did not shine.

"You been spendin too much time in the ron, Miguel."

"You spend too much tiempo con su madre, Pedro. You no longer have the cajones. They all shrivel up."

Pedro straightened and looked as if he might pick up the chair next to him. "Wait," another man said. "If we take her with us, who get to keeps her?"

"We all do," Miguel said. "Just like tonight."

The men looked at her, still sprawled on the table. "Um um um," someone said.

"I'm gone," Pedro said. "If I see you I don know you."

"You don know anythin," Miguel said. "You don know anybody."

"I leavin with Pedro," another, older man said. "You look for trouble, Miguel."

"Ah," Miguel said, "and I find it too!"

"No brains," Pedro said, and he and the older man left.

"Put her clothes on," Miguel said.

The men laughed. "She didn't hardly have none," one of them said. Miguel laughed from deep in his chest. They took a large shirt from a peg on the wall and put it on her. The shirt reached almost to her knees.

"We take her to my brother," Miguel said. "He can get a truck."

<hr />

Ted Jenkins sat in the corner of the barroom, at first leaning back against the wall and then sitting forward to prop his head with his hands. He put his elbows on the table and his palms in an attitude almost of prayer, a small temple made from his fingers, which he brought against the bridge of his nose.

Anita, he whispered.

He tried to think of something, of some strategy that had as yet eluded him, a plan the policeman had not bothered to consider, but his mind and body betrayed him and he slumped forward against the table in anger and exhaustion, as if he'd been waiting up for his daughter since she turned fourteen. He began to dream before he was asleep, his mind roiling with worry, a crowd of useless information and confusing images. Floating above the table, he found that he was at sea, rising and falling, day after endless day, with slim hope of survival. He was Daniel Foss, of Elkton, Maryland, shipwrecked from the seal hunting brig, *Negociator*. But in the unsleeping dream that now overtook him, he played the part less of Daniel Foss than of the ship's surgeon who had ended in the lifeboat with him. Of twenty-one men who had gone into the boat, only three remained, Daniel Foss, the surgeon, and one other. Now the last of their food and water dwindled away, and they faced death by starvation. Daniel Foss cut three strips of cloth from his thin coat, one marked with a brown thread. With trembling hands each man drew a piece of the cloth from a hat and looked for the sign, for the strand of brown like dried blood. The surgeon had the thread. He must have stared at it intently, doubting his own sight, wondering if he were really the one to die. "I am a native of Norfolk, Virginia," was all he had said. "If you should live, tell my wife and children of my wretched fate."

Ted dreamed that the time might come when he would draw the brown thread. Would he have the courage to slit his wrist, as the surgeon did, and let the others, the survivors, drink his blood?

Is this what, as a father, he would be asked to do?

When he woke from this half-sleep, he filled the coffee cup with more water and placed it in the microwave as T.C. Burgess had done. Microwaves excited the molecules, a kind of magic, even for an engineer, and he wished that he could take in some of that energy, the cells of his body excited to some new action.

What was it that drove parents to protect their children against the unavoidable perils of a free life? He worried about Karen, not only tonight, but forever. She had always been "out of bounds" as a girl, and her mother's death, when she was only fifteen, further spun her into erratic orbit. He feared that she would end on drugs, promiscuous, ultimately alone and lost. He feared that she would suffer.

Gulping down the hot and plastic-tasting instant coffee, he set out again in the dawn light, thinking briefly of breakfast but determined not to eat until he had some news of his daughter. At the same time, he felt the raw awareness of the sleepless, a colliding frame of mind somewhere between the Zen-like being-in-the-world that Anita had tried to teach him and an aching, out-of-control anxiety that screamed his daughter's name. In Belize, in Boston, everywhere, looking and watching for Karen.

———

Walking toward the center of town, Ted eyed the blank fronts of narrow silent buildings. At the far end of a narrow street he at last spotted someone, a suspicious figure skulking along in the dawn shadows. Ted thought to question him, but as he approached he could see that it was Burgess, creeping along the edge of the street. A hand moved. Was he signaling him? At that same instant he saw four men emerge from a door and between them, sheltered by them, wrapped in a red plaid shirt too large, was a girl, a woman, his daughter, Karen. She had not yet seen him. She appeared drunk, drugged.

"Jenkins!" he heard Burgess call from across the street. Odd that he should be yelling at him, when these four men were the ones, they were the ones to be yelled at. He was almost upon them already.

Miguel saw the American coming at him, and was not surprised. He had expected trouble, and the American was not even armed. He pulled his machete from his belt as the American drew near and stuck him in the chest. The machete at first struck bone, but this did not surprise him either. It was not the only time he had stabbed a man.

T.C. Burgess had not expected this, though now so much seemed predictable. He knew the men would have their knives, perhaps even guns. He knew they would have the woman and would use her as shield and hostage, making it impossible for him to fire, and without question they would threaten to kill the girl and make him drop his own gun. And then they would all be at the mercy of these men from the interior. No, he was not surprised that this had become a bad situation. He had felt some premonition from the very moment the phone had rung and the sergeant had told him about the tourist.

But he had not expected Jenkins to show, not at all. And now everything had changed. The men were distracted. They were not looking at him, but at Jenkins, who still stood, only a few feet from his daughter, with the machete at his chest. The rigid steel held him where he was, at arm's length. There was no time to call for back-up, so Burgess did what he hated to do. He aimed his heavy and awkward revolver at the hand of the man with the machete and pulled the trigger. The old gun made an awful sound as it discharged, and the man next to the man with the machete jerked his shoulder sideways and fell against the wall. Burgess prepared to fire again, but feared hitting the girl, so ran toward them as he aimed, to get closer. As he did so the man pulled the machete from the American and wheeled toward the girl, just as Burgess knew he would, and so he stopped and fired again, straight at the man's trunk, the largest target and the least chance to hit something else.

Miguel flung his arms back like a puppet, eyes bulging. "Ahhh!" he yelled, and then staggered forward, grabbing the girl with his free hand. He stood holding her, but it soon became apparent that it was she who was supporting him, because his legs began to wobble. The other two men turned and ran, and Burgess fired two warning shots that accidentally hit one of them in the leg, bringing him down to the pavement yelling and cursing and grasping the back of his thigh. When Burgess came closer Miguel swung the machete right at his neck, but his reach was short, and losing his balance he dropped to his knees, one hand on the machete and one arm around the girl's leg. She blinked, then reached down and placed her left hand on his head. As he looked up he smiled, a trickle of blood appearing where he had bit his lip. She pushed hard, and he fell into the street.

Burgess stood over him with the revolver aimed at his head, but he did not fire. Miguel lay on the stones trying to move his mouth.

"Karen," Ted Jenkins said, and they both turned to look at him. He kneeled on the cobblestones examining his own chest, where he had pressed one of his hands against the wound. He looked up and spoke again, but she could not tell whether he said "Karen," or something else. "It's my blood," he said.

"Yes," she said.

Burgess dropped to one knee and pulled Ted's shirt away from the wound. The cut was deep, and the girl's vacant stare unnerved him. "Snap out of it!" he yelled. "Your father is bad hurt."

She said, "I know." Then she knelt down as well. "Hi, Daddy," she said. "I knew you would save me."

Burgess finally pulled his walkie-talkie from his belt and told dispatch to call an ambulance first and sergeant Matthews second. Either way, he didn't think they could come in time.

—

Karen Jenkins arrived at the Belize City airport five weeks later, on the twenty-third of May. She blinked in the bright Belize light, the sun's rays vertical. Only a week away from hurricane season.

She had the cab take her to the police station, where she knew T.C. Burgess waited. As soon as she saw him, with his dark leathery skin and piercing cat eyes, everything came back in a rush. She brought her right hand to her temple.

"Mr. Burgess," she said.

"Just Burgess."

She asked him about the boat. "Don't worry, it's fine. We been keepin a eye on it. Around at the dive dock. They aren't charging you nothin for it."

Together they walked to the waterfront. From the hotel pier a boat took them to the marina where *Last Chance* sat safe in a slip. As they walked down the dock to look at her, the cutter rocked in a wake and pulled at its nylon lines, restive. A boat for a dreamer.

"Is your Daddy gonna make it?"

She turned to see Burgess looking at her. "He's going to have another surgery. They're trying to fix his lung."

"He's with his family now," Burgess said and then felt awkward. Clearly Karen was his family.

"Yes. After we flew to the hospital in Miami, after the first operation, we took him back to Connecticut. His sister still lives there."

"He was cut pretty bad."

"Yes."

"Won't be sailing this boat again I don't suspect."

"Oh he will. Once we get the boat back to the States, and he gets better."

Burgess looked at her, lit by sunlight. "And you think you want to take this boat by yourself?"

"I know I do. I've been sailing all my life."

"Don't you need to . . . recuperate?"

"This is . . . "

"What?"

"I said this is my recuperation."

Burgess shook his head and looked down at his feet. He had forgotten to put on his shoes. "Who'll be your crew?" he asked.

"The boat's rigged for single-handing. I don't need a crew. My father rigged it that way."

"Must be a good sailor, your father."

"Damn good," she said. "They don't . . . "

"What's that?"

"I said they don't come any better."

"Um."

She had been thinking, lying in the overly soft bed in her aunt's house in Hartford, of her father's words that night. When he said her name, "Karen." Or was it "carin'" or "caring"? What had he meant about the blood? In any case, he had saved her. He and Burgess.

Burgess kept looking at her. Her skin had paled, her hair had less light in it now, and deep circles carved shadows below her eyes. She seemed older than when she'd left, that day when the ambulance had taken her with her father from the hospital to the plane.

She turned toward *Last Chance*. The old cutter now held

more of her father than did the house where they'd lived in New England. The house he'd sold to buy the boat.

"I'll be here for a few days, getting ready. Drop by, Burgess, before I go. Maybe you can help me get some diesel."

"I will, honey." Now he looked away, embarrassed at the tone he heard in his voice. They stood looking at *Last Chance*. "It's big water out there," he said.

"Yes," she said. "It is."

The Goddess of
Going Around Again

A CLATTER OF HOOVES, and a gray horse trotted down
the beach at the water's edge, moving across her field of
vision, left to right, like a sentence. The dark-haired young man
seemed to lean too far back in the saddle but otherwise appeared
at ease. Turquoise light and white wind. She had meant to live like
that, on the verge of breaking bone, wind in her hair and eyes
focused straight ahead on what was coming, fast. And perhaps
she had, riding around the rim of the Caribbean Sea, that great
watery track, and now on the home stretch she found herself
slowing and unwilling to end the race.

Like the palm fronds beside the balcony, her heart lifted in
recognition of the east wind. Carol Burns, trained as a biologist,
thought how any book will tell that the trade winds blow east in
this low latitude, but there comes a different learning through the
skin, through the heart. And she had learned and learned about
this east wind. Perhaps because it came from Africa, womb of
human kind, she felt some kinship with this wind. Its memory of
the Sahel was distant, as remote as her own evolutionary memory. The wind spawned so many waves, nameless offspring, from
Africa's dark coast.

She and her husband Terry had left their careers to contend
with those waves. They cast off their jobs as staff scientists for a
federal agency and took to the sea. Their boat, *Endeavor*, had

shouldered its way east, past the Turks and Caicos, past Hispaniola and the south shore of Puerto Rico, past the Virgin Islands. All that way they worked upwind, against the waves.

Now that same band of waves broke against the shores of the Yucatan, where she and Terry had stopped to feel (as he said) the tension on their life-line. Just as a fisher might place a finger on the taut leader to question its resistance. Is this merely the tide, the undertow? Or the great fish, preparing to pull them in? Or perhaps they were simply dawdling here. She thought of her nieces and nephews who would think of any excuse at the unlooked for hour, a drink of water, a trip to the bathroom, to avoid that thief of dignity, surrender.

She felt the great circle closing. She was a fish, watching the ring of net draw tight. Her fingers ran through dark brown hair touched with silver. She sipped her coffee. No, she was making too much of this. This was only the circle of life — of their life for the past three years, from Florida clockwise around the Caribbean, down the Windward and Leeward Islands, to Venezuela, Colombia, up past Panama and Honduras. She loved the beautiful Bay Islands, hunks of emerald rising from the sea. She wanted to return there.

They'd continued north to Belize (the placid warmth of Placencia) and now the Yucatan, one country shy of the behemoth they called home.

On a whim they accepted an invitation to use this beachside cabana near Playa del Carmen for these few days in May, while their friends, the Cerrillos, took a trip to Merida to visit family. They left *Endeavor* resting in a slip on the nearby island of Cozumel. It had been a long time since they'd been on land. She found herself on the western rim of the emerald sea, looking straight into the mirror of their voyage. She watched again as they ticked a coral head in Rum Cay, as they made their way in total darkness along the north shore of Hispaniola, tacking in close to the steep-to rocky shore, avoiding the open sea, wild and crumbling.

She had not intended this retrospection. They had sailed, she and Terry, dawn to dusk to dawn, following routines of day and night, seamless and without separation, with no sense of stopping. Now she had stopped.

She sat in a white wooden chair looking at a sea grape tree and its stubby oblong leaves, glossy green. She had felt those leaves before and found them rigid but more succulent than a magnolia's leaves. The leaves shook, then a black bird hissed at her. Stark and shadowy as a raven — she identified it as a Great Antillean grackle. How could the bird have found her at this latitude and longitude, waiting to hiss its question: What have you learned?

Live and learn, she had often quipped, repeating the words of her mother, but the other alternative also held sway: live and not learn. Live and live, and not learn.

Her sister Tracey had learned much. A professor of anthropology at the University of Maryland, she had published article after article and then book after book. She knew so much, her sister. The history of the Aztecs, the Toltecs, the Maya. It must be wonderful to love your career that much.

She looked at the horizon, at sharp white shapes that showed where Cozumel and their boat lay, a mirage. So many times at sea the horizon had played tricks, islands building on the retina, only to dissolve again into waves. But when at the wheel they could never stop staring, watching for real hazards. The Samana Cays, Glover Reef, the Silver Banks.

Out of this, what had she learned? Only a sense of the east wind and its memory of Africa. The meaning of the shift from turquoise to dark blue as the boat slipped from each island's sand hands and found deep water. The kindness of the katabatic breeze as it flowed like vapor down the great mountain slopes of Hispaniola at night and helped them on their journey east. The hospitality of people like the Placentes on Little Farmers Cay, who took them in and fed them. I have learned all these things, she told the hissing bird that now whistled in mockery or amazement, but whether these vague lessons would help her or even stay with her once she returned home to the States she could not say.

She looked across the great emerald crater of the Caribbean.

Near shore a man stood at the bow of a skiff and pulled a long anchor line. The skiff had white sides but the inside was turquoise, like the water itself, and so he seemed to rise and fall on water, in water, of water. His black hair took the wind like a sail, and the muscles of his back flexed with the knowledge of the sea, the coast. Mayan memory. She was the stranger here.

She had trouble sleeping on land. Strange dreams. The first night here, as she luxuriated in the wide bed, the memory surprised her of searching for sleep in Silver Spring, before they'd left their jobs and sold their house to take this trip. Silver Spring. Cenote de Plata. For her it had been the seat of government, or at least the seat of bureaucracy, where she had labored for more than a decade for the National Oceanic and Atmospheric Administration, before the "reductions in force" began. Before politics threatened to suppress the agency's good work.

It was also the place where she'd begun to feel sick, her energy and strength draining away. She even spent a week in the hospital while they tried to figure out where her spirit went. Around that same time she and Terry hatched this plan to sail around the islands. Her energy started to return, a tide creeping up its shallow bay.

She did not like the way she'd begun to think of her home, the United States. Something had crept into her image of that great country and sat in shadow, an unease, an anger. She looked up the beach to the north, as if she could see the great continent that appeared to spread its influence even here, in the form of giant cruise ships. She pictured the urban centers of the east — Boston, Philadelphia, New York, Baltimore — calving chunks of themselves like glaciers, floating bits of urbia: steel and electricity set drifting on the sea.

She and Terry left the silver spring and what many called the highest standard of living on earth. Some might think them small people, with small assets and small influence, small plans. Some might think them dreamers, living the lie of romanticism. It was true that they had spent much of their life savings.

Last night Terry looked depressed and went to bed early, leaving her in the hammock to stare at her favorite star, Canopus. She had watched the star flash red and blue and green and began to dream, hypnotized. She dreamed that there were planets there, circling the star, and that they were all named Canopus, and that all their moons were named Canopus. Further, she dreamed that people on all the worlds were named Canopus, all tribes the same. All day on Canopus green and red and white clouds drifted overhead, and at night the moons and stars glittered pink and turquoise. Depression and anxiety, she dreamed, were not known on Canopus, nor greed, nor worry. They have a thousand names for red, two thousand for green. If she had not held to the edges of the Mayan hammock, she felt certain she would have flown there, to that star.

Today she felt uneasy. Terry was not doing well. He seemed unable to see Canopus or to feel the cleansing breeze. He was often silent or fixed on odd information. He had ruefully described to her the Mayan gods — like Ik, the god of the wind. And the other god he had told her about. Ishtab. Or Ixtab. What god was that? She couldn't remember.

In Tulum the wind had indeed seemed like a god, unwilling to relent against the ancient white stone. They had seen how the old temple, built facing the sea, served as a lighthouse, torches placed in recessed windows on either side of the tower, both lights visible only if one came straight through the break in the reef. So they must have conceived this lighthouse function from the very start, she thought, to build the temple in precisely that spot, and then to measure out the town and the symmetrical stone walls from there, everything keyed on the break in the reef.

Here in the trade wind belt what a powerful and ever-present god Ik must have been, even now pressing back the curtains with invisible hands. She put down her coffee cup and the dime novel she was not reading, rummaged through her green backpack for the Yucatan guidebook. The book's glossary listed Spanish and Mayan words — chul (flute), tunkul (drum), and chohom (dance performed during the month of Zip, related to fishing). She saw the word mayacimil (small pox) which the glossary defined literally as "easy death." And there it was: Ixtab, goddess of the cord and . . . of suicide by hanging.

For a moment she held the book as if it were a divining rod, her eyes shifting left and right, seeing everything and nothing, looking for water. Gradually the book indicated the door.

Where had he said he was going? To use the telephone, of course, to call home, to begin that slow and painful process of re-entry into his former life, or to find out perhaps that there was no place for him, no opportunity, no way back. She tossed the book on the bed, grabbed the room key, itself strung to a long blue and now ominous cord, and hurried through the door. She remembered he said he would buy some line.

"Señora. Señora. Aqui. Aqui." The Playa merchants called from their booths, holding up the ends of rugs, of shawls, of hammocks, all tediously made from strangling cord. "Señora. Mucho trabajo." It had been much work, this great circle around the Caribbean, maybe too much work. She walked to the ferry dock, as if to return to the scene of their coming, their arrival from Cozumel where their boat still waited. She walked down a narrow street, startled by a man holding an automatic carbine, sinister, inimical — here was the police station, an armed guard standing at the ready, perhaps because of the unrest in Chiapas. But then she always felt the threat of this harsh authority in Mexico, careful to look away from the eyes of the uniformed men, seated at a table just inside the open window, their cigarette smoke mixing with the seabreeze.

Back on the main street she looked left and right along the line of colorful stalls, people everywhere, their feet powdered with dust, mortal ghosts. Here the lushness of the tropics gave way to a sudden aridity, and water — for drinking, for bathing —

seemed in short supply. Only the wind, partly blocked by the town's low buildings, robbed of its humidity, still blew from the ancient east.

Where would he do this thing if he were to do it? No, do not think it. If you think it, it will happen. You can will it, accidentally. No, she thought, I am not a superstitious woman. Not superstitious? The Mayan figure on a blanket, bent beneath some invisible weight, stared with fixed and perpetual glee.

"He feels the Earth Comer is upon him," the man behind the booth said.

"I am looking for my husband," she said.

He smiled. He was clean shaven. "What will your husband like?" he asked. "This rug? Three hundred pesos."

"No," she said. "I'm not looking for a gift for my husband. I am looking for my husband."

"You lookin for a husband?" the man repeated, confused.

"No, I am not looking for a husband. I have a husband. He is lost." Was he? Was he lost? She had often thought of that possibility: lost at sea. She had not thought of this: lost at land.

She felt hopeless. There was no chart for this place, no compass course. She could not run a search and rescue pattern. She could not jibe and follow the reciprocal. There was no buoy, no rule of the road, no tide table, no notice to mariners. Only a crowd of apparently aimless people, wandering, running, leaning, talking, staring. Staring at her. "Never mind," she said.

"Two hundred sixty pesos," the man said.

She stopped at a cafe with tables along the roadway-walkway. If she sat here, she could see who passed. He could pass. She could see him. As long as she was having a beer she might as well have some arroz con pollo, so she did. It was as if she were celebrating, but it felt like a wake. The parrot in the corner squawked a grating requiem. A blonde man, an obvious American, watched her. After a while he sauntered over, carrying his Corona beer by his thigh like a revolver. "Hey," he said. "You're too pretty to be sittin' here all by your lonesome."

"Lo siento mucho," she said. "No puedo hablar engles."

The man looked at her for a long time, but she met his stare, as if waiting for him to answer in Spanish, which he did not do, lifting the beer bottle toward her in a kind of salute, then fading back toward the bar's other side.

She pushed her fork through the chicken and rice. She thought of poor Mrs. Beaman.

An endurance test, that's what Mrs. Beaman had called it. They had met the Beamans in San Salvador, heading east and south. Mr. Beaman, gray-haired and erect, had sold his pharmacy in Madison, Wisconsin, and bought a sturdy but clumsy fiber-glass sloop and had set out with his wife to discover a dream, to drift into a wondrous retirement. What they drifted into were the west-marching waves, each one an unlooked-for insult to their progress, slap slap slap. Dropping from crest to trough of one steep swell, their boat buried its bow and flung Mrs. Beaman to the cabin sole. A cracked rib and spreading bruises. She said the bruises looked like dark paint, spilled. Patting with nervous hands her permanent-wave blue-gray hair, now windblown, she revealed how hard all this had been for her. Less the pain of the cracked rib than the continued relentlessness of waves that simply would not leave them in peace. "It's nothing but an endurance test," she said, her blue eyes going gray and misty. "It's the men's dream, isn't it, dear?" she had said. "Not ours."

"Oh no," Carol had answered, "it's mine too. I mean this trip. I wanted it just as much as Terry did. Maybe more."

Mrs. Beaman had glanced away, pursing her lips, as if hearing something rude. "Well," she said, "you may be deceiving yourself." Mrs. Beaman looked oddly prim, except for her wind-whipped hair, her damp and wrinkled blouse.

"It's my dream too," she had said again. "Terry and I are in this together."

She looked up, worried that she had spoken aloud. Where was he?

La cuenta, she said. She handed the waiter a generous tip.

Though the beer and chicken felt solid in her belly, when she joined the drifting crowd her anxiety returned, cleaved to her like an abandoned child. Soon she would have to return to the cabana to see if he was there.

She wandered back toward the ferry dock where they'd lifted a large tent, for whatever festival this was, and like a circus goer she drifted in on loud music coming from speakers, almost expecting to see clowns or elephants. What she saw, in the makeshift spotlights lashed to tent poles, were his legs, Terry's legs, dancing in the wind.

He spun around and around, wanton in his white shorts. In each hand he held the hand of a child, and he was turning in a great circle, laughing. The dark-skinned children with bright smiles laughed at him, and they turned like a living circus ring. A length of line lay coiled across his shoulder. He seemed an animal trainer, unshaven and going gray at the temples, celebrating the greatest show on earth. The children were jaguars.

She walked across the floor — he hadn't seen her — and broke into the circle. Then he saw her, watched her turn and turn around the space they surrounded, the children shy but smiling.

"Did you call?" she said.

"Call?"

"You know."

"Oh, yeah. I called all right. Not good."

"Not good?"

"No. Not good at all."

They turned and turned, only now the children became unruly and charged in and out of the circle, as if to break it up.

"I know," she said. "Let's circle back the other way."

"Yeah," he said with a broad smile, whiskers lit by the harsh light. "Let's."

The children lunged in the opposite direction, and the goddess Ixtab let them dance. Terry was with her. She would not need to fly to Canopus alone.

Night Sea

H ER SHORTWAVE RADIO had gone out, and now she had lost the world. Every night, as the sun raced for the horizon, as if to abandon her, Jessica Roth would switch on the shortwave and listen for the BBC. And with the dark of the ocean dropping its veil around the boat, she hung on every word about Africa and the Mid-East, all the war-torn world, as if she had some connection, as if she could do something about it.

But now the radio had gone out — completely. The switch did not even spark the lighted dial, the dead radio now one more victim of the sea's corrosiveness. So she stood in the silent cabin, bracing her hip against the bulkhead as she lit the propane stove and began to heat hot water for the long night ahead. No not silent, but a continuing rush of water that reminded her of her position somewhere in the Gulf Stream, heading back toward America. Endless sound, and yet a quietness, sometimes soothing, sometimes ominous, like the stillness that precedes a great catastrophe. Freighters, for example, made no sound before they hit.

Tightening the teapot between its metal tongs, she climbed the companionway and poked her head above decks to check the self-steering gear, and to make certain no monstrous thing had suddenly taken shape on the sea. There was nothing, only that vast expanse of slag heaps melting toward the western horizon, their hilltops turning silver in the final light of dusk. How the heart could sink, with the light going, as if she were losing her sight for good.

That first needling wave of fear had almost passed now, and she forced herself to perform the routines of twilight. Reluctant to go forward but knowing that she should check the rigging before dark, she clicked her harness to the jackline that ran along the starboard deck, and with one stride moved around the dodger, its synthetic canvas held skintight by rods and snaps, and stepped into the wind. Here she could feel how the dodger had shielded her. Spray lifted from the face of waves, exploded from beneath the bow, and sent a white curtain of water off the leeward side to her right. The sound of the wind and the rushing water now filled the air as though someone had turned up the volume, and standing unprotected in the wind she felt more keenly her complete isolation, here in the center of a world of water. Holding to the handrails, she walked herself along the cabin until she reached the mast. There she looked aloft, as she had been taught years before, hoping not to see anything wrong with the halyards, the cleats, the sails. She knew she would not get a good look at the rigging again until the sun came back. The double reef and storm jib made for good balance, and the little 31-foot sloop, *Jessie*, handled the twenty-five-knot wind nicely. If the wind built any higher she would have to reef again — the third and final reef — and she did not relish the thought of doing that, especially not in the dark.

For a moment she leaned against the mast and looked across the darkening ocean, in some way lashed there by her own thoughts. From her place on the cabintop she stood above most of the spray, and with the small boat plowing diligently through wave after wave she felt for it an unexplainable fondness. Like a mythical steed — Pegasus or Shadowfax — it bore her faithfully toward the dying western sky and the coming night.

Tugging at the dock line that secured the half-deflated dinghy to the cabintop, checking its tension, she took a final look around at the monotonous and magical waves and then made her way back to the cockpit's relative quiet. Once safe behind the dodger she unsnapped her life harness, then quickly resnapped it to the cable they had run along the cockpit kickpanel. She remembered when Joel had installed the cable, through-bolting it and backing it with wide stainless steel washers. He had run the jacklines along the deck as well, port and starboard, using shrouds left over after they had replaced, as a precaution, the standing rigging. Shroud. She remembered how, as a teenager, she had found that word so strange, a death word. Then habit had erased the strangeness from her mind — until now, when she thought of it again, as the cloak of death.

"I have lost my husband." The words came to her lips though there was no one there to hear. She remembered saying the sentence for the first time at the marina in San Juan. The phrase was familiar enough: she had heard other women say it, women of her grandmother's and then her mother's generation. She had never expected to say it herself. Her hands gripped the top of the dodger and she watched the dying deck, the dying waves, the dying sky all smudge and blur into oblivion until she closed her eyes, not wanting to see.

If the shortwave radio had not gone out she could listen to the news and try to imagine all the world's mourners, the refugees, the displaced and dispossessed, the widows. She felt as though she had lost touch with her family, starved for news of her sisters in Darfur, Baghdad, and everywhere that death unfolded its dark shadow. And so now she was completely alone.

In this aloneness, almost as if part of it, like the snake in Eden, she heard a hissing, and for an instant she thought that something — or someone — had caught on to the side of the boat and was hanging there. A barb of adrenaline pricked her heart, but then she recognized the noise: the stove. She flicked the switch at the side of the companionway, cutting off the supply of propane from the tank, and lowered herself down to the galley, where steam draped heavy drops of condensation on the bulkhead above the tea kettle. One of her rules was never to leave the stove unattended — she did not trust propane — and the fact that she had forgotten about it entirely broke her confidence. A fire here, at sea, the dinghy and the life raft burned . . . unthinkable.

Now she became herself again, the navigator, the mate, the captain and began to perform one action after another, methodically. She poured hot water into the thermos for the night's coffee and set it in the sink next to the companionway. She switched on the red night light for the knotmeter and the depth finder and the red light over the chart table. She checked the VHF radio as well (the only radio that still worked), even pushing the soft button for the weather channel, though she knew that the closest radio station now lay miles behind her, in Puerto Rico, or miles ahead, on the mainland. She switched the dial to channel 13, with a double watch on channel 16, in the event that any freighters might try to call — which they never did, coming out of the dark like black soundless mountains. Still, she turned the squelch knob until the radio squealed, as if to see that it still lived, then turned it back slightly.

The GPS receiver gleamed its greenish light, and she wondered what she would do if it went the way of the shortwave. She had a sextant on board, and had taken a class with Joel at the local community college near where they had lived in Falls Church, Virginia, several years ago, before they had set sail, but she had never used it underway and every time she took out the worksheets to practice she ended by stuffing them untouched back into the chart table drawer again, slightly nauseous. Double-checking the Greenwich Mean Time, she plotted her position (or at least what the GPS gave as her position) on the large chart half-folded on the chart table. The southwest North Atlantic. Tiny Xs with circles wandered up from San Juan in a long arc toward the massive continental coast of the U.S. She looked at the coastline, at Georgia, which had once been her home, and wondered if she really wanted to return.

If the chart were big enough, it would show more tiny Xs trailing around the eastern end of Puerto Rico to Culebra, and from there a twisting and turning path through St. Thomas and St. Johns, Tortola and Virgin Gorda and down to St. Martin and

Martinique and Grenada. And even now, on this very chart, she could see the first line of Xs, darker and larger than hers, marking the voyage down, over two years ago, mostly in Joel's hand. Those Xs led from Florida, where they had bought the boat, to Grand Bahama, and then down the Berry Islands to Nassau and the Exumas. They had planned to go as far as Venezuela, but ran out of time and money in Granada. A shame, too, because they had been so close. Then Joel had come up with the idea about working in Puerto Rico, and had gotten the name of someone in San Juan. God, she wished that they had never taken that turn.

Spreading the long legs of the dividers, she reached out to the continent from the most recent X on the chart, bringing the far point down on the Savannah River light. Several people had told her not to go into Savannah, because of the tides and traffic, but she wanted an entrance she could maneuver in day or dark, and she had already decided to keep the boat at Thunderball marina, at least until she figured what to do next. Maybe she would take the boat north on the intracoastal to the Chesapeake Bay, near where they had lived before. Or maybe she would live near her sister now, in Atlanta. She wasn't sure.

Too much time had passed since she'd looked around, and she forced herself back into the cockpit, taking the binoculars. The darkness — suddenly so complete and unrelenting — almost panicked her. No matter how many nights she spent at sea, the darkness always took her breath away. She raised the binoculars and tried to peer directly ahead, as if this were a car, to see if there were something in the road. Only darkness, only endless water. She scanned the horizon then, looking for any hint of a freighter's range lights. Because she would gradually be closing with the coast, freighters became an ever greater worry. Nothing so far. The waves hissed and rushed up on the port side and then disappeared to starboard in a long heaving sigh, the wind out of the south now, so that she sailed almost on a beam reach, dipping and lifting with each wave that came at her with the warm wind, as if following her from the islands.

————

She stood in the narrow guardhouse and looked through a slit in the stone toward the sea. Waves rolled against the rock shore and exploded, racing among the crevices of stone and spilling back into the next wave that hit. The fort at old San Juan rose beside the harbor entrance, and the guardhouse, cylindrical, exotic and medieval, seemed to thrust out over the very sea itself, oblivious of time. For a long while she stood there, as if herself on some kind of guard duty. Joel, who had complained of feeling tired, sat outside the door, leaning against the stones and nodding. He had been working hard, hired as a civil engineer through a contact he had in San Juan, Phil Werner. She knew the job wore him down, not only because of the work, but because of the peculiarly hectic or at least disjointed pace of San Juan and because of the switching back and forth from Spanish to English. Much of his Spanish had come back since they had landed here, and she felt proud of the way he seemed to adapt.

Between two stone jetties a tug, painted bright red and black, headed out to sea with its ponderous barge, laboring against waves that rolled in a widening arc into the harbor mouth. At first the tug made slow progress, but once it cleared the jetties and began to take on the swell of the north shore, it appeared to lose momentum altogether, plunging up and down, up and down, evidently going nowhere in its bath of foam. The barge, barely moving now, began to drift sideways, bearing down on the spray-covered eastern-most jetty. The tug changed direction only slightly toward the west side of the channel, to keep tension on the towline, and continued its languorous and laborious plunging into the swell. She felt she were watching an insect pursue a mindless and fruitless task, and the whole benign purposelessness of life settled over her like salt spray, the repetitive tedious harmless futility of it. She could not imagine, at the moment, setting out into that swell, which had been formidable enough behind them as they sailed into San Juan. She knew that going out under the power of their throbbing diesel engine they would look very like this tug, plunging up and down, a slow parade, with a thousand miles to go.

When she finally stooped down in the sunlight, Joel's eyes opened, and there he was, seeing her, his brown hair moving slightly in the wind, his face-skin tan and tough from their time at sea, his broad nose looking forever like it was about to peel or had just peeled or both. He blinked and stretched and said, "Ah, Jessica." They agreed that they would take a cab back to their boat now.

Joel had put on some weight during the past three months in San Juan. Before that, when sailing from island to island, he had become wiry as only people at sea become wiry, his skin worked over like leather, his muscles not so much large as hard and knotty. He had had a wispy beard most of their trip, but now he had shaved it off, and he did look younger, even his brown eyes, which seemed to have gotten darker. She felt him take her hand as they neared the street, and they each raised their free hand when a taxi approached. Her Spanish had not progressed much, so sitting in the San Juan traffic she strained to hear as Joel tried to talk to the cab driver, or rather as he tried to listen, since the driver did all the talking — and too fast, because she could hardly understand a word. From his gesturing, she could see that he seemed riled up, complaining about his family, or maybe the government or the police.

When the cab stopped by the marina, the heavy chassis of the big American car rocked forward and backward on its springs. They climbed out with some relief, happy to be near their boat again, for nearly three years their home, their safe haven. "What was he saying?" she asked, as soon as the cab pulled off.

Joel looked at her. "I have no idea," he said.

A light breeze ruffled her hair as they walked toward the right side of the marina, where *Jessie,* her sails neatly furled, waited in her slip.

"Su dinero." This much she understood. One of the two young men who stood in front of them, blocking their way, had said this.

"No tengo nada," Joel said. She looked at him in his khaki pants and white shirt with a flap over the pocket. He looked handsome to her, but she knew that to the two young men he looked only rich. She wanted to explain to them that they had put all their money into their boat, that in many ways they too were living on the edge.

"No tengo nada," the closest man said, repeating Joel's words with a sneer. "Tiene una mujer guapa," he said, not smiling.

"Basta," Joel said, taking her elbow and starting to walk toward the other side of the marina, to avoid challenging the two men. She was not too afraid: it was broad daylight, and the marina generally had very good security, patrolled by a heavyset man named Rudolpho. Where was he now?

"No," the other man said, "not basta. Not enough."

"You speak English," Joel said.

"No. No es verdad. English pig," he said.

They had tried to quicken their pace, determined to circumnavigate these two young men they'd never seen before (she thought, looking at them, how they might have looked in the old fort, two hundred years ago, perhaps wearing the rags of day laborers, with that same sallow skin, those same vacant but precarious eyes), but the men kept circling in front of them, so they seemed unable to go anywhere. Where was Rudolpho?

"Su dinero. Pronto," the first young man said again, and this time his voice hit another register. Joel must have heard this tone in his voice as well, because he suddenly stopped trying to walk and took his wallet from his back pocket. He opened it slowly and deliberately, so they could see inside, where there were only a few bills. These he took out begrudgingly and handed to the first man, holding them at arm's length so as not to shrink the distance between them. The young man, who seemed now to be drunk or drugged, looked at the money with apparent disgust, then grabbed it and stuffed it in his pants pocket. And then, not quite as an afterthought but as an act lightly considered and dispensed, the second man stepped forward with a short knife and stabbed Joel in the chest. The knife appeared to miss a rib and sank down to the handle. "Mujer bonita," the first man was saying, then the two of them walked away, not running, disappearing back into the streets.

Joel's legs gave way and he sank to his knees. "Help!" she yelled. "For God sakes help!" Her voice sounded queer. The afternoon was so heavy and quiet, the sun so warm; her cries sounded out of place, overly dramatic, hysterical. "You'll be all right," she said to Joel, who was now leaning back on one arm, his other hand on his chest, as though to hold the blood there and not let it spill out on his shirt. It looked as if the knife had hit the heart. "Help!" she screamed again, rising to her feet, and now a heavy-set man in a tank-top shirt turned to look at her from across the marina grounds. "Call the police!" she said. "Call an ambulance!" The man frowned and stared at her. He was beginning to understand that something was wrong. He looked at Joel and squinted, trying to see from a considerable distance why he would be lying on the ground. She screamed again, no longer using words, simply screaming. The world had become like the tugboat, slogging tediously out to sea, and nothing could happen quickly. Everyone appeared to move so slowly, as if in a half-sleep. Even the traffic stopped and the gulls stood still on the pilings beneath the great weight of the sun. Only Joel seemed to be leaving, the light going from his eyes.

～

The sloop rose over a sizable wave and then settled into the next trough, sails snapping with that spanking sound they made in a stiff wind when they luffed and filled again quickly. Instinctively she looked up to see if the sails were well trimmed, if they were drawing as they should, but of course she could see nothing in the dark.

They had, she mused, spent almost their entire life savings on this boat, not only for the boat itself, but to equip it with so many indemnities against catastrophe: extra water tanks to defend against thirst, an extra fuel tank to bring them back to safe harbor, and all the electronic equipment: the knot meter, the depth finder, the GPS, the shortwave . . . It was as if they needed the security of all these human contrivances before they could let go of the land — as they had let go, that dawn when they had motored out of the inlet at West Palm Beach, heading for no clear destination other than one island after another. But then catastrophe had found them anyway, not on the edge of a coral reef, nor at the colossal bow of a six-hundred-foot freighter, nor beneath the savagery of a storm at sea. No, calamity had found them on dry land, near a crowded roadway, other people within shouting distance, and their boat tied safely in its slip, a three-quarter-inch nylon dockline secured to each of four well-spaced pilings.

She emptied a packet of instant coffee into the cup she had bought in Martinique, a heavy, brightly painted mug, and bracing herself beside the coaming she poured steaming water from the thermos. Then, with the same methodical movements, she replaced the lid, reached around the bulkhead and lowered the thermos into the galley sink below. With her head part way inside the cabin she noticed the eerie green numbers of the GPS. She seemed to be heading in the right direction. How odd that the one black box she never trusted, the one filled with who-knew-what space-age circuitry, the one she thought would be the first to fail in the corrosive salt air, still worked: the little box that spoke to satellites whirling high and invisible overhead, whispering those miraculous bright green numbers, telling them over and over where they were.

Telling her. Where she was. Where he was now she could not say. Was he in that plot of ground in Virginia where she had labored to travel, accompanying, she said, her husband, as though he were sleeping, and at other times escorting a corpse, the way she could only have imagined happening to someone else, the corpse less like the body of her lover, now cold, than a piece of freight to be labeled, processed, tracked, and claimed. Or was he not there at all, not in the Virginia earth, nor hovering in anger or remorse over the scene of his death, near that dry dusty spot where his blood was pumped clear of his body by his dutiful but misdirected heart? Having surrendered forever his association with blood and bone was he now released, drifting like pure spirit, unrelated to the corpse, the cadaver, the coffin — like the wind?

She stood and peered over the blue dodger, almost as if she could already see the Savannah light calling her from far ahead. She felt the wind massage her hair with spirit hands. It seemed certain that he was here, with her, in the wind. Perhaps that defined what wind was: the spirits of the dead, moving over the dry land, over the sea, carrying with them the mist and the rain, never leaving earth but remaining, staying, just as dying fish and waterfowl feed whatever grows on the ocean floor. Not quite closing her eyes, but focusing on the darkness where the Savannah light would finally appear, she surrendered to the company, to the fellowship, of the wind.

Some Nautical Terms

backstay – Cable that supports a sailboat's mast from the back (the stern).

backstay tensioner – Device that adjusts tension on the backstay for better sailing performance.

beating – Sailing at a close angle into the wind, generally harder and slower than sailing sideways to the wind (reaching) or before the wind (running).

binnacle – Stand, often at the ship's wheel, that holds the compass and other instruments.

beam reach – Sailing with the wind directly on the side (the beam).

boom – Horizontal pole that holds the bottom (foot) of the mainsail.

bow – Forward end of a boat.

bowsprit – Short pole or platform that usually supports a cable (forestay) for a jib (see jib) and may also provide a place for a boat's anchors.

bridgedeck – Raised seat or deck that protects the bottom of the companionway (see companionway).

broad reach – Sailing with the wind on the corner of the stern (the quarter).

Bruce anchor – Type of anchor with a curved metal scoop that digs into sand or mud.

CQR anchor – Type of anchor with a metal plow that swivels to bury into sand or mud.

cant – To lean a boat to one side, often using an anchor, for example in an effort to raise the keel off the bottom; hence the terms "cant the hull" or "cant the boat."

caprail – Rail, traditionally of wood, that covers or caps the sides of a boat above the deck.

chock – Metal guide through which a line passes, for example on the bow (a bow chock) or the stern (a stern chock).

cleat – Two-pronged fixture around which a line is secured, usually in a figure eight pattern.

close-hauled – Sailing at a narrow angle to the wind, which requires pulling the sails in tight. See "beating."

coaming – Raised section that surrounds a boat's cockpit; it both protects the cockpit area from spray and provides a backrest for sitting.

companionway – Main opening that leads below decks, usually by way of steps or ladder (companionway ladder).

cutter – Sailboat with two forward sails (jib and staysail).

dodger – Protective canopy, usually of a canvas-like material with plastic windows, that covers the companionway and shields the cockpit from spray.

EPIRB – Emergency position indicating radio beacon, usually powered by a battery, which sends automatic radio signals to identify the location of a vessel in distress.

forestay – Cable that supports a sailboat's mast from the front (the bow). See headstay.

furl – Roll up or fold a sail when not in use. The mainsail is usually furled on the boom; a jib may be furled around the headstay (roller furling).

genoa jib – Large jib (foresail) used in light to moderate winds.

GPS – Global Positioning System. This electronic system depends on an array of satellites to establish one's position virtually anywhere in the world.

ground plate – Metal plate attached to the bottom of a boat's hull to provide a negative ground for the boat's electrical system and to help prevent electrolysis.

halyard – Line used to raise a sail, for example the mainsail (main halyard) or jib (jib halyard).

hawse hole – Hole in the bulwark or deck through which a line passes, usually for docking or anchoring.

headstay – Cable that supports a boat's mast from the front. See forestay.

heave to/hove to – To trim in the mainsail and tighten the jib to windward (called backwinding the jib). This keeps the boat moving slowly forward at a close angle to the wind, even with no one at the helm (the helm is lashed down).

heel – To lean. When the wind puts sideways pressure on a sail, the boat heels.

jackline – Line, often run the full length of the boat, to which one can clip to prevent being lost overboard.

jib – Triangular foresail, usually attached to the forestay.

katabatic winds – Winds that drop down the sides of high mountains due to a cooling effect, usually at nighttime. Sailors since Columbus have taken advantage of this phenomenon, for example when sailing upwind along mountainous coasts (as on the Dominican Republic, which has the highest mountains in the West Indies).

ketch – Sailboat with a jib, a mainsail, and an aft sail (mizzen) that is positioned in front of the ship's wheel (the helm).

lazarette – Hatch placed in the rear (stern) of a vessel.

lee/lee shore – Downwind side of a vessel, or a shore that is downwind and therefore dangerous, since the wind pushes boats in that direction.

leeward – On the downwind (lee) side, or moving downwind (leeward movement).

lifeline – Cable that runs along the sides of a boat's deck, usually all around the boat, to help secure people onboard. Also a line (usually nylon) that runs from a chest harness and clips to a jackline, to prevent a crewmember from being washed or thrown overboard.

LORAN – Long Range Aid to Navigation, a system that relies on signals from multiple radio towers to establish one's position. To do this the system uses time difference (TD) of the signals, shown as "TD lines" on special charts. LORAN predated satellite-based GPS.

luff – Front edge of the sail, for example the edge of the mainsail nearest the mast, or the edge of the jib nearest the forestay. The luff is the first part of a sail to flap when a boat heads into the wind. To luff a sail is to bring it into the wind, causing it to flap.

mainsheet – Line used to control the mainsail.

packing gland – Seal around a boat's engine shaft, traditionally wrapped with cord and forming an interface between the inside of the boat and the water outside.

port – Left side of a boat. Also an opening to let in light and, if it opens, air. And, of course, a harbor where boats and ships come and go.

prop – Propeller used to drive a boat forward.

propwash – Water roiled behind or beside a boat by the spinning propeller.

reef, reefed main – To reef a sail is to reduce its size by lowering it, usually to pre-set reef points. A sail can be double-reefed or triple-reefed to reduce its size further. A reef is also a place where coral grows.

rhumb line – Navigational course set directly toward a boat's next destination point. Because of wind and currents, sailboats traveling long distances are rarely right on their rhumb line.

rode – Line used to attach an anchor, an anchor rode. The small aperture in the deck through which this line passes may be called an anchor rode hole.

sat nav – Satellite navigation; satnav originally referred to the use of transit satellites, which predated the more continuous and dependable GPS system.

scupper – Drain or opening, in the cockpit for example, that allows seawater or rainwater to empty out of the boat, often through a hose that passes through the hull via a metal fitting (seacock).

sheer – Line of a boat's hull as it rises from the rear (stern) to the front (bow). Many traditional sailboats have a gracefully lifting sheer.

sheet – Line used to control a sail (a mainsheet for the main, a jibsheet for the jib). Also used as a verb; for example, to sheet in the main.

shrouds – Cables attached to a sailboat's mast from the sides. See stays.

single-hander – One who handles a boat alone. Joshua Slocum was the first person to sail around the world solo. Also used as a verb: single-handing.

sloop – Sailboat with one mainsail and one jib. (A cutter has two foresails.)

snubber lines – Short lines, usually nylon, used to hold an anchor chain and to absorb the shock of a boat's rising and falling at anchor.

stanchion – Short metal post, usually stainless steel, that holds up the lifelines.

starboard – Right side of a vessel.

stays – Cables that hold up a mast; a general term that can include the forestay, the backstay, and the shrouds (which are essentially side stays).

staysail – Small triangular sail, often a foresail run on an inner stay.

stern – Back end of a boat.

steep-to [shore] – Shoreline where the land drops off suddenly to considerable depth.

stuffing box – See packing gland.

tack – To shift back and forth into the wind in order to make progress toward an upwind destination. The tack is also the corner of the sail where the bottom of the sail (foot) meets the sail's front edge (luff).

taffrail – Rail or trim, traditionally wooden, that runs across the back (stern) of a boat.

toerail – Raised trim that runs around the edge of a boat's deck, to help prevent people and objects from slipping overboard.

vane/windvane – Device that uses wind direction to steer a vessel by means of a steering oar. On most models, the steering oar does not steer the vessel on its own but pulls lines that are attached to the boat's wheel or tiller.

vang – Device, either rope or rod, used to hold down the boom and keep it from lifting in the wind.

whisker pole – Thin pole, usually aluminum, used to hold out a jib when sailing downwind.

windlass – Geared winch, historically manual but now often electric, used to haul in anchor chain or rope (rode).

Afterword

I have many to thank. First, my wife Bobbie and my son David, without whom I could not have written these stories nor lived the experiences that inspired them. My sisters and life-friends, Anne and Nancy — who kept our dog Sam while we were at sea for a year. My nephew, John Stevens, sailor, friend, and reader of this manuscript; and Jeff Packer, who helped us cross the Stream. Christine Drewyer, who introduced me to the work of Kevin Fitzgerald, and Pam Wilson, who read drafts of these stories. The Mayo Gang: Spencer, Tim, Viki, Debbie, Jim, Annie, Ken, Vicky, Amy, Ian, and in memoriam, Mary Jo. Our good friends, Tom and Carol Howie. My friends and colleagues at the University of Maryland, beginning with Dr. Rita Colwell, who granted me the year's leave that led to many of these stories, and Dr. Don Boesch for his steadfast support. I owe a deep debt of gratitude to my co-workers at the Maryland Sea Grant College, who have been my family for more years than any of us would like to admit. In particular I want to thank Jonathan Kramer for his friendship and support, and Doug Lipton, Dan Jacobs, Jeannette Connors, and my other colleagues at Maryland Sea Grant for their enduring friendship. I have been especially fortunate to know and work with a very talented group of writers, Michael Fincham, Erica Goldman, and Jessica Smits, and one very special designer, Sandy Rodgers. Most of all I must thank Merrill Leffler, my colleague, friend, and mentor, poet and publisher, who has helped so many writers, without whom these stories would not have reached their final form.

Finally I want to thank those who taught me how to sail,

especially Bill Pearsall, who first handed me a tiller, and Pen Shiflett, who showed me the ropes when we were both teenagers.

Abraham's Bay, in Mayaguana, is a very real place, but even though my wife and I sailed to Mayaguana in 1990, the setting I describe in my story is a fictitious one. Mayaguana has been a remarkable — and remarkably remote — destination, and for me one full of mystery. Now the Bahamian government is apparently working with American investors to develop the island. Like so many places that once seemed so far away, the island is changing, and once developed will in some way cease to be that distant place of mystery.

I hope for Mayaguana and all the world's islands that they find the right path between economic development and the preservation of nature. The sea preserves us all in ways we don't understand. It is the mother of life.

About the Author

Jack Greer grew up on the Chesapeake Bay and has been sailing since childhood. He and his wife Bobbie have lived aboard their 30-foot sloop, and during one year-long voyage left their land lives to sail to the Dominican Republic and beyond. Director of Communications and Public Affairs for the University of Maryland Sea Grant College, Greer has written hundreds of newspaper and magazine articles, largely about the Chesapeake, and for some years authored the *Bay Shore Report*, a weekly column published in newspapers around the Bay. He has been recognized for the quality of his writing and environmental work with citations of merit from the Governor of Maryland. In addition to writing fiction — he has twice won awards for his stories from the Maryland State Arts Council — Greer is also a poet and the author of *America & Other Poems*. He lives with his wife Bobbie in Annapolis, Maryland.

Abraham's Bay & Other Stories
was designed by Sandy Rodgers and is set
in Sabon, an old style serif typeface designed
by Jan Tschichold (1902-1974). The typeface
was released jointly by Linotype, Monotype, and
Stemple type foundaries in 1967. Design of the
roman is based on types by sixteenth century
typographer Claude Garamond and named for
fellow printer Jacques Sabon. The italics are
based on types designed by Robert Granjon,
a contemporary of Garamond. The book
was printed on acid-free papers by
Thomson-Shore in Dexter, Michigan.